The

Troublemakers

Part of Hyades Wars,
Book 1 in the Humans series,
Book 2 in the Orc series

Michael Ryan

Hyades Wars Publishing
Hyadeswars.com

ISBN-13:
978-1-7329292-1-0

ISBN-10:
1-7329292-1-0

Body of Work

Path to the Gods
book 1 in the Orcs series

Darkster, Even the Gods Tremble
book 3 in the Orcs series

The Troublemakers
book 1 in the Humans series
book 2 in the Orc series

The Troublemakers, Halfling
book 2 in the Humans series
book 4 in the Orc series

Schula and Downs, Love Triangle
book 1 in Life's Mysteries

Tales of Hyades Wars
book 1 in Short Stories

Acknowledgments

This book is dedicated to all my loved ones that supported me in my endeavors to overcome, not just writing and completing this project, but the inherent impediments in my personal life, without whom this piece would not have been possible.

Special thanks to Zefanya Maega for Artwork created, based on my designs. Font for cover page was created on cooltext.com.

This book has been edited by Sandra Ely from Polished Pearl Author Services.

Content

Prologue

A wheel in the cog, the works of which were usually hidden from civilians, was all too ready to turn on its unsuspecting officers within its military machine and roll right over them.

Lieutenant Colonel Jonathon Valor entered the spacious room as he passed a number of armed guards. His eyes followed the red and gold carpet that ran the length of the corridor and was cut into the center of marble flooring that softened beneath his feet. Being somewhat unorthodox, he had stridden next to the carpet, alongside his commanding officer, Colonel Vance Parker. This distance from his military training was further enhanced by his boots that went from a rhythmic clicking to a muted stomp as he entered the room.

As the two men left the corridor, they were met with an ornately, yet stately space. The carpet was easily overshadowed by the massive marble columns and travertine inlaid walls that were decorated with statues and paintings. Furthermore, the sense of insignificance was cast upon the two as they were dwarfed by the scale of the ceilings that consisted of beautifully crafted stonework. The architecture rose to a pinnacle of more than fifty feet, at which an immense dome eclipsed the men below.

Colonel Parker stopped before a large mahogany desk. It, like the room, was at a scale that was larger than necessary in a practical sense. However, it did convey a sense of importance. It was a dated piece, probably a thousand years old, yet it shined, highlighted by the accents of light that danced across the hand-crafted wood details that enveloped it. Jonathon Valor came to a halt at Parker's immediate left. The two faced the desk in a uniform military stance and waited for someone.

Parker made sure that he took a moment to carefully instruct his inferior officer to behave and to look sharp. He also reminded Valor about a few of his last embarrassments and that he should be careful not to make the same mistakes here. This meeting was as important as it got. Parker didn't want any screw ups.

Valor asked, "Have I ever let you down?" Then, he smiled.

"Too many times, Valor. I hope this meeting isn't another assignment for you and your Troublemakers."

Valor chuckled under his breath. "Don't worry. I will only respond to questions directly. I have done this more than I care to remember, Colonel."

"As have I."

The conversation was cut short by the appearance of the Commander in Chief of the Armed Forces. This title and responsibilities were those of Orson Korgue. He had gained them by election of humanity within the star cluster known as Hyades. More than thirty planets had given their votes to pronounce him as such. He easily won because of the blunderings of the past Commander in Chief.

Korgue closed the door behind him and turned to face the two officers that were waiting. He returned their salutes in kind and instructed them to be at ease.

All three sat down at the impressive desk' Korgue sat at one side, and the officers on the other.

Korgue shuffled some papers and cleared some things from his desk. He casually pushed a button on his desk and asked for java from the feminine voice on the other side of the call. He thanked her after she brought a cup of hot java, complete with cream and sugar. All the while, he didn't make eye contact with the officers. He knew that they would wait for him at his convenience. He almost seemed careless in the amount of time he took, dismissing the importance of the individuals that sat before him. They were simply rank and file beneath him, regardless of how friendly their past interactions were. Yes, they would simply wait.

Valor took note of Korgue's actions. He thought that Korgue was somewhat pompous in his deliberate disregard for others. He had seen this before. Furthermore, he noticed that Korgue was not as clean cut as he was accustomed to seeing. His attire was that of a king, however- not the dress of an elected official. His mustache and beard were considerably longer than Valor had seen since their last meeting. Valor thought that he just didn't fit the look of a prototypical politician.

After a while of shifting things around and taking loud slurps of java, the leader of humanity addressed his subordinate, "Colonel."

"Sir?"

"I want you to organize a mission. I want the Troublemakers to sort out some things in the Plenna System. I think we may have pirates, or aliens, or gods knows what out there. Carboncrete production is down forty-seven percent."

"Yes, sir?"

"One moment Colonel." Korgue flipped through some pages and began reading one in particular. After a minute or so, he continued with, "No collateral damage this time, Colonel."

"Sir, with all due respect, maybe the Troublemakers shouldn't go on a mission like this."

Korgue's tone put Parker in his place. "With all due respect, Colonel, this is exactly the kind of mission the Troublemakers were primed for. I haven't even told you the details of the mission yet and you are opposed?"

"Yes, sir. They seem to have side effects that might hinder the mission."

Jonathon's ears perked up. He was waiting for the colonel to say something derogatory about him or his men. None of them asked for what happened. None of them wanted to be used for the gains of their people. It was forced upon them. No, Jonathon would be damned if his idiot colonel would badmouth any of them.

Korgue raised an eyebrow. "What side effects?"

"Well, take Leroy Hardy for instance. The guy seems too trigger happy if you ask me. And Harry Starke has all kinds of flashbacks and blackouts."

Jonathon Valor leaned forward in his seat, ready to pounce.

Parker went on with the reasons why he claimed that he didn't want the Troublemakers to go on this mission. He continued, "And those are the semi-competent ones. Lieutenant Colonel Valor has almost no control of these two. He has no control over Rabbit Harrison. That guy is a menace to all. He is a loose cannon who listens to nobody. I wouldn't even let him do garbage detail."

"Excuse me, Colonel! You are out of line," Valor exclaimed in defense of his men.

Parker stood up and challenged Valor. "You watch your mouth, Lieutenant Colonel, or I'll bust you and have you thrown in the brig."

Valor shut his mouth for a second. But, soon, he turned to Korgue and questioned, "May I speak candidly, sir?"

Korgue responded with a question of his own in a bit of a smile. "You don't agree with the Colonel?"

Valor didn't hesitate in his reply. "No, sir, I don't."

"Why is that?"

"I believe his facts are incorrect and skewed by his want to exact revenge against me and my men."

Korgue explained the quandary that Valor was potentially putting himself in. "I will allow you to be candid, Lieutenant Colonel, but you are treading on very thin ice. Be careful."

Parker attempted to intervene with, "But Mister President."

Korgue waived his hand to quiet Parker. "Let him speak."

Parker sat back down, obviously displeased with Korgue's decision to allow Valor the opportunity to give a piece of his mind.

Valor began, "Mister President, Colonel Parker doesn't like me or my men. It isn't our professionalism, or lack thereof, as he suggests as the real reason he doesn't want us to take this mission."

Korgue leaned forward, "I'm listening."

Valor went on, "First of all, I must defend my men, not because they are my men, but because their heroic actions warrant it. I'm not sure about what the colonel is referring to when he mentions blackouts and being trigger happy. These men have never faltered when it counted. And I, for one, appreciate soldiers who will fire their weapons under the most difficult circumstances. Also, I have a great working relationship with my men. My style of leadership doesn't appeal to the colonel and I am just fine with that. We get the job done."

Valor explained his plight further. "But, when the Colonel bashes Rabbit Harrison, I have a real problem with it. He may be the best soldier, the best pilot, and the smartest guy I have ever known. He has my back and I have his. He listens to me. He isn't a loose cannon."

Korgue sat back in his chair. He nodded as he thought for a moment and turned his eyes from Valor to Parker. "Colonel, your thoughts please?"

"I'm sorry, Mister President. I simply disagree. Rabbit Harrison alone is a detriment to humanity."

Valor stood up. "He is a good soldier and you know it, Colonel."

"I know no such thing. He has been cited a dozen or more times for disciplinary actions."

"Yes, by you, Colonel."

Parker stood up and faced his accuser. "What are you trying to say, Lieutenant Colonel? That I have an ax to grind?"

Valor looked at Korgue. "I'm glad he said it."

Parker took a step forward until he and Valor were eye to eye. "That's it, soldier, I am busting you and you will be demoted."

Korgue intervened with, "Not so fast, Colonel. I want to hear why you might have an ax to grind. I find it rather odd that you would use that terminology." Then, he directed Valor to continue.

Valor did. "We have a long history together. It goes back some time and there have been some run-ins between our troops. My men had gotten credit that they deserved, but the colonel felt that he was the deserving officer. At least, that's how it started."

Parker disagreed. "You take too much pride in your pathetic little group. The amount they contributed to that invasion was minimal."

"But, see? You do have a problem with me and my men getting the accolades we did."

"Lieutenant Colonel, although I think your little group shouldn't have been praised, that is hardly any reason for me to make an attempt to stop a mission like this."

"I agree. But there is more...Like the rumors that Rabbit Harrison slept with your daughter."

"I am aware of the alleged rumors. Do you have anything of substance?"

"Well, if it was me, and a young, good-looking guy that I didn't like was potentially screwing my daughter, I'd be pissed."

Parker was getting visibly irritated at this point. "The man is an animal. He is the reason General Amadas is dead. He broke tradition and rank. He decimated that whole planet."

"There is some truth to that. Actually, General Amadas had taken it upon himself to attempt the construction of a super army. I was there. I was a victim, as was my little group and fifty-eight other humans that were tested on. Plus, how many thousands of orcs, Colonel?"

Now Parker was infuriated. "General Amadas was my commander. He was the best in the galaxy. Rabbit Harrison killed him. He also killed an entire division of my men. He should have been hanged."

"But he wasn't. He was acquitted of all charges. That was it, Colonel. That's why you have an ax to grind, isn't it? Rabbit Harrison killed General Amadas, your personal friend."

Parker was seething. His cheeks were flushed, and his eyes were fiery. "I change my mind, Mister President. Please, send these Troublemakers to the Plenna System. Isn't it right next to Cypra?"

Korgue appeared puzzled by the sudden change in his colonel's decision. "It is."

"Good. Orcs are on those planets. Since the Troublemakers' debacle on Cypra, they are hated by orcs and their fellow human soldiers. This should be interesting." Parker looked at Valor and sneered.

Valor spoke up. "Troublemakers are up to the task, Mister President."

Korgue was satisfied. "Then, it is done."

Parker added, "No screw-ups this time, Valor. You have no room for error. I bet your Troublemakers are out partying as usual."

Valor stood at attention. "No, sir. If I know my men, they are fast asleep and ready for duty."

One
Call to Duty

"This round's on me!" Harry Starke's announcement was music to the drunks' ears, and accordingly, the room erupted in cheers. Harry smiled and raised his glass. He left his seat in the corner and got to his feet. He stumbled toward the bar to get another set of drinks for his mates.

Compared to his mates, he wasn't as good looking or as muscled. But he knew how to have a good time and he always gave to his friends. He was probably considered the nicest one in the bunch overall. He had a kind of "boy next door" charm about him.

Harry stopped at the jukebox. It was here that Rabbit Harrison was leaning on the machine while chatting up two attractive women. Harry found himself leaning as well. This way he was able to listen to Rabbit's tales without falling over. He heard much the same as what he usually heard.

One of the women, a brunette, asked, "Really? You want to take both of us to bed?"

Rabbit didn't hesitate. "Of course. How could I not want to be with the most beautiful women I have seen tonight?"

The brunette laughed. "You're drunk."

"Well, a little. But it hasn't changed my eyesight or my innate sense for beauty and art."

The brunette smiled and said, "You are too cute."

Harry laughed.

Rabbit turned to see his more than intoxicated friend standing behind him. He wasn't sure what the laugh meant. It didn't matter. His concern for Harry caused his curiosity to peak. "You okay, Harry?"

"Yeah, I'm good."

"Oh, okay. You made a funny noise. I was just checking."

Harry nodded and responded, "Yeah, man, I'm good. I just laughed."

Rabbit was waiting to hear the joke. He instinctively smiled. "And?"

"Well, these women *are* beautiful."

The women both smiled and approached Harry as they said, "Thank you."

Harry replied, "You're welcome," followed by a slight burp. He straightened himself up and continued. "It's just that it reminded me of those robot chicks you picked up on Steller1. Remember?"

The women turned their heads to Rabbit to hear his response. They weren't satisfied with his answer of, "Yeah, I remember."

The blonde asked Harry, "What robot chicks?"

Harry was slurring and spitting all over himself, even through the wet cigar that seemed permanently lodged in the corner of his mouth. He didn't mean to throw Rabbit under the bus. He was simply too inebriated to know that he might be causing irreparable damage. "Oh, the girls that were robots. Or they were sort of robots."

The brunette got involved. She had actually thought about having sex with this Rabbit guy. "Did these girls have bionic limbs or something?"

Rabbit closed his eyes and shook his head in a "no" motion.

Harry laughed. He explained that Rabbit was so drunk that night on Steller1, that he took a group of cyborgs to bed. He went on to explain that Rabbit had ripped one of their arms off by accident during sex.

The two women turned and just stared at Rabbit.

Rabbit smiled. "Well, she was a prototype. I guess she wasn't built as well as I had hoped. Tell ya what...I wouldn't have her as a maid to vacuum my place. Damn straight." He downed his drink and winked.

The brunette now had a "what the hell?" look on her face. She didn't know what to say. She finally asked, "You fucked a cyborg?"

Rabbit explained, "No, a handful of them. That one was just defective or something."

The blonde laughed. "Oh my gods!"

The brunette laughed, too. "You aren't serious."

Rabbit corrected her with, "No, I'm sincere. And yes, I fucked them. There was a pause due to disbelief. Finally, Rabbit exclaimed, "They were hot!"

All four of them were in stitches for a couple of minutes. The blonde kept making computer and buzzing noises. The brunette fought to get out the words, "What did you do when her freakin' arm came off?"

Rabbit muttered something to the effect of, "It tasted just like chicken."

Harry was showering everyone with shlogger from his mug and shlogger from his mouth. Finally, he excused himself and made it to the bar. He had a duty to fill a few pitchers with shlogger and to do a round of shots. He wouldn't disappoint.

Rabbit talked to his new female friends as if nothing was wrong. His chiseled, boyish features complete with piercing, baby blue eyes that sat beneath a wonderful flock of golden hair, gave him some confidence. His lean, muscled body that sported six-pack abs didn't hurt either. It was really his countless, intimate experiences with women that gave him his true confidence. He had a world of experience in that category. Actually, more accurately, he had worlds of experience.

The blonde, still giddy and not as bright as her brunette counterpart, was still caught up in laughter. She blurted out, "You haven't had sex with guys, have you?"

Rabbit smiled. "Not intentionally."

The women were laughing. They couldn't believe what they were hearing. Rabbit was either totally lying, or he was brutally honest. Maybe he was something in between. Either way, the women were intrigued. The brunette asked, "Not intentionally? What does that mean?"

"Well, Harry and I have sort of crossed swords a few times. You know, while we were being taken care of by women."

At this time, a red-headed bombshell walked through the front door and waved to the women that Rabbit was talking with. She came over and introduced herself as Marla. The brunette introduced her to Rabbit, and soon, she was laughing hysterically, too.

After a few minutes, Rabbit and the three women left for a night of pleasure.

Harry had made his way back to the corner booth where he found Leroy Hardy. Leroy had been drinking for the last few hours, like the rest of his mates. He wasn't into shlogger like the other guys though. He liked the hard stuff. This usually seemed to exacerbate the chip on his shoulder that he carried around with him, but tonight, he was happy. He was going to call his family in a bit. It was a long time since he spoke with them last. He felt good. That is, he felt good until some Marines came to the booth looking for trouble.

Seven Marines from Alpha Company had heard that the Troublemakers were back in town. If the rumors were true, then the marines hoped to find them in one of the local bars. After three bars and twice as many drinks, Alpha Company found what they were looking for. The anxious men spread out around the booth.

Harry was plastered and was in no shape to fight. After sitting down, he had gone through another pitcher of shlogger. He had lost count after the first three. Then, he went through a few rounds of shots at the bar. He couldn't even stand at this point, but he still clung to the soaking cigar that wasn't much more than a stump in his mouth.

One of the Marines tapped Leroy on the shoulder. "Hey."

Leroy looked straight ahead. He was still thinking about his family. He was drunk, too, and his brain didn't allow him to turn his head at the moment. He just asked, "What's up?" He downed another drink and yawned.

The Marines were laughing at these two Troublemakers. They were nothing more than lousy drunks. There was nothing special about them, certainly nothing menacing.

The Marine spoke again. "Where's Rabbit Harrison?"

This time, Leroy looked up. "Who's askin'?"

"I'm Sergeant Dutchstag. Where iz he?"

Leroy struggled with the sergeant's name. At least, he appeared to. "Douche, douche, wait…douche what?"

The sergeant affirmed his name as, "Dutchstag, like ze mountainz."

"Oh. Well, Douche Bag, I don't know where Rabbit is."

Patrons seated at nearby booths and tables laughed. This began to anger the sergeant and his men. They quieted down when a few of the Marines walked around the patrons to show their dismay and to display their power.

The sergeant put his hand on Leroy's shoulder. Unlike how he tapped Leroy the first time, he held it there as he leaned on him a bit. "I don't sink you heard me correctly. My name iz Sergeant Dutchstag and I am looking for Rabbit Harrison."

Leroy calmly stated, "I heard you the first time. Like a mountain of douche bags and I don't know where Rabbit is. Sit down and have a drink, dude or fuck off."

Immediately, the sergeant began to throw hard punches to Leroy's face. Harry's face was an instant target, too, even while he slept. The other six Marines poured into the corner. The space was tight. Still, the two Troublemakers were taking a beating.

Leroy pulled his right arm from two Marines, who were holding it from behind. He punched the sergeant in the face. It was only a glancing blow, but enough to knock the man back a few feet and onto the floor.

Then, Leroy broke free his left arm from one Marine and flipped another over the booth and the table. The Marine flew through the window and landed heavily on the sidewalk outside.

Leroy desperately attempted to stand several times as his feet tried to escape the confines that kept him close to a sitting position in the booth. He couldn't fight while his legs were stuck under the table that restricted his motion. So, he fought to clear the booth and finally succeeded. One Marine took a jaw breaking shot to his face. Another felt the cracking of broken ribs.

The marines that were assailing Harry got worse. Leroy unloaded on them. This was payback for their attacks on Harry's limp, drunken body. Leroy pulverized two of their faces. He wasn't done either, not by a long shot, but he was stopped in his tracks by an order from his commanding officer.

"That's enough, Lieutenant," rang out from Jonathon Valor's mouth.

Leroy straightened up and wiped his bloody nose. "Yes, sir."

"Don't give me this 'sir' shit. Come on, Leroy. I left you guys alone for three hours. Three hours. What the hell happened to Harry? How did he get so messed up?"

"Drunk, Jon. They beat him while he was like asleep. He didn't fight back."

Jonathon Valor lowered his tone as he glanced around the room. "Okay, what happened?"

Leroy looked around and found the sergeant sitting on the floor. "Well, Sergeant Douche Bag over here" …Leroy was cut off.

"It iz Sergeant Dutchstag."

Leroy continued, "Yeah, Douche Bag, like I said. Him and his guys were looking for Rabbit. I didn't know where he was. So, they started hitting us."

The sergeant snarled at Leroy.

Jonathon begrudgingly smiled. "Is that the best story I'm gonna get from you?"

Leroy half-grinned. "If I wasn't so drunk, I could give you a better one. It would include fairies and unicorns."

Jonathon helped the sergeant to his feet. "Is that about right?"

The sergeant rebutted, "Not exactly."

"Okay, so you guys came in here looking for Rabbit Harrison. You weren't getting anywhere with my smart-ass lieutenant, so you started a fight. Is that closer to what happened?"

The sergeant was silent.

"I'll take your silence as an admission of guilt. I outrank you. Get your men out of here, now."

The sergeant stood up straight and answered, "Yes, sir." Then, he and Jonathon helped his broken Marines out the door. Jonathon coaxed him to fork over a few hundred bucks for the broken window and the Marines were on their way.

Jonathon came back to the booth. Leroy was sitting next to Harry, as opposed to across from him, like before. Whereas Leroy looked like he was in a fight, Harry looked like he had been in a war. He had gashes over each eyebrow, his nose was bloody and swollen, and he was missing some teeth in the front. The nub of a cigar clung to his bloody lip. He was either sleeping or unconscious.

Jon asked, "You think we need to take him to the hospital?"

Leroy replied, "I don't think so. It happened pretty fast. So, I don't think he was hit that many times. And they only hit him with their fists."

"Okay, but any brain damage is on you."

Leroy retorted, "If I had a dime for every time somebody told me that..."

Jon laughed. "So, where is Rabbit?"

"No. I really don't know. He was talking to some chicks over there before."

"Well, it's just after three now. We can give him a few hours, I guess. He's probably upstairs, getting laid."

Leroy grinned. "Probably?"

Jon agreed, "Yeah, right? Anyway, we have a new mission in the Plenna system. What do you know about it?"

"Seriously?"

"Yes, seriously. Why? What's wrong with Plenna?"

Leroy scratched his head. "Aren't there settlements of orcs out there?"

"Yeah, but we have dealt with orcs before."

"Not these orcs." Leroy sighed.

Jon was puzzled. "Damn, Leroy, orcs are orcs." He nervously laughed.

"No, not from what I have heard. The ones in Plenna are the big, nasty ones. And some of them are real smart, too. They are like the ones on Cypra. Plus, orcs hate us anyway. They hate us as humans, because we tested on them on Cypra. They really hate the Troublemakers, because Rabbit nuked their whole fucking planet. Cypra is the closest system to Plenna. You do the math."

"Well, math isn't my strongest suit."

Harry mumbled, "Kevlar makes for a pretty strong suit." Then, he drifted back to sleep. Jon and Leroy laughed as they shook their heads.

***

"In the vastness of space, many ships have been lost. Most have disappeared, never to have been seen again; for space is harsh and unforgiving. Without technology to move through it and to shield travelers from its many dangers, hopping from star to star would be impossible. But now, Crystal Technologies

Incorporated has engineered a way to double the distances that we can travel."

These words were being spoken by the renowned scientist, Adolph Gruber. He stood at a podium before world governors, CEOs of major companies, and other scientists. The room broke into applause.

"Furthermore, Crystal Technologies Incorporated has found ways to enhance the human mind. No longer will we have to depend solely on mystics to channel their psychic powers for interstellar travel. Now, people without the extreme abilities of mystics can power our wormhole actuators. This is the breakthrough of our time!"

The crowd got to its feet in an even more thunderous applause than before.

When the noise began to drop, Gruber spoke, "And now, I give you a man who found the funding for these projects that I have been working on." He whispered into the microphone and continued with, "Because without him, I wouldn't have a job."

There was some laughter and clapping in the room.

"It is my pleasure to introduce my boss, the Chief Executive Officer, and majority shareholder of Crystal Technologies Incorporated, Arthur Krump."

Krump walked to the podium and shook his lead scientist's hand before the accepting crowd of seven hundred plus. He waved his hands to them. "Thank you. Thank you. No, please. Thank you." He began in earnest after several minutes of fanfare.

"Without the likes of Adolph Gruber and his fellow scientists, none of this would have been possible."

***

Rabbit was sitting at a computer console aboard the *Outcast* at the other end of the room from where Harry sat. He had just sat down after piloting his ship out of the atmosphere and hooking up with the *Outcast*. Now, his and Leroy's fighters were attached to the bigger vessel. While Jonathon and Leroy piloted up front, Rabbit and Harry caught up on some stuff here.

Rabbit asked his mate, "Harry, you see this Gruber guy?"

"Um, Gruber? No."

"He just talked about some pretty radical breakthroughs."

"Really? No. Hey, what are the two dominant species on the planet called Gorinth?"

Rabbit answered, "Tolkienz and Harem."

"Which ones are the little fuzzy guys?"

"The Harem. What the hell are you doing?"

Harry looked over his shoulder in disgust. "Doing my freakin' rank tests. I build bombs and work with explosives. Why do I even have to know this shit?"

"I know, buddy. It isn't like any of it matters when you are shooting 'em."

"Right? Okay, so...Tolkienz are little orcs then?"

"Yeah." Rabbit switched his screen from the Crystal Technologies conference to his social networking site. He began to respond to some of the women he had recently been intimate with. Some that responded to him had sent naked pictures of themselves to his site.

Leroy entered from the bridge and walked up behind Rabbit. "Didn't you get enough of that stuff last night?"

Rabbit smiled. "Is it ever really enough?" After he chuckled, he went on, "These are old flings. Some are friends with benefits. This is good, actually. I can see which ones are in any of the systems we are traveling to. So, if we have free time, well, you know."

"Yeah. Live up to that name, Rabbit." Leroy began heading toward Harry.

"Leroy".

Leroy rubbed his face and shifted his head to crack his neck. It popped in gradual steps from bottom to top, each vertebra's trappings freeing a little knot that grabbed at him. "Yeah?"

"Did you get to call your family last night?"

"No."

Rabbit gritted his teeth and sighed. "Sorry, man."

"No worries, dude. I busted some Marine heads though."

While Rabbit went back to his correspondence, Leroy came up behind Harry. Leroy remarked, "Those gods awful tests?"

Harry responded, "I hate 'em. A complete waste of time. Where the hell is the moon of Tarnice?"

Leroy laughed.

Jonathon entered the room. He saw his three men. Two were sitting and one was standing. They were all wearing some derivative of what *were* military uniforms, but none were completely to code. He thought for a moment that perhaps Colonel Parker was right. Maybe he had no control of his men, but the more he thought about it, the more he realized that he simply didn't care about such insignificant things. They were still warriors and damn good ones, too.

Still, as he passed behind Rabbit, he took note of Rabbit's computer monitor which displayed a number of naked women. Rabbit was typing away while wearing his gray army utility pants, drab green tee shirt, and combat boots. Although in slightly mismatched clothes, he also wore chains around his neck and wrists. His ears were pierced, and his hair wasn't military cut. He was obviously unshaven from the last few days. Jon jeered, "I see you are perfecting your correspondence skills while getting them to undress, too. Nice job, soldier."

"Thanks, Jon."

As Jon walked toward Leroy, he saw that Harry was taking his required tests. He observed Harry's side profile, which gave view of a disheveled man in a light gray warcoat that hung loosely over a tightly-worn, buttoned-down fatigues shirt. Harry was fairly well-built, although not as lean and cut as Rabbit, nor was he as bulky as Leroy. He sported a bit of a shlogger gut that was somewhat hidden by his wrinkled clothes. Harry sat with his boots off. This displayed different colored socks; one of which had a hole that a big toe had found its way through. Lastly, he sucked on a half-smoked cigar. The damn thing wasn't even lit. Jon thought for a moment and decided that he almost never saw it lit. Then, he chuckled to himself as he found it hard to understand how a shirt that was so small on Harry's body could still be wrinkled. This somehow defied the laws of physics, or physical properties, or something.

Leroy saw his commander walking toward him. "Hey, Boss."

Jon gave a quick nod and glanced at Leroy's thick, muscular arms that were crossed. They were easily visible as they bulged beyond the cut of his guinea tee. His face wasn't cleanly shaven, but trimmed to outline a goatee with connecting sideburns that formed a nontraditional "chinstrap" facial feature. Other than this, he seemed to adhere to military policy; at least as far as dress wear was concerned.

Jon stopped his mind from sizing up his team and got to work. "Okay, guys. We have four and a half days till we get to the first wormhole. I calculated three jumps to Plenna. So, the trip will take around a month. Rabbit, what do you think your prison orc friend might know about Plenna?"

"Hmm. I don't know. But we can find out."

"Cool. Then, let's do this; we will stop for that and at each station or actuator to refuel, get supplies, or whatever. Any questions?"

Harry looked up from his monitor and exclaimed, "Yes! What is the density ratio from carboncrete to graphene?"

Two
Orcs

Leroy didn't mind that the prison was dark and cold. He didn't mind it nearly as much as the call he was going to make to his family. They had been somewhat estranged over the last year. Leroy had initiated some small talk, but mostly kept busy with the military to avoid contact that inevitably led to uncomfortable conversation. He decided to bite the bullet and call home. It wasn't all bad. He loved his family and wanted to check in. The time that it took the transmission to travel millions of miles gave him a few seconds to think about what he would say.

"Hello?"

Leroy instantly recognized the voice. It was that of his brother. "Hi, Lenny; how are you?"

Lenny sounded surprised, but happy. "Hey, Leroy; what's going on? How are you?"

Leroy sighed quietly as he slightly backed his mouth away from the mouth piece of the phone. Then, he stated confidently, "I'm okay. How's everyone doin'?"

"Good, good. Well, you know. I'm able to stay home for a few more months on my partial pension. So, I have some time to work on some battleship models." Lenny nervously laughed.

Leroy wondered if Lenny was embarrassed to be putting together plastic toys like one might perceive a child to do. Leroy didn't care about such things.

Besides, he wished that he could be home doing the same thing. He briefly thought about the models they had worked on together as teenagers. They had played simulated tabletop war games, too, among other things. Leroy missed those things. Finally, he said, "That's good. It's better than flying the damn things into battle, huh?"

Lenny acknowledged, "Yeah, no kidding. Lou's legs are still all messed up."

"Awe, that sucks. When do you think he will be cleared to command again?"

"I don't know. He's doing pretty good. He still has some pain, but I see him doing stuff around the house now. He's getting better."

Leroy was picturing Lou, his oldest brother as Lenny spoke. While he saw Lenny as fun-loving, he depicted Lou as being more complicated; a bit solitary or distant. He was intelligent and cunning; still fun to be around, but different. Whereas Lenny was just older than Leroy, Lou was over five years his senior. Leroy quickly dismissed any distance between them as being more related to the age difference than what he briefly tossed around as character traits. He always looked up to Lou, even now after adulthood smeared the gap of their five-year difference into something that felt more common. Any distance now, he reckoned, was due to his own issues.

Leroy's mind settled upon his youngest brother. "Any word from Larry?"

Lenny kept the conversation upbeat. "Not really. I mean, he checks in like you. He's doing good from what I hear. He's supposed to get his own command soon, too."

"Wow, that's quick. He's only been in the academy for three years or so. Good. That's good. Tell him I said hello when you talk to him again."

"I will. So, what's up with you?"

Leroy admitted, "Well, I just shipped out."

"You got the *Renegade* back?"

"No, no, no, no. I'm with the Troublemakers. Checking out some lost production in the Plenna System; probably nothing."

"Yeah? So, why are they sending you guys, then? Why a team of specialists?"

"That's a good question. I don't know what we will find." Leroy wanted to get off the phone for two reasons. The first was that he wanted to see how Rabbit was doing with the orc prisoner. The second, and most important, was that he was extremely uncomfortable with himself. He was crawling out of his own skin. He hated himself; he hated his appearance. He didn't want it to come up in conversation. He just wanted to see how everyone was, so he could get off the phone. He made his final attempt with, "So how's Mambi?"

Ah, Mambi…His loving mother and head of the family. She was so kind and so loving. Like a true matriarch, she was the glue that kept her boys honest. But Leroy couldn't help the fact that her look of shock was overwhelming when they last saw each other. It was a memory that haunted him over the last year.

Lenny was more than happy to chat. It seemed that all of Leroy's preconceived notions about his family may have been concocted out of his own imagination. Nobody cared about Leroy's appearance. It was weird, certainly…but not the kind of thing that should tear a family apart. He figured he would answer and then, he'd ask the inevitable question. "She's good, Leroy. We are all good. But how are you?"

Leroy abruptly said, "Good, man. Well, you know…it's different being part of a crew, especially when I'm back in a fighter again. I kind of miss having my own crew, but since Cypra, I'm not sure I'm fit to lead again."

Lenny joked, "It's like riding a bike. You could do it."

"I don't know if I'm up to it emotionally. Things have been different for me. It's hard to explain and I got a lot going on right now. Maybe some other time." Then, he sounded rushed, so Lenny might think that he was speaking the truth. "Hey, that's for me. Gotta go. Send everyone my love."

"Okay. Good to hear from you. Call again, any time."

***

Leroy sat down with Jon and Harry at a small wooden table. He could view an orc through a large glass window on the other side of the table. Beyond that were the bars that kept the orc contained. Leroy, like the other two noticed the dark block walls and rusted bars. Their eyes took in the view of the orc's confined area as their brains determined its minuscule size. "Did I miss anything?"

Jon shook his head. He leaned forward and put his elbows on the metal table in front of him.

Harry spoke in garbled English as he fought to enunciate with a soggy cigar and a wad of gum in his mouth.

Leroy couldn't believe that someone would do both at the same time. "Who the hell smokes and chews gum at the same time?"

Harry looked indignant. "I'm not smoking, stupid. I'm just holding it in my mouth."

Leroy was tempted to explain that he had something that Harry could hold in his mouth, but he stopped himself when he saw Rabbit come into view.

Harry retorted, "Anyway, I said that the orc looks a lot bigger and stronger than Rabbit."

Jon commanded, "Sh, sh."

The orc sprang from his tiny cot and threw his own body against the bars as hard as he could. The sound of the crash was colossal. He didn't stop there. He screamed at the top of his lungs and continued to slam his trunk against the bars as his hands reached through. His arms flailed violently as they sought to rip Rabbit apart. But this was all for naught.

Rabbit, on the other side of the bars, had just strolled down the poorly lit corridor. He came to rest upon a squeaky, wooden chair that sat across from the vicious orc in the narrow hallway. After sitting, he put his feet up on some crates and rocked back and forth. He put his hands behind his head and locked his fingers as he displayed his small balancing feat.

The orc was not impressed. He was too busy fighting against the laws of physics, reality, and common sense. He smashed and smashed. He screamed and screamed. His mouth found its way around a bar as he bit down as hard as he could. It was a mighty, but feeble attempt to free himself from the cell that held him.

Jon commented, "He's a determined fucker, isn't he?"

Harry chuckled. "Yeah. They have no brains. They're all stupid."

Leroy grinned and rebutted, "No, not all of them."

***

Work was moving ahead at full bore. Yes, progress was made, but there were still problems. Flaws existed that could be disastrous, at least, hypothetically. All the kinks needed to be ironed out and quickly.

Crystal Technologies, Incorporated had released its plan to the masses. It was on a deadline to produce the fastest interstellar travel options ever. Delays could mean losing the necessary government contracts, and worse, all the tax benefits and incentives that such a scientific development company relied on to pad its pockets.

What would happen if the hypothetical questions became reality? What if lives were lost? What if massive corporations took heavy losses? Crystal Technologies could be bankrupted; forced into submission by class-action lawsuits. What if the unthinkable happened? What if the military, as opposed to civilian or commercial entities, experienced losses? Crystal Tech would be finished.

Still, the announcement at the Interstellar Conference was deemed necessary. By announcing the breakthroughs in both actuator technology and brain development, Crystal put itself at the forefront for future government considerations. The perception of its control in the industry was hoped to decimate any competition by showing its dominance in those fields.

Now, dominate it did. Not only did Crystal Technologies have a lead scientist with the most experience, but they had the laxest regulations when it came to their research. Crystal hid behind loopholes to conduct experiments that would be illegal under their proper designations. Furthermore, they took unnecessary risks when it came to testing. This, too, was hidden behind false premises.

Crystal Technologies, Incorporated was a monster, in more ways than one.

***

Rabbit tried to calm the orc that spewed saliva from his mouth as his hell-bent attempts to rid himself of the prison cell and Rabbit were unsuccessful. "Ucktock, c'mon."

The orc continued, unfettered in spirit only.

"We can do this all day, my friend."

Ucktock finally used words as he screamed bloody hell. "We not friends!"

"Sure, we are. I came to break you out."

These words seemed to further inflame the wild orc. "You not Ucktock friend! I killa you!"

Rabbit released his hands from behind his head, kicked the crates away from under his feet and leaned forward in his chair. He extended a hand with his palm face up. This didn't calm Ucktock. It instigated him further.

After a minute, Rabbit waved to an orderly that was waiting down the corridor. The orderly showed up with a cart that whined and whistled as its small, rusty wheels bound against the concrete floor. Rabbit removed a cloth that was covering its contents. A full, hot meal was revealed. Rabbit said again, "I'm your friend."

Ucktock didn't even hear him in his frenzy. Rabbit waved his arms over his head to get the orc's attention. Any closer and they may have been bitten off. Orcs, typically being of little thought and very aggressive, particularly picked up on sudden movements to defend themselves. Rabbit's movements worked just long enough for Ucktock to see the cart.

Rabbit tried again to reach the absent-minded monstrosity before him. "If we aren't friends, then why did I bring you food?"

Ucktock's nostrils flared. He stopped everything and began to sniff the air. He looked at the meal as it smoked. He saw the rare meat, the golden gravy, and the large container of Shlogger. His eyes went from the cart to Rabbit and then, back to the cart. "Dat fo' me?"

"Sure. I'm gonna break you out."

The orc tried to think. Normally, this prospect was difficult enough, but with the aroma of a wonderful meal further distracting his mind from its important functions, he struggled more. Finally, he said, "Wait one second. You try to break me out once befo'. We got caught."

"Yeah, but I was stupid. This time I thought our escape through." Rabbit winked to convey a sense of secrecy between him and Ucktock.

"No way! You are too squishy, too."

"I'm not squishy."

Ucktock didn't think that he was smarter than a human, but one thing was for certain. "Yep, humans are too squishy."

"Ut uh. I'm not squishy."

"Proves it den."

This was Rabbit's chance to finally show his strength instead of hiding it. Eighteen months of ducking the media and Marines that were gunning for him had built up frustration that he hid well. Now, he could check his own strength against a well-known quantity, an orc. Rabbit pulled a crate over to the bars and rested his right elbow on it. "Okay, I will. Let's arm wrestle."

Ucktock's eyes lit up. Not only could he flex his muscles and prove his own strength, but this was a favorite competition in Orcdom. Plus, he could rip the arm off this puny human. His smile showed a crooked row of sharp, gnarly teeth on the top. The bottom teeth were equally crooked and jagged, but two tusks protruded upward some four inches from the corners of his mouth. His smile stopped as concern gripped his face. "What if I rip you arm off?"

"Oh, it's okay."

Ucktock was satisfied. He had the approval he needed to show this human. It didn't matter what authority granted such a thing. In his mind, everything checked out. "Ok."

He eagerly placed his arm opposite Rabbit's. The two jostled their extremities for position. Ucktock was getting the sense that Rabbit might be a little stronger than he had first anticipated, for when he pushed his arm to gain the upper hand on the crate, he was met with fairly equal resistance. He quickly dismissed this thought though as he knew in his mind that humans were, indeed, squishy.

Rabbit asked, "You know how to count Ucktock?"

"Yep, I do."

"Okay, then. You count to three and we will start."

"Ok."

"If you win, you can probably rip my arm off."

***

The other Troublemakers looked at each other in disbelief. Jon said, "Maybe I should stop the idiot."

Leroy hesitated before stating, "He's pretty smart, Jon. He must know what he's doing. You think he will win?"

Jon disagreed, "I don't know. Orcs are real strong. I've faced them. Me and my guys sedated them first. Have you ever had an encounter with one?"

"No. I have heard that they are like apes; like, I don't know, three times stronger than a man; five, maybe ten, times stronger? I mean, I'm pretty big now and Ucktock's arms are bigger than my legs. He is a big son of a bitch. I guess, we will see."

"They are so strong," Jon began. He continued, "I once saw one rip a guy's leg off like it was nothing."

Leroy asked, "Did he eat it?"

"No. He started beating the guy with it."

"I hope Rabbit keeps his legs," Leroy half-joked.

Harry switched out his wet, disgusting stub of a cigar for a new one. He chuckled. "Light 'em if ya got 'em boys."

They continued to watch.

***

Rabbit began, "If I win, you rush with me to the ship and we will try to get those files that we couldn't get the last time. Deal?"

Ucktock smiled a devilish smile. "Deal!"

Rabbit finished the conversation before the orc's fun began. "Okay, big guy, you count to three. Then, we start. Cool?"

"Ok." Ucktock had to think about his numbers for a minute. He usually counted on his fingers and toes, but one hand was busy. He would have to improvise and so he did. After a brief pause he counted. "Wun, two, anda," he screamed, "free!"

The muscles in Ucktock's broad shoulders and back popped. They bulged into large bowling balls that were wrapped in green leather. His veins pulsated just beneath the surface of his skin. He snarled as his uneven teeth gritted. He bore down to use his immense power.

Rabbit was puny compared to the orc. His muscles were long and lean. They lacked the mass and bulk of the orc, but they tensed and tightened to hold back the orc's strength. They held while the two made very little movement in either direction for almost a minute.

What was thought to be true about orcs *was* for the most part. They were much stronger than humans. In essence, humans were comparatively "squishy." Humans were taller. Actually, if orcs stood at their full height, they would be as tall as, if not taller than, humans. But their posture caused their heads to appear attached to their chests. They hunched with their long, massive arms barely scraping the ground as they walked. Their arms and legs were pretty close to each other in length. They were tightly packed animals with immense strength and power. They needed these advantages to compensate for their relatively inferior brains.

Rabbit was struggling with his larger foe. His brows were furrowed, and they began to bead up with sweat. Still, he held his own. "Not so squishy, huh?"

"I shocked, Rabbit. You do goods." Ucktock was happy to be in any kind of competition. His cell was the same thing day in and day out. Even if he lost, which he was pretty sure he wouldn't, things weren't all bad. He was intelligent enough to know that if he lost, he would attempt to escape this Hell hole. No, it wasn't that bad. But now, it was time to beat the human and collect an arm as a prize. Ucktock turned his body and grabbed the bars of the cell with his left hand. This gave him a decided boost of strength from using leverage.

Rabbit complained, "Not fair," as he began to lose some ground. "You big, ugly, cheating bastard!"

Ucktock smiled. "Tanks!" He was rarely complimented so thoroughly.

Rabbit turned his body as well. But before his right arm could be pushed down to the crate, he unloaded on Ucktock. He threw a hard, left jab that slipped between the bars and landed against the orc's jaw. Ucktock was stunned enough to loosen his grip on Rabbit's right hand. Rabbit quickly forced Ucktock's right hand to the crate. "I win!"

Ucktock was not happy. "You cheated! You no win. Dat not fair!"

"Hey, you cheated first."

"You no win. Gimme you arm so I can rip it off."

"Nope."

"Gimme."

Again, "Nope."

This time Ucktock screamed at the top of his lungs, "Gimme you arm, so I can rip it off!"

Rabbit was unaffected. "No. You lost."

"You a big, stupid cheater!"

This time, Rabbit replied, "Thanks."

"I mean you lil, squishy bastid."

"Yeah, whatever. You wanna get out of here or not?"

"Yep, but I gotta punch you in da face, too."

Rabbit wasn't so sure about this proposition. The ladies liked his face. He wasn't sure how his own strength compared to his being able to take such a powerful punch. Either way, it was going to hurt like Hell. Then, something occurred to Rabbit. Ucktock's arms were too thick to fit through the bars. He would have to be freed first. This might present a problem if Rabbit was knocked unconscious. By the time the other troublemakers came to the aid, Ucktock might be in his ship and out to space.

After some thought, Rabbit asked for insurance from Ucktock. "If I let you out, you can punch me."

Ucktock smiled.

"Just once, and you won't try to escape if you mess me up?"

Ucktock stopped smiling. He was confused. "Aren't we gonna both escape?"

"Yes, that's the plan. So, you won't try to escape alone?"

"Nope."

"Okay, my friend. I'm gonna trust you, then. Oh, don't hit me in the nose though. Hit me in the jaw like I did to you." Somehow, with superior brain and all, the human was as satisfied with the orc's assurance, as was the reverse.

***

Jon argued with the air around him. "Are you fucking kidding me?"

Leroy had to admit, "Maybe he isn't so smart."

Harry said, "He did beat him arm wrestling, though." He smiled.

Jon and Leroy both replied in unison, "He cheated!"

Harry made an obvious statement, "Well, he seems just as strong as the orc. How bad can an orc punch be?"

***

Rabbit flew fifteen feet. His back and shoulders smashed the concrete block wall behind him. The impact of his body left an imprint of his squishy body in an almost perfect outline. The light green tile had cracked and fallen in small pieces, leaving exposed concrete and structural rebar in its wake. Rabbit slumped to the floor. When he looked up, Ucktock was standing over him.

Ucktock whispered, "You ok?" He was fighting back laughter.

"Yeah, I'm fucking perfect. You just caved in my head. How do I look?" Rabbit rubbed the back of his head and turned to see the damaged wall behind him. He looked down at the blood in his hand from whatever wound he sustained to the rear of his noggin.

Ucktock puffed out his bottom lip as he checked over the little human. Overall, he nodded to himself that Rabbit looked okay...Well, for the most part. He explained, "Well da side a you head is like two times bigga dan it should be. Oh, anda you ears be bleedin'."

Rabbit thought to himself, *Not good*. These were sure signs of head trauma. He got into a slouched sitting position and leaned back against the crumbling wall. He closed his eyes and hoped to get rid of the awful pain between his ears. He opened his mouth wide, held his hands on each side of it, and popped his jaw. After a jolt of pain gripped him, he found some comfort. His jaw had been dislocated. His head wasn't all that swollen either. His misshapen jaw was unhinged to the side. He still had some blood in his ears, but his vision was clear, and he hadn't lost consciousness. He urged Ucktock to enjoy some of the food that was brought while he sat there and hoped to feel better.

Jon, Leroy, and Harry were making their way down a corridor that ran perpendicular to the one where Ucktock's cell was located. Upon seeing them, Rabbit waved them off. Luckily, Ucktock hadn't seen them as they were around the corner and out of his view.

Rabbit spoke so Ucktock thought that he was being spoken to, although in truth, he did so to alleviate his team's concerns. He was loud and clear. "I'm feeling a little better, Ucktock." With that, Rabbit stood up and dusted himself off. He nodded to his team to reassure them that he was fine.

The Troublemakers removed themselves as fast as they could and ended up ducking into the security room. There, they found the prison warden and some security officers. Monitors were at various locations. On them were live action pictures of locations in and around the prison. One was located in the corridor just outside where Rabbit had been smashed.

The warden pointed to the screen that showed Rabbit walking over to Ucktock. He looked puzzled, and somehow, a bit annoyed. He sternly questioned the Troublemakers, "How did your friend withstand that punch?"

Jon shook his head to show what he hoped would be recognized as disbelief. "I have no idea. We ran down to check on him and he waved us off."

The warden continued to interrogate, "Because it looked like he reset a dislocated jaw."

"Are you sure? I didn't see that. I guess we were on our way to him." Jon coughed lightly and looked away.

"My wall has been smashed by his head and body. How is that possible?" The warden folded his arms and raised an eyebrow, anticipating some stupid excuse.

"I don't know. But, he will do whatever he has to to accomplish the mission.

The warden wasn't sold. "You expect me to believe that we didn't witness something that couldn't possibly have happened?"

Jon wasn't sure what he should say. He thought of a quick response though. "Do you have facilities to take x-rays and a doctor on staff? He's probably hurt. He just doesn't know it."

"Is the mission really this important that you could lose one of your men?"

"I can't lose him. He's the best. It is never an option. I can't believe that he let the orc hit him. He just has to hang in there now."

The warden seemed to be persuaded to think that Rabbit was lucky…Or maybe unlucky and dead on his feet. Either way, the hope was that he dismissed any thoughts of extreme feats of strength by the punch-drunk jail breaker.

Just then, Jon pointed to the monitor that showed the corridor. Rabbit and Ucktock were on the move. "Let's go, guys."

The warden cut in, "There is the small matter of my damaged wall."

Jon smiled. "I will take care of it. Maybe we can get some info from the orc for you, too."

"I hope so."

"Get your men ready, Warden. I have dealt with orcs before. As you know, they are a handful."

Three
And the Award for Best Actor Goes to...

The skies were green and turbulent on the Planet named Plenna Four. The red giant star and dark gray thunderstorm clouds produced a tumultuous melting pot of swirling vortexes. The dark green clouds dipped in places where torrents of rain and tornadic winds plummeted from the fifty thousand-foot tops.

This was of no consequence to the thousands of orcs that barreled down the ramps of their landing crafts and spread out into the marshes beyond. They wore blue uniforms and leather boots. Their green skin was like that of the dangerous sky. However, they were perhaps more dangerous, certainly to those whom came across their path. They had no worries about the weather. By contrast, it was exhilarating to them. It further pumped their blood and got them ready for any battle that lay ahead. They came together in groups by designation and rank. Their equipment, although heavy and strong, blew around or tipped in the heavy wind gusts. Everything was soaked in a matter of seconds.

As more ships landed and replaced those that had already unloaded troops and material, the largest in the group landed. All eyes came to rest upon it, for it belonged to the leader of these troops. Not that their leader didn't own everything that they saw, but this was his personal ship; it *personally* belonged to him.

The doors opened, and the ramps engaged, meeting the saturated ground. A hundred or so troops disembarked and assembled into groups like those before them. They, too, turned and watched as their leader came into view.

The leader was also dressed in blue. While his uniform, plain and virtually unadorned, wasn't much different than that of his troops, it was much larger than theirs. His immense frame was equal to his stature. His head was wrapped in cloth and he wore black, leather gloves with holes cut out for his large fingers.

As he stepped from the shadows of the dark, metallic ship, he walked heavily down the ramp. The steel of his boots gave rise to awe as his weight drove home his size by virtue of sound. Even more impressive were his battle scars. Although he was young, scars that marked his face, ears, neck, chest, and arms were visible. He was a true warrior and a great leader. His troops would go into battle and die for him. He was quickly met by one of his commanders.

"It looka goods so far. We stopped da humans on da ridge and in one a der factries."

Nuttybomb responded happily, "Great, Booma. Da days of humans treatin' orcs like dawgs is ova."

Booma was Nuttybomb's oldest brother. He wasn't as brilliant, nor as skilled in the ways of war, but he had learned enough to be effective and worked tirelessly to provide his brother, his troops, and his species with what they needed and deserved.

Nutty had picked up tactics and logistics easily. He was promoted as a child to protect his town during an invasion. Within weeks, he had crippled the enemy's chances to invade, and also racked up a number of unlikely kills against impressive and formidable foes. He had become a legend to his troops and word of his accomplishments had spread beyond his home system.

Now, he stood on a new world, committed to promoting the welfare of his species. It didn't matter that the orcs on Plenna Four didn't know him. It didn't matter that he didn't know them. He knew enough about them as orcs to know that they were a dominant species, albeit handicapped by intellectual deficiencies. They were proud and strong. They weren't to be tested on and then exterminated like those on Cypra. He wouldn't allow it! He began giving orders to carry out his directives as such.

***

Rabbit made his way down the dimly-lit corridor, passed the security room where Jon and the others were, and made his way toward the exit. He took notice of an overhead camera and thought briefly about the possible consequences of surviving an attack from an orc virtually unscathed. He and the other Troublemakers were loathed enough without the knowledge of their super soldier status. Although he was happy, but not totally surprised at his wherewithal to withstand such a vicious strike from one of the most brutal species in the star cluster, he was concerned about anyone else having witnessed what should have been total carnage. Not only might it hinder him from completing the immediate task at hand, but it could lead to the revelation about what had truly occurred on Cypra.

It was quickly decided by Rabbit to fake stumbling a couple of times. His hope was to appear more seriously injured than he really was. He didn't consider himself the best actor, but he wasn't playing to billions over live broadcast. He just thought that there might be a few suspicious eyes upon him and any look of symptoms would suffice. As he and Ucktock reached the exit door Rabbit fell to his knees. Ucktock grabbed him like a doll and bolted outside. There was the first act.

As Ucktock cleared the eight-foot stairs with a thunderous landing in one jump, Rabbit's body limply hung in his arms. Ucktock ducked and dodged for no apparent reason as he ran along the back side of the prison loading area. He was an orc and did such things to hide his ridiculously massive proportions. Fortunately, nobody cared that he was doing so. He was being watched the whole time. However, he didn't know that. He thought that there was no sense in being overly cautious. This was a rare trait in Orcdom. It was too bad to be wasted unnecessarily.

Rabbit came to somewhere near a high barbed wire fence. He yelled for Ucktock to put him down, and upon being released, he cut through the fence with unparalleled efficiency. Then, he and the orc dashed toward the east side of the prison. It was here that vehicles, items, and other belongings from inmates were stored during the their stays. Rabbit pointed and said, "There," referring to Ucktock's ship. He saw

Ucktock's lips rise in their crusty, green corners. Rabbit smiled in return.

This was the time for Rabbit to take a breath and evaluate where the two needed to be at certain times for this attempted escape to go off without a hitch. He went over a few things with his large companion and made a break for the spacecraft. Rabbit followed Ucktock across the fenced field that was dotted by other vehicles. While Ucktock did his typical ducking and dodging as he weaved in and around vehicles, Rabbit filled his mouth with some food and drink that had been on the cart in the corridor. He hoped to use these to persuade Ucktock if they were needed in the future, but he made the decision to make use of them now.

Soon, they were inside Ucktock's old space fighter. Rabbit caught the look of pride and yearning from the orc as he gazed so fondly upon his ship. This had been his home, his baby, and his life support in the harshest areas of space. Rabbit felt a little sick to his stomach. He gave some instructions as well as a disc to Ucktock, and then spewed chunks of vomit all over the main console. He fell to his knees again and held his head in pain; act two.

"Ucktock, give me the disc as soon as the information is on there."

"How you know orc space fro' here, Rabbit?"

"I spent time on Cypra. It had orcs on it."

Ucktock looked puzzled at Rabbit. "I know Cypra, too. Dat wer all da orcs die."

"Yeah, humans, too."

Ucktock seemed satisfied as he rolled his eyes and scratched his head while he thought. He had no reason to draw a correlation between the orc deaths and Rabbit. Finally, he affirmed it with, "Ok."

When the disc was done Rabbit took it from Ucktock and said, "Watch the cameras, my friend. My eyes are too blurry. I think you messed up my head."

Ucktock laughed.

It was Ucktock's turn to give commands, not because he was the captain of this vessel, but because he simply knew where everything was. He fired through a checklist that Rabbit went along with. Ucktock shouted out in his deep voice, "Drive one?"

Rabbit responded with, "Drive one, check."

"Drive two?"

"Drive two, check."

Ucktock was elated. He might finally escape the prison cell that had become his home over the last seventeen months. He hadn't even done anything wrong. All he did was wander into an area of space that was quarantined by humans. He had no way of even knowing. Regardless, he was treated as a criminal. Even worse, he was treated as an orc prisoner. Orcs were no more than dogs in the eyes of humanity.

Rabbit was feeling even sicker than before. He leaned over the console and fell to the floor. He had seen the cameras. They revealed prison security forces closing in and beginning to encircle the ship. Rabbit snapped at Ucktock, "What's moving on the cameras?"

Ucktock jumped. He hollered, "Prison mens! Dems comin's!"

Rabbit continued his acting. But this was for Ucktock not to know that he was a pawn in a much larger picture. He threw a disc to Ucktock and yelled, "Block the door! I don't know how well I can fight."

Ucktock wasn't happy with Rabbit for a brief moment. Orcs never avoided a fight; never! They never even mentioned that they might not be up to a fight. Fighting's what they did. Ucktock looked at Rabbit in disgust and then secured the door the best way he knew how. This was done by pulling a heavy electronics case and putting it in front of the door. It didn't occur to him that the door opened to the outside, and that his meager attempt to keep the security detachment from pushing the door open, was useless. Rabbit felt so sorry for the poor orc.

Rabbit had to do it though. He had one more thing to do in order for Ucktock to give up to the security force without a fight. He hit his own forehead and calmly stated to Ucktock, "Oh no."

"Oh no, what?"

"Ucktock, with the ship in this new holding area, we can't get fuel. I thought of everything but that."

Ucktock thought for a minute. His mind had to confirm what his heart already knew. He and his newestest, bestest, dedicatedest, and mostest funniest friend weren't going to escape. They couldn't without fuel. But this attempt was better than the one six months before. This time they made it all the way through the checklist. Still, Ucktock's disappointment was replaced by elation. Like a child, his emotions took over and he began to laugh. He was so happy that

Rabbit, the superior intellect, had failed. He had failed, not by virtue of physical frailty, but by some kind of deficiency of intelligence. He gloated, "You so stupid, Rabbit!" He held his belly as he laughed. He pointed his sausage-like finger at Rabbit and his eyes bled tears of joy. He slid the huge electronics case away from the door. He lumbered over to Rabbit in defeat. "Now, what?"

Rabbit turned from his slouched position and dropped to a sitting position up against the helm computer console. "I will get us out of here, my friend; not today, but the next time."

Ucktock did his best to console his friend. He dropped down on the deck with a loud thump and sat with Rabbit. His tone was uncharacteristically compassionate for an orc as he spoke. "It ok, Rabbit. Sumptimes, Ucktock maka mistakes, too."

"What irony," Rabbit thought. While the two were supported by an inanimate object called a console, an orc, who wasn't known for doing so, was in the act of supporting his friend by using a form of the same word. Rabbit felt terrible. "I will get you out of here, Ucktock. I promise you. I'll go out and surrender." With that, he patted Ucktock on his left bicep and stumbled to the door.

No shots were fired, and no punches thrown. Rabbit and Ucktock were shackled. They were separated and brought to their respective areas for interrogation.

The warden began asking Rabbit questions. "I hope so," Rabbit responded. "I preprogrammed the disc to pull everything related to traffic in the systems of Cypra and Plenna. Ucktock has the disc."

"I already retrieved it from him and made a copy." The warden handed the copy to Jon. Then, he resumed his interrogation of Rabbit. "Did the orc say anything of importance?"

"What?"

The warden asked again, but this time he did so louder and slower. "Did the orc say anything of importance?"

Again, Rabbit asked, "What?" He shook his head from side to side and swayed a bit on his feet.

Jon grabbed Rabbit under his right arm. "Hey, man, are you okay?"

Rabbit pushed Jon's arm away in a show of defiance. He exclaimed, "Stop! I'm fine. I'm just a little dizzy."

Jon engaged in conversation with the warden. "Can we get him to your medical area?"

"We can. I just have a few more questions."

Jon was visibly annoyed. "Really? Dammit, Warden! I know this was a huge favor you did for me, but he took a hell of a shot to the head."

Rabbit intervened, "No, Jon! I said I'm fine."

Jon's eyes met Rabbit's with a look of discontent. "Fine, Rabbit." Then, he addressed the warden once more, "Sorry, Warden. Go ahead."

With that, Rabbit put both hands around his head and dropped to his knees.

Leroy cried out, "Rabbit, what's wrong?" But Rabbit didn't respond.

Harry asked, "Rabbit?" Again, there was no response. Rabbit's eyes rolled back, and then, his body rolled back into a lying position on the floor.

Jon instructed Leroy to grab his arms and Harry to get his feet. The two fumbled like idiots as they appeared to struggle in lifting him. Once Rabbit was firmly in the air, Jon hastened the interrogator to respond with, "Warden?"

The warden reluctantly gave in. "Follow me."

The group of men hit the hallway that led to the medical area. Harry dropped one of Rabbit's legs. The group had to wait as Harry fought to bend over without falling, while trying to lift his comrade's foot from the floor. Had Rabbit's condition not looked so potentially severe, Harry's actions would have been borderline comical. As it was though, nobody saw the humor that he did. He smiled when he regained his composure and the group continued.

Rabbit was fully acting out his third part at the behest of his prison audience, even though they didn't know that they requested such a performance. He began to moan and move around in Leroy's and Harry's arms. He yelled out, "Where the hell are you taking me?"

At that moment, Ucktock could be heard telling somebody about his escape attempt. He was boasting, "We hads to give up cause da squishy Rabbit fogots to get fuel!" He was laughing hysterically.

Rabbit yelled out, "Shut up, Ucktock."

"Rabbit?"

"Yeah."

"Hiya, Rabbit!"

***

Most of the guys in the group chuckled. Harry said, "Awe, you have a nice friend, Rabbit."

Rabbit sort of smiled without looking too healthy. He yelled back to Ucktock, "Hi, Ucktock."

The orc happily responded, "Wer are you?"

"They are carrying me away."

"Dems bastids! Don't worry, Rabbit. You aren't squishy. You can take 'em."

Without missing a beat, the warden slowed from his leading position of the group until he could make eye contact with Rabbit. "Are you done with your friend?"

Rabbit nodded.

"Good. You are going to the medical area, Rabbit." He expected an argument from Rabbit. This would be the response of someone who didn't want to get examined. Maybe it would be from someone who had something to hide.

But, Rabbit wasn't stupid. He knew what was going on. He needed to put the warden's suspicions to rest. "Oh, okay. What happened?"

"You blacked out," Harry hastened.

The warden began walking and the group kept pace. He assured Rabbit that there should be no trepidation with, "It's just precautionary, Rabbit. I understand that you have a long trip. A scan will show what is causing your symptoms after taking such an unbelievable blow from that green monster."

From a distance, Ucktock's words could be heard. "You ok, Rabbit?"

Rabbit played along. He didn't answer Ucktock. "I hear you, Warden. I shouldn't have hit him first. It's a good thing my back took most of the hit against the wall. And the orc respects me now."

"Yeah, right. Here we are, gentlemen." The warden led the men into the only clean room in the prison. It had commercially tiled floors and some sort of smooth, plastic-coated walls. It was bright and obviously non-friendly to germs. Everything was white, except for the metal table and some tools.

Jon instructed his two carriers to, "Carry him over here."

Rabbit began to fidget. "Put me down, you morons. I can walk."

Jon didn't agree. "Well, after you fell down, I think I am more capable to make that decision than you, Rabbit."

Rabbit broke an arm free. "Dammit, I'm okay. I can walk!"

As Leroy and Harry brought Rabbit to the scanning table, Rabbit thrashed around until he was free. In the process, he and Leroy knocked the warden into the portable scanning control unit that operated the scanner. The unit tipped and crashed to the floor. The warden fell hard on his back. He bounced so hard that his little, round eyeglasses flew from his face and slid across the room.

Jon raced to the warden's aid. He knelt down and quickly asked, "Are you okay, Warden?"

Although shaken, and somewhat embarrassed by landing on his ass, the warden shook his head and said, "Yes." He jumped to his feet to somehow lesson the embarrassment in the eyes of those around him.

Jon screamed at Rabbit, "What the fuck, Rabbit? Is there anything else you want to break that I have to pay for?"

"I said I'm fine."

"Really? Then, why is the whole side of your head swollen, bruised, and probably the reason you are losing consciousness? You have blood in your ears and the back of your head looks like roadkill."

Rabbit shrugged his shoulders.

Jon stood next to the warden. It was his turn to act. Rabbit was carrying most of this orchestration alone, but probably wouldn't be able to close the deal on the warden without help. He looked at the warden before speaking to Rabbit. "What are you afraid of? Is there something you are hiding?"

Rabbit's mouth hung open.

Jon shook his head, showing that he couldn't believe what his subordinate was making him look like. He sort of half-laughed and sighed to the warden. "He is difficult to control sometimes."

The warden concurred, "I have heard some rumors to that effect."

Jon turned back to Rabbit. "Well?"

"I don't want anyone touching me."

"That doesn't seem to be a problem when women are involved."

Rabbit snapped, "Shut up!"

Jon rushed at Rabbit and stopped so the two were face to face with their noses touching. "Captain, I am going to make believe that I didn't hear that because I strongly feel that your errant actions are due to an injury. You have never talked to me like this before and you can be sure that you never will again. You better tell me what the hell is going on."

Rabbit screamed, "I can't! I can't do it! Nobody is gonna do things to me like back on Cypra! Now get the fuck out of my face, Jon, while you have a face!" Tears began to pour from his eyes and his breathing became quick and constant. He clenched his fists.

Leroy and Harry jumped between Jon and Rabbit. Leroy tipped his head to the side and sympathetically begged, "Jon."

Jon stepped back. He looked at the warden. He tried to show hurt in his eyes. But for a moment, he could only think of the warden's ties to other branches of the military and key politicians. Jon appeared like he was trying to think of what to say to the warden, but in the end, he decided that it would be better to show compassion for his suffering soldier. He halted his aggressive posture and said quietly, "I know, Rabbit. I was there." He corrected himself, "*We* were there. Just let the doctor take a quick look. You won't stay here. We will take you with us."

Rabbit shook his head "no."

"I was tortured, too, Rabbit. We are a team. We are all in this together." Jon was pretty sure that he wasn't breaching any significant secrecy when it came to this information. He was betting on the warden's back alley knowledge of this fact. At the very least, he was banking on the warden's feeling that he was being included in some top-secret information. Gaining favor by opening up to the warden might prove fruitful down the road. Jon turned to the warden and firmly stated, "Warden, don't share this with anyone. You didn't hear this from me. Do you understand? The events of Cypra are top secret."

The warden was pleased to receive top secret information, even if he did already know it. He did trust the Troublemakers a little more now than just a bit earlier. "I understand, Jon. It will stay with me. You have my word."

Jon extended a hand to the warden for a hand shake. "Thank you, sir. I can't tell you how much I appreciate your concern for me and my men. It means a lot." Jon assumed that a little more buttering up couldn't hurt.

"Sure. No problem. Let me get a doctor in here." The warden looked at Rabbit. "He will just examine you, Rabbit; no tools or devices."

Rabbit agreed.

In the end, the doctor had determined that Rabbit's jaw had been dislocated, but assumed the soft tissue hadn't been torn. He implied that a concussion was probable, although Rabbit's eyes didn't show it. Rabbit's sensitive rib cage was probably due to a crack here and there. He was bruised up and down his back, but overall, he was miraculously healthy. It was further suggested that he was amazingly lucky.

During his brief examination, Rabbit thought about how he had given Ucktock a blank disc while the two were aboard the vessel. Rabbit kept the one that Ucktock had put information on. Rabbit, then, supplied the orc with a blank dummy disc. Nobody was any the wiser. The warden, getting a disc- blank or otherwise-wasn't disappointed at all. On the contrary; he was happy to have made some headway with these Troublemakers. It was another feather in his cap when it came to his long list of political and military allies.

Rabbit thanked the warden up and down repeatedly for all the help that was provided. End of act three; exit stage right.

***

The warden interrogated Ucktock and didn't find anything that was disconcerting. Furthermore, there wasn't anything of value that he could use. This brief questioning didn't include the typical torture used to obtain answers as it had been applied to the orc to date, but the warden was sufficiently gratified that the results were spoken in truth.

Aside from getting nothing out of the green animal, he thought that the meeting with the Troublemakers had gone well. As he had hoped earlier, he yearned to have earned their confidence. He certainly seemed to.

However, he, too, was a bit deceitful when it came to his visitors. He did have powerful friends throughout the star cluster and he would pull any strings necessary to advance his career. He instructed his secretary to open a line of communication with an old friend. Upon doing so, she let him know and the conversation began.

The warden said, "Hello. The Troublemakers are on their way."

The voice on the other side whispered, "Did they get what they wanted?"

"I don't think so. We retrieved a blank copy of a disc from the orc that they wanted to get codes from."

"And this orc...this is the one that was picked up in Cypra?"

"Yes, sir."

"Okay, my old friend. Perhaps they didn't get what they are looking for, but they may be getting close."

Four
Hacking

Jon looked to Rabbit for help. "Hey, can you break the code to get me into a higher rank file?"

Rabbit came from the adjoining computer area. He lowered his head as he stepped into the short, wide corridor that connected the computer area and sleeping quarters. He had seen this corridor so many times that he paid no attention to the gray walls and carboncrete beams that supported and ribbed the area. Jon used this as a personal, makeshift computer room on the starboard side of the ship for his own needs. The room he slept in was just beyond. There were two other rooms that were accessed from this area as well. For now, they were packed with additional stores of food and supplies.

Rabbit responded to his commander, "Wow. I don't know. That stuff is really well protected. I can try."

"Yeah, 'cause it'll help me get a better idea of what we might be up against."

Rabbit was more than happy to oblige Jon. "Sure. What am I hacking?"

Jon pulled up the site and stepped aside so Rabbit could access it. Rabbit saw the content and gave Jon a concerned look, but that was quickly replaced by a broad smile. He went to work, trying to cross reference log-in information that was consistent with other military sites. It took about fifteen minutes for him to break the lowest level access points. The stricter access points would take longer, but at least Rabbit had figured out the patterns.

Rabbit asked Jon, "You want the good news or the bad news?"

"Oh, boy. I hate when those options are presented." Jon smiled and then continued, "Just give it to me."

Rabbit laughed. "I usually hear that from women." Rabbit went on to explain that it would take a while for him to get into more sensitive areas. Some areas he might never be able to access. Hacking and computer espionage weren't his strong suits. They were just something he played with while attending the academy.

Jon instructed him to do his best and stick with it. They had a little more than a day until their first jump. The whole trip to Plenna was estimated to take just over a month. Any information that could be gathered before arriving would undoubtedly be helpful in completing the mission.

Jon turned his attention to a workstation next to Rabbit. He logged into the computer and began searching. He looked at the systems the Troublemakers would be traveling through. He planned where to stop and refuel. He estimated times. He thought about contacts along the way that might help him, contacts like Ucktock. Ucktock's coded ship logs were essential in determining traffic patterns that came in and out of Cypra and Plenna. As the two were neighboring systems, they had a connecting wormhole. Contacts like this were essential.

After roughly a half hour, Jon found himself looking at recruiting records. They led him to his own men. This was partially by chance, but also, he was curious about what the official records indicated. He never doubted his team's abilities or questioned their dedication. But did anyone else? Were there blemishes on their records that the top brass saw?

By this time, Leroy and Harry had found their way to Jon and Rabbit. This wasn't very difficult as the *Outcast* wasn't very big. On the contrary, it was rather cozy. The center of the ship had two levels; the top was the computer area with sleeping quarters to each side. The bottom had a food space and cargo hold. To the rear of the cargo hold were the powerful Strenu engines. Above them was the engine room and small medical area. The front of the ship's bridge and helm were connected to the computer area on the upper level by a corridor. The fighters of Rabbit and Leroy were docked above the corridor. Some guns and access ports lined the outer hull in other locations. These weren't whole levels, but rather smaller, individual spaces.

Harry settled behind Rabbit. "Whatcha doin', Rabbit?"

Rabbit smiled. "That's a damn good question. I'm asking myself the same thing."

Harry's eyes widened. "Oh, shit! That's some serious stuff, man."

This caught Jon's attention. "You in, yet, Rabbit?"

"No, not yet, but I think I'm close. You find anything?"

"Actually, yeah. You guys want to hear your recruiting info?"

The unanimous decision led Jon to begin. "Okay. Leroy, you were in the academy for two years; recruited into the officer program. You won the best pilot award once and recorded highest officer scores twice. Impressive. You went on to command the *Renegade* before going to Cypra. Hmm…the rest of this stuff is top secret. Well, that's Cypra for you."

Jon found Rabbit's information. "Rabbit, you were recruited after winning the Humania Legends Martial Arts Tournament three straight years. Not bad."

Harry questioned, "No shit?"

Jon went on. "Six years in the academy…top of your class…best pilot award three times. Wow! You scored a perfect two thousand on the Intelligence Qualifier?"

Harry interjected. "Does it say he slept with hundreds of women, including Colonel Parker's daughters?"

The men laughed.

Jon continued sarcastically, "No, it doesn't mention that. Hey, I didn't know that you made a citizen's arrest of the Rebel Sons?"

Leroy chimed in. "What's the Rebel Sons?"

"A pirate ship. Well, not just any pirate ship. It was *the* pirate ship on the fringes of the rim. Rabbit, who helped you?"

Rabbit shrugged his shoulders. "Nobody, why?"

Jon pressed, "You took them in alone?"

Rabbit didn't see the big deal. "Yeah. They were harassing my family's trade in the area. The freakin' corrupt police weren't doing anything. It probably wasn't the smartest thing to do, though. My family had to leave anyway under pressure from the fact that I cut into the pockets of corrupt bureaucrats. We ended up on Cypra. The rest, well, you know…" Rabbit hung his head. He was still deeply damaged by Cypra; he lost all his loved ones. He thought to himself that he would probably never be the same.

Jon tried to boost his hurting crewman's morale. "You have unbelievable credentials, Rabbit. I'm sure I can get you a job as a janitor or a garbage man somewhere. Just ask for a reference and it's yours."

Rabbit smiled at the light-hearted counterpoint of his superior officer. Jon was a good leader, fair and understanding, and he was a great friend. "I thought those were my jobs on this mission? You always have me removing the trash and cleaning up your mess." He seemed okay, at least on the surface.

Jon now focused on Harry. "Um…Very weird. Your academy history is sketchy."

Harry elaborated, "Eh, I drank a bit in those days." He chuckled. "Favors usually got me out of trouble. I found that it got crap off my record. Anything good in there?"

"Actually, yeah. Looks like you were in the academy on and off for eight years. Top explosives candidate once and became a munitions trainer at the academy. You served under Leroy on the *Renegade*; no surprise there. Then, you led the engineers in setting up Cypra, regarding the power, electrical, and weapons systems."

"I guess you can thank me for Cypra, guys."

Leroy cut in to alleviate any of Harry's blame in the Cypra matter. "Hey, dude, I supplied the defense from space. My brothers and I let ships in and out. I think there were other people that were part of this, too, Harry."

Jon added, "Hey, I coordinated Special Forces on the ground and even rounded up most of the orcs that were tested on. I didn't know why...just following orders. But, I did more than my share, too."

Everyone nodded. Rabbit finally gave his own admission of guilt. "I only killed fifteen million humans and orcs. You think my hands are clean?" They fell silent.

Jon, feeling that the wind had been sucked out of the room, tried to reel his men in. "Look, we didn't know what was going on...and we all had jobs to do. It's not like they don't throw you in the brig or hang you for treason if you disobey orders. You guys had jobs to do and you did them admirably."

Rabbit, mostly angry at himself, lashed out, "Yeah, we did our jobs and we looked the other way. We all knew that something stunk there, but we were busy living our own lives and just doing what others thought we should. At least, that's what I did...And I was stupid, so stupid. I should have known that there would have been a massive explosion. I knew there was ammonia and hydrogen variants in the air, not to mention a number of others, but I still lit the whole damn thing up."

Harry interjected, "Whoa, whoa, whoa. I'm an explosions expert and I didn't know. How could you?"

"I don't know. I don't make mistakes like that."

"Yeah, well guess what...you're human. You couldn't have known that with the difference in atmospheric pressures, the explosion would cause a flashpoint and burn at those temperatures. That place was a powder keg just waiting to go up."

Jon agreed. "He's right, Rabbit. You are brilliant, but you couldn't plan on something you hadn't learned, yet."

Leroy laughed. "Why didn't anyone tell me he was brilliant?"

Harry summed things up, "Well, we all got what was coming to us anyway, huh? What does it say about you, Jon?"

Leroy prodded, "Yeah, Jon."

Jon obliged. "Okay, okay. I also won the Humania Legends Martial Arts Tournament three straight years. It was right before Rabbit started winning them. Then, I went into Special Forces Training. I excelled there; trained for two years before going into the field. I have some stuff that is classified and really not that important. Then, it goes on to list stupid team comradery in sports and being the leader of them. Whatever."

Rabbit wanted to know more. "What about that top-secret stuff you were part of?"

"Oh, it's not important."

"Okay, so tell us then."

Jon looked at his men's eyes, craving for some great story, or maybe something he had done that was amazing, but he didn't have something so riveting. "This stuff isn't really important to us. It's mostly Harem stuff."

This caught Leroy's attention. "Harem stuff?"

"Yeah, like they are the ones who developed cloaking for ships. I got some inside stuff. They don't need Mystics to use wormholes. They have a technology that is far above ours. Anyway, I broke in to find out some stuff that might help humans. For instance, they have mastered wormholes to protect themselves, not from us, but from getting lost in the void between wormholes. I don't know, it seems that their whole existence is based on that. That's it, nothing sexy to tell you guys."

Harry questioned, "The void, huh? No, not very sexy."

Leroy dropped his head and sighed, "Come on, Harry, let's finish that game of cards. Besides, we should leave these two to work."

Rabbit jeered, "Somebody has to."

Leroy and Harry left Rabbit and Jon to their tasks. They settled in the wide corridor beyond the computer area that mirrored the one they had just departed. It was here on the port side that some tables, chairs, and extra cots had been arranged. The men sat down and picked up some cards and began to squelch their boredom.

Around asking how many cards would be drawn, the two engaged in some personal conversation. The stuff that Jon read to them had them thinking about who they were and what they had done. It seemed to bring up things that they hadn't discussed in a while. Even as close friends and brothers in combat, they hadn't learned everything about each other.

Harry reluctantly asked about Leroy's falling from grace. Leroy had lost command of the *Renegade* and been demoted to corporal. Harry was careful not to upset his friend. "So, how do like being on the *Outcast*?"

"It's okay."

"Kind of small compared to the *Renegade*," Harry stated.

Leroy admitted, "Yeah, I miss it. We had good people there."

Harry pressed a bit. "You think we will get her back? I mean, that you will get her back?" He chewed on his soggy cigar.

"Who the hell knows at this point? Losing my Captain's rank doesn't help my chances. You know, I pilot a fighter now, but it has some perks."

Harry queried, "Yeah? Like what?"

Leroy tried to put his pesky friend's mind at ease. "I only worry about myself. I mean, I fight alongside you guys, so I look out for you, too, but I don't have hundreds of men under me to worry about."

"You are a pretty good fighter pilot, too, Leroy."

"Thanks. I do okay."

Harry was curious. He always wondered who was the better pilot, Leroy or Rabbit. His inquisitive mind needed to know. "So, you're a better pilot than Rabbit, right?"

"Are you kidding me? No way." There was no hesitation.

Harry was shocked to hear that. He had been second mate on the *Renegade* under Leroy's command. The *Renegade* had done amazing things. He had also witnessed Leroy fly his fighter in combat. He assumed the answer to be closer than Leroy's factual tone and quick response indicated.

"Well, what about your brothers?" Harry asked.

"Compared to Rabbit? Or do you mean all of us compared to each other?"

"I don't know. I guess all of you together."

Leroy obliged, "Wow. Well, there is Rabbit and then there's everyone else."

"Seriously?"

"Well, you asked. I guess my brothers and I are close. There are maybe, I don't know, a hundred other pilots like us in the star cluster. But who knows? And, that's just humans, too."

Harry nodded in satisfaction. Leroy had adequately answered his question.

Leroy decided to ask how Harry was doing. "Hey, you have any seizures lately that I don't know about?"

"No. No blackouts either, I don't think." Harry smiled.

"Oh, good."

***

Rabbit finally broke some of the codes to get into the areas that Jon wanted access to. He told Jon and left him to do what he needed to. Rabbit went to lounge on his cot for a while.

Jon looked through the Cypra survival names list. Rabbit had brought up most of what he sought. Maybe he could start putting together enough information to solve the puzzle that was Plenna. He read:

Rex Wiler, Male- age 37, deceased. After seven failed suicide attempts, the eighth was successful due to a self-inflicted, high-powered rifle shot to the head. Former expert sniper. Survived by wife, Carmella.

Marcus Deshanti, Male- age 26, deceased. After three failed suicide attempts, the fourth was successful due to an unassisted jump off of the sixteen hundred-foot Quawatha Falls. Former intelligence officer. No known family.

Tyrus Biggs, Male- age 28, deceased. After three failed suicide attempts, the fourth was successful due to a self-inflicted, high-powered shotgun shot to the head. Former demolition expert. No known family.

Jon read further. Cal Dykstra, suicide. Sacres Alumini, suicide. Benjamin Hostler, suicide. All three had multiple suicide attempts on their records. There was maybe a dozen more that had committed suicide. All except for three of them had died by their own hands after several suicide attempts.

The picture was becoming clearer. Yes, the torturous experiments on Cypra were enough to break most men. Sixty-two had initially survived, but for many, dealing with the aftermath was even harder. Jon felt lucky to have the strength to cope after the experiments and the following year and a half. He further knew that he was lucky to have minimal affects after the initial events on Cypra. Up until recently,

Harry had still had seizures and blackouts. Leroy had become a different man, at least physically. His oldest brother, Lou, was still suffering from damage he sustained on Cypra.

Then, there was Rabbit. Physically, he was strong and seemed unharmed; unchanged. But, he carried with him the deaths of fifteen million souls at his hands. He now lived his life without care. Those not close to him were sure that he had a death wish. Those close to him prayed that he wasn't hiding the possibility of something so tragic. Jon wanted to get inside his head, but to this point, was unsuccessful in his attempts. He simply gave Rabbit some space and offered a friendly chat if necessary.

Jon scrolled through the list of names until he found those that were still alive. He and his Troublemakers were listed as well as a few of Leroy's siblings. He read further:

Zen Furer, Male- age 30, active. Top secret commander of covert operations team, The Electus. Former expert rogue assassin.

Max Dullus, Male- age 26, active. Top secret corporal in covert operations team, The Electus. Former expert sniper.

Thomas Matthews, Male- age 26, active. Top secret corporal in covert operations team, The Electus. Former expert martial arts and weapons specialist.

Interesting, Jon thought. Who were these Electus guys?" He hadn't heard of them before this. Then again, he was kept in the dark about a great many things. Only what was relevant to each of his missions was divulged, and even then, he wondered how much sensitive information was actually revealed. There were a few more names included in The Electus as well. Jon researched further.

***

Time seemed to move quickly as the Troublemakers worked on the things that might bring them closer to Plenna, not just as far as crossing the distance, but the solution to the problem, too. The first task was preparing to move through the first wormhole. They readied the ship and themselves. An error, a miscalculation by them or the Mystic, or an actuator malfunction could be fatal.

In fact, there were ships that never survived the jump. Some disappeared forever, never to be found. Others were rumored to appear randomly; their crews totally insane. Legend told of their meeting huge, blue/gray aliens on the other side. The other side was commonly referred to as the void. It was an alternate universe that ran parallel to the one that humans and other species shared in what they considered the real world. The fact that wormholes manipulated the fabric of space made the belief of such a thing entirely plausible in the minds of many.

The *Outcast* and her crew jumped through the first wormhole. There were no errors or miscalculations. There was no void with blue/gray aliens. No, the ship and men survived the trip and found themselves a mere two days shy of the next jump. The actuator that would move them to the next location was on the outskirts, just beyond the asteroid belt that eclipsed the planets. They were one step closer to Plenna.

Leroy informed Jon of their position. "Jump successful. All readings are normal. We are one hour from Dextra."

Jon smiled as he checked the settings that he read on his console. He typically sat in one of the two forward chairs instead of his command chair which was located up and behind the main console. He felt close to his crew and didn't share the same ego that other commanders did. Many commanders differentiated themselves by deliberately sitting above their men, but this wasn't the case with him. "Dextra sounds good. Just keep an eye on the other two for me."

Leroy chuckled. "Well, Rabbit's gonna do his thing. I'll try. You will have to tell him that we don't have enough time for him to have sex with a roomful of women."

"Dually noted. You keep Harry away from the slots and the bottle, then."

"Okay, I'll do what I can."

"Thanks."

No sooner had Jon verbalized his appreciation when Rabbit poked his head into the bridge. Rabbit looked like a kid in a candy store. "Is that Dextra?"

Leroy said, "Yes."

Jon said, "No."

"Well, which is it?"

Jon clarified, "Yes it's Dextra. No, you can't have sex because we don't have the time."

Rabbit showed his disgust toward Jon's apparent handling of the situation. Jon didn't know for sure what Rabbit was thinking and why he was excited about Dextra. It actually bothered him more that Jon was right. He exclaimed, "Fine," and ducked back out of the bridge.

Rabbit stopped in the corridor as Harry approached. Before Harry asked, Rabbit told him, "Dextra."

Harry's eyes lit up. "Really?" He passed Rabbit and, he too, poked his head into the bridge like Rabbit had before him.

Jon turned around to see Harry. "Everything good in the engine room?"

"Never better. So, we are landing on Dextra?"

"Yeah. Leroy?"

Leroy did a double take when he caught Harry's lively facial expression. "No gambling, Harry. Oh, and stay off the booze."

Harry was surprised. "What?"

"You heard me. We don't have time and we can't get in trouble here."

Harry was annoyed. Was it that clear that he wanted to have some fun? How obvious was it? He didn't even say anything. He retorted, "Fine," before walking away.

He caught Rabbit in the corridor. "No gambling? What the hell?"

Rabbit thought for a second. He chuckled. "So, no women for me and no gambling for you. Well, they didn't say no sex for you and no gambling for me, right?"

Harry half-smiled.

***

There was little left to secure. Most of the area had been cleared of humans. Nuttybomb's troops were a model of consistency and efficiency. However, this wasn't common among most orc armies. Many worlds where orcs lived were in disarray. It took great leaders and a cohesive effort to bring such a barbaric species under control. Furthermore, this was usually done with the use of brutality. Armies under other leaders were bands of warriors that even fought amongst themselves. This wasn't the case under Nuttybomb.

Nuttybomb was informed of the situation by one of his favorite underlings named Arc. Arc was a student of Moonoak, a shaman that helped Nutty in defeating another dangerous orc with necromancer like abilities. While Moonoak used his powers and spells to primarily heal others, Arc had developed the use of spells to attack his enemies. He was always kept in close proximity to Nuttybomb, and although trusted, he was under constant watch. Orcs had a funny way of misusing power at times. It was felt that an orc wielding these types of powers could be very dangerous. Still, keeping him close was just precautionary.

Arc told his leader about the small human fighting force that was beaten. He explained that they were guarding a series of caves that were beneath huge generators and other mechanical devices. He went on to give details about huge smokestacks that pumped billowing plumes of acrid material into the sky. The caves, mechanical devices, and smokestacks were as yet unimpeded. But the humans that survived the battle were taken prisoner.

Nuttybomb was pleased. He had little knowledge about humans though. He got the impression that they were particularly dangerous, probably more so than Arc and the rest of his orcs. This was mostly because they were highly intelligent and had mastered technologies; technologies that he wanted to learn about.

He had obviously heard about the events that transpired on Cypra. He didn't know why the whole atmosphere had been incinerated. He didn't know why fourteen million orcs had been killed. He knew they were tortured, but wasn't sure why. He *did* know that he would try to stop humans from doing these horrible things.

But again, among the most problematic thoughts he had was about the humans' abilities. The technology that the humans had that could vaporize everything above the ground was astounding to him. He thought if humans had this ability to annihilate whole worlds, he was probably outmatched.

Nutty pushed these thoughts aside. He had to do what he had to do. So, he followed Arc and a few guards to the encampment that housed a dozen humans.

The humans wore uniformly brown and tan garments. They were outfitted with boots, belts, and straps that weren't very much unlike Nuttybomb's orcs. The men were dirty and some of their uniforms were torn in places. Some had blood and soot on them. All of them stood behind a tall wire mesh fence. Their eyes widened at the sight of Nuttybomb. They had never seen such a massive and menacing orc.

Nuttybomb stopped at the fence. He questioned, "Wut are humans doin' in da caves?"

The men didn't answer him.

He tried again. "Anywun know why der are mens in da caves?" This time he leaned on the fence as he spoke, causing the fence posts to bend from his weight.

A man spoke out. He was a commander of the group that was being held. He thought it best to be the one that the enormous orc killed, if need be. He hoped to spare his men. "No. We just protect them."

Arc laughed. "You mean you try to protect dems."

Orcs in the area laughed and slapped each other on their backs.

Nuttybomb issued a "Silence," command. It became utterly quiet. He asked the human, "Wut are da machines and chimneys dems have?"

"I don't know."

"You don't know, or you don't wanna tell me?"

The human looked around at his men. Then, he turned to Nuttybomb. "I don't know. I really don't. Please, let my men go. They don't know anything either."

Nuttybomb puffed out his lips as he blew some air through his mouth. He rubbed his chin in thought for a minute or so. Then, he addressed the human. "Ok, human. You tells me what you know bout da stuff dat happened on Cypra."

With substantial reluctance, the human finally spoke. "Um, okay. I don't know much. What happened is classified so only the big leaders are allowed to know.

I'm just a fighter. But I know that..." He paused. He realized that he almost endangered him and his men by saying that orcs were tortured. He fumbled for the right words and was as careful as he could be. He was extremely nervous under the circumstances. "Bad human leaders hurt orcs and humans. We weren't there. But the bad leaders were trying to do science stuff. I don't know what science stuff. They didn't tell us. Anyway, somebody found out that orcs and humans were being used for this science. I don't know what happened next or why, but a human blew everything up."

Nuttybomb already knew about most of what the human had said so far. The information to this point was somewhat useless. It *did* mean that humans were developing stuff through scientific methods though. They were crafty little bastards. Furthermore, it was confirmed that they didn't have much use for life. They seemed to be just as brutal as orcs. Nuttybomb didn't approve of it. He was an orc. At least, orcs were brutal to your face. They didn't experiment on humans. They just killed them outright. Lastly, he knew how humans perceived him. He didn't care. He asked, "Wut human blowed up da planet anda why?"

"Well, I don't know why. Really, I don't"

"Wus he tryin's to hide all da orcs dat were hurt?"

"I don't know."

Nuttybomb wanted to drive home that he was in complete control of the humans' lives that he held in the camp. He held their families' hearts as well. He wasn't sure how family-oriented humans were. They were vicious enough to hurt their own, but he wanted answers. If he miscalculated the importance of these men to their loved ones, so be it. He hoped that their own lives might be enough to give the information he wanted. He began with, "Who blowed up da planet?"

The human looked around at his men. He knew what was at stake. The pressure on him was immense, but for a second, he reasoned that he and his men would probably be killed anyway. He lied, "I don't know."

Nuttybomb wasn't convinced by the poor acting that came from the squishy human. He, now, worked from his position of power and tried to manipulate the little bastard. "I can let you mens live...I give my word. Or I can killa dems all. Der lives be in you a hands. Anda what 'bout you families? Dems will be heart broked." He lowered his head and took up an attack stance. He bared his teeth and lowered his voice. "Dis lil fence no way stop me fro' killin's you anda all you a mens. I ask fo' lasta time. Who blowed up Cypra?"

The human was terrified. He didn't even know why he would withhold the name of the guy who incinerated Cypra's atmosphere. It was his duty not to tell, but good soldiers had already died. The soldiers on Cypra, and now, some of his own during the recent skirmish with the orcs that captured him. He decided to do the right thing, regardless of his oath to his superiors. "Rabbit Harrison blew up Cypra."

Nuttybomb growled, "Anda wer is dis Rabbit Harrison?"

Five
Karma

"Come on seven," Rabbit hollered as a crowd gathered around him.

The dice stopped, and the dealer stated loudly, "Seven. We have a winner."

Rabbit yelled, "Yes!" The women on each side of him gave him kisses on his cheeks. They were quite bubbly.

Jon interrupted all the fun though. "Rabbit, let's go."

Rabbit tried to explain as he laughed. He pleaded, "But I'm on a hot streak."

"Sorry. Let's go." Jon walked away.

Rabbit gathered his coins and stood up. One of the women couldn't believe that he would jump at the other guy's command. She asked sarcastically, "You do everything he asks?"

"Yup."

"Seriously?"

"Yeah."

She took it a step further. "Oh, so it's like that?"

Rabbit looked her in the eyes. "Have you ever seen him with his shirt off?"

The crowd became silent. Rabbit flipped a coin to the dealer and said, "Thanks. That's for you." Rabbit smiled wide at those that stood around the table. Then he walked away and met Jon at the door to the casino.

Rabbit still needed to explain his plight to his superior officer and friend. "You know, one of those women was for Harry, too."

"He'll be fine without her. Listen. Did you meet your friend here, yet?"

"No. She might be avoiding me."

Jon seemed perplexed. "Why? I thought all women loved you."

"No Jon, not all...not when they catch you in bed with two other women."

Jon smirked. "Oh."

Rabbit shifted the conversation. "Wait. That's her over there."

They stood there as the woman made her way across the room. She was dressed to kill. Most men in the room noticed, even those who were married caught a quick glimpse behind their wife's back. As she approached, Jon caught wind of her consuming aroma. She used just the right mix of body wash, creams, and perfumes to go along with her goddess-like beauty.

Rabbit spoke. "Wow! Evelyn, you look amazing."

She briefly acknowledged him, "Rabbit," before her attention was drawn to Jon. "Hi, I'm Evelyn."

Rabbit apologized and remembered to introduce them. "Oh, I'm sorry. Jon, this is Evelyn. Evelyn, Jon."

Jon was intrigued by her very presence. "Hi. Rabbit tells me that you have some experience on Plenna."

Evelyn looked at Rabbit; then, at Jon. "Jon, I have experience on a few planets."

Jon could feel the tension between Rabbit and her. It was a little uncomfortable, but he didn't really care. He had a job to do. Everything else took a back seat. He simply responded, "Okay. But my real concern is about Plenna. I..." He found himself being distracted by two women that were standing at a table where people were playing a card game.

Rabbit asked Jon, "Are you okay?"

"Yeah. Are those women looking at me?"

They were immediately recognized as the two whom Rabbit had just left at the dice table. "Oh. They are probably just thinking about what you look like with your shirt off."

"What?"

Evelyn blurted out, "Everything is sexual with him." Then, she found the nerve to ask a question while throwing a dig at Rabbit. "You able to keep your zipper up these days?"

Rabbit replied without any pause, "No, no. I use Velcro. It helps me to pull it out at a moment's notice. Very useful." He smiled.

Evelyn put her hand on Jon's bicep and directed him out the front door to the casino. She taunted Rabbit with, "Ever heard of karma?" She used her sensual body motions to tease him while flirting with Jon. "So, Jon, I hear that you have a very, very big," she licked her lips and continued, "problem."

Jon played along in the banter. "Well, let me tell you, Evelyn, it isn't my problem that is so big. It's my...well, kind of hard to give a real description without showing it to you."

She was very playful at this point. "You will show me?" She hugged his arm now and looked at Rabbit.

"Yes. The only way to see it is up close so you can get a real sense of every detail." He smiled.

Rabbit said, "Okay. You two have a good time. I'm heading back to the ship to get everything ready."

Jon responded, "Yeah, you do that."

Evelyn stuck her tongue out at Rabbit. Then she tipped her head to the side and smiled. She said giddily, "Bye, Rabbit."

Rabbit smiled and looked into her eyes. He needed her to know how truly sorry he really was. Sex to him was just that. He never wanted anyone to get hurt who may have developed feelings for him. "Evelyn, can I talk with you for a quick minute?"

"Um, no. I'm good."

"Please. I'll make it quick."

Jon jumped in with, "Hey, I need a minute to get some papers anyway. I'll be right back." Teasing was teasing. Jon had Rabbit's back, no matter what.

Evelyn put her foot down. "You have one minute."

"Then, I'll make it quick. I'm really sorry about, well, you know."

"I knew going in. But I told you how I felt."

"I know, I know. Look, this probably doesn't matter. But I donated everything to the kids you were sponsoring."

She was surprised. "That was you?"

"Yeah. I don't know. I had a revelation or something."

Evelyn snarled. "Well, you're right. It doesn't matter."

Rabbit understood. He decided to compliment her one more time before leaving. "Well, anyway, I'm sorry. You still look great."

She shook her head. "Do you think that I can forgive you because you gave to those kids or that you said sorry, so you can keep me from sleeping with your friend? Ever heard of karma? You're still a bastard."

"No, that's not why. I'm really sorry and now, I guess, I am legally a bastard."

"What? Not funny, Rabbit."

"Come on, Evelyn. I sent you countless messages."

"I blocked you. Rabbit, your dad died?"

"Yeah."

"I'm so sorry. When?"

Rabbit sighed. "About eighteen months ago."

"How is your mom handling it?"

"She's not. She's dead, too."

"Oh my gods, Rabbit! I didn't know, I swear."

"I understand. I hate the whole social networking thing anyway. I use it to keep in touch, but I hate all the religious and political stuff that ends up on there."

Evelyn didn't know what to say. As much as she disliked him for having sex with other women, she was a compassionate person. She tried to give him a bit of happiness, to find a silver lining, to expose a glimmer of hope. "What about your sister? Did she finish college?"

"No." Rabbit hesitated. Evelyn was the last person he wanted to open up to, but he didn't want to lie to her either, not again. He had done that once or twice in the past. He finally said, "She's gone, too."

Evelyn couldn't help herself. "No way. Now, you're just being an asshole." She backed up and crossed her arms. Her face had a snooty look to it.

"Evelyn, you don't understand. They're all dead...all of them. My whole family." Rabbit needed to be careful what information he told anyone, especially an unhappy ex with a grudge. "There was an accident on Cypra."

Evelyn cupped her hands over her mouth. Her face was stricken. She gulped. "So, it's true? The things; the rumors about you are true? The things they say are true?"

"Um, I don't know what things *they* are saying about me or what rumors, nor do I care. All I can say is that there are parts of our government that are corrupt. They did terrible things. I tried to fix stuff and I fucked it all up. After I found my family dead, I went on a warpath; I lost it. I took out the whole facility. The rest happened by accident as a result of that. I don't know what to say or what to do. I struggle with it every waking moment. Okay, I've said too much. Anyway, I'm sorry." Rabbit kissed her on the cheek and walked away.

At that time, Jon walked up to her and saw tears in her eyes. "Are you okay?"

She briefly glanced at him and nodded. "Yeah. Let me get you those ship logs and registers so you can cross reference stuff." She stared at Rabbit as he

90

walked off in the distance. She perked up momentarily when she saw him turn around in her direction.

Rabbit talked loudly enough so she could hear him. "I almost forgot to answer. Karma…yeah, I get it. I understand karma." He rubbed his forehead, turned and walked around a corner.

***

Colonel Vance Parker paced back and forth in front of the Capitol Building. He was usually calm and collected, but he always seemed a bit rattled when it came to the damned Troublemakers that he felt cursed to command. Their name was fitting, ironically chosen as a top-secret file name that just happened to stick. Who knew that it would turn out to be so profoundly prophetic and poetic?

Parker imagined the grass being flattened beneath his feet. Bright green and lush with liquid, it had a natural spring to it. But this new-found, high-traffic area was beginning to show signs of wear. Each step lessened the rebound of the tampered blades. For a moment, the colonel envisioned Jonathon Valor being each blade. During that same moment, the sweet smell of grass was replaced with the bitter taste of defeat.

It wasn't like Jon ever beat Parker at anything in a head-to-head match. Actually, they were always part of the same team; working together to enhance the well-being of humanity. However, Jon did seem to best him in the President's office not long ago. Plus, there was the real issue of the Troublemakers killing General Amadas. Colonel Parker just couldn't get passed his suspicions when it came to his own handpicked team. He couldn't be too careful.

A man approached from the east and he caught Parker's eye. It wasn't his sharp suit or dark sunglasses that drew attention. No, it was his swagger; he walked with a certain air of confidence. From a distance, Parker guessed that he was tall, based on his gait. His wide shoulders and posture gave a sense that this man could take care of himself too. Parker had stopped his pacing and stood still, anticipating the meeting that he was waiting for.

"Colonel Parker?" the man asked as he engaged his superior officer.

"Yes. You must be Zen Furer."

Zen agreed with a nod and saluted. "Sorry for the delay, sir. I didn't know if you were the colonel or not."

Parker smiled. "It's quite alright, Captain. I don't like to dress in uniform on Sundays."

"Killball, sir?"

"As a matter of fact, yes. It does my heart some good to see men struggling physically against what should be humanly impossible. It reminds me of basic training days when I was a sergeant. But I'll miss a few televised games today. Let's walk."

"Yes, sir."

The two discussed the mission at hand. This discussion was primarily one sided though as they usually were between a commanding officer and his subordinate. Furthermore, for the most part it was top secret. Zen assured Parker that his team was ready, available, and up to the task. He also assured the colonel that the Troublemakers were outclassed by the Electus. Parker urged the Electus to use caution if confronting the Troublemakers; obviously they were armed and dangerous.

After a few minutes, Colonel Parker sent Zen Furer on his way. Then, he pulled a phone from his pocket and dialed Colonel Gary Taggart. Like Parker, Taggart had served under General Amadas, too. The two colonels competed for their superiors' favor. There were other colonels that vied for the same recognition, but Parker and Taggart were fairly high on the list of those considered for promotion. However, the debacle on Cypra hurt their chances. This call was to update Taggart about the mission.

"Hello?"

"Gary, hello."

"Who is this?"

Parker chuckled, "It's me, Parker."

"Yes, I was expecting your call."

"It is done, my friend. Things have been set in motion. It will be led by ZF and his group, as we discussed earlier."

"Understood. So, he will report to you, then?"

Parker explained, "Yes. I have the resources on this side to make sure things are carried out."

"As long as we don't have another Cypra type incident."

"I don't think that is even possible."

"Thank you for the call, Vance. Enjoy your Sunday."

"You too, Gary."

***

The computer area was bustling with activity. It wasn't moving in the way that a commander would be

93

proud of his crew, though. It was sloppy and celebrative over something that would irritate most commanding officers. The laughter was loud and continuous, the ribbing nonstop.

Jon came in from the bridge with a smile on his face. The initial sound of raucous laughter was infectious and contagious. His face couldn't help but conform to those that caught his attention with their silly smiles and happy go lucky applause marked with cheek to cheek grins. Jon simply asked in his own uncontrollable chuckle, "What the hell is so funny?"

Rabbit turned a monitor, so Jon could see it.

Jon saw a picture of a few guys on Harry. His memory quickly kicked in as he recognized the setting. He knew it as the last place him and his men had drinks; the same place where Leroy and Harry were in a fight. It struck him that none of his men took photos of the fight. So, who did and how were his men able to view them? His stomach told him first that something didn't sit right. His brain and his temper would soon affirm it. He was no longer smiling when he asked, "How did you guys get pictures of this?"

Rabbit said, "One of my girls sent it."

Jon lightened up for a moment. "Oh, okay. I thought we made the news again."

Rabbit visually cringed and Jon saw it.

Jon pressed, "What is it, Rabbit?"

"Well, the girl got the pictures from the news."

Jon interrogated in a pissed off tone, "What news?"

Leroy jumped in. "We weren't laughing at the news Jon, just the pics."

"Let me see the news," Jon commanded.

Rabbit minimized the pictures and typed in some search criteria. Within a few seconds he had what Jon had requested. Rabbit turned the screen in Jon's direction.

Jon wasn't happy; in fact, he was far from it. Maybe Colonel Parker was right about him and his men. Jon was tired of catching flak for his guys. The repetition of defending them unnecessarily was exhausting. Unfortunately, this thought of how reckless they were and how little control he seemed to have over them kept surfacing. He stood inside the entrance from the bridge hallway and planted his feet shoulder's distance apart. He spoke firmly.

"Listen up. It seems that our little incident on Rigar has become news for those that have nothing better to do than look for shit to write about, just in case you three didn't notice over your laughter. I am sick and tired of looking like idiots with our peckers out blowing in the wind while we are bent over with our pants around our ankles."

Leroy seemed amused. "Now, that's a picture I won't forget."

Rabbit and Harry smiled, but only briefly.

Jon snapped, "Shut the fuck up, Leroy, before I drop your ass off at the next space port and leave you there! I'm done fucking around! Don't you guys get it? We are supposed to keep our abilities hidden. Our missions are top secret, as is all the crap surrounding Cypra, but every time we are in the news, attention follows us for weeks. And you guys keep us in the headlines. Why?"

Rabbit tried to clear his name and expunge himself of any blame. "I didn't have anything to do with that one, Jon. I was upstairs with those girls."

Jon frowned and shook his head in apparent disgust. "Of course, Rabbit."

Harry tried to do the same. "I was sleeping. I didn't even know I was in a fight."

The guys couldn't help but chuckle over that line. The stupidity of the comment almost left Harry unaccountable by way of honesty and humor.

But it didn't. Jon gritted his teeth. "Look at this picture. You are getting beat senseless while you are passed out drunk and you still have a cigar in your mouth!"

Leroy didn't help him or Harry. He probably should have said nothing, but that simply wasn't his way. Besides, the chip on his shoulder due to Jon's hostile tone and words had grown. He spoke with a bit of sarcasm in his voice. "Hey, those were expensive cigars, Jon. I bought those on Rigar. It's good Harry hung on to one during his sleeping beating." He glanced at Harry to his right and nodded in assurance.

Jon turned to Leroy and scowled at him with a look of death. Again, he gritted his teeth, but this time his tone had more of a growl to it and was much quieter as he fought to keep his composure. "Maybe you should have thought of that before you got into another fight, Tough Guy."

Leroy's chip was weighing on the muscles in his neck. His facial expression was that of a strained weightlifter holding hundreds of pounds above his head for an extended period of time. He needed to get rid of the chip and its weight before it caused him to explode on his leader and friend. His anger was now obvious, but he also showed his reluctance to challenge Jon. He did know his place amongst his shipmates. In the end, he clenched his fists and blurted out, "Oh, like it's my fault that Harry is always drunk, and I end up fighting everyone that hates us."

Harry didn't care for Leroy's remark, nor did he like his own place among his shipmates. It wasn't like he minded doing his job or helping his friends, but he didn't like the perception of his place and what seemed to be an attack on his character. His own chip came to light and his thoughts were revealed. He fired off, "Sure, Leroy. You go and fight everyone because your attitude sucks! Rabbit, you go and screw anything that walks!"

Rabbit calmly responded, "Hey, I share."

"Jon, you go on and take every gods forsaken mission to prove that we aren't the troublemakers that we have been dubbed. Maybe, just maybe, we can live up to your expectations and you can get an accommodation. And yeah, I'll drink until I can't see. I drink because the press has called me the fat, drunk troublemaker. I'm the sloppy, cigar-toting dope that apparently follows you guys around and wipes your asses. You know what? Fuck all of you! On any other ship, on any other team, I would be the leader and a damn good one. I'm a genius with a pretty good body and I'm handsome, too. The women like me, Rabbit. And I have exceptional skills. I scored as high as you, Jon, on the officer intake exam. In fact, I'm the best in my field. I am a gifted genius, stuck behind other geniuses. So, I'll drink if I want to, Leroy. Jon, drop me off at the next space port. I resign my post."

Rabbit waited for his irate friend to stop talking before he did. "Whoa, whoa, whoa. I never said you had a bad body."

Leroy added to Rabbit's comment, "I think he has a rather nice body."

Jon took a deep breath and relaxed his posture. "At least his clothes were on for this photo. I don't know what the hell he was doing naked with the cigar in his mouth in that last one." Jon looked at Harry. "We are all geniuses, huh? I don't know about that. What I do know is that, Harry, you're a good man and a fine soldier. I'm not dropping you off anywhere and I won't report this, but here's the thing...cut back on the booze, period."

Jon turned to Rabbit and added, "And you...cut back on the women. Spend more time with your team. Maybe if you three were together, trouble would steer clear. There is safety in numbers."

Jon wrapped up by addressing Leroy. "Man, you have to lighten up. I don't know what the hell is going on with you, but enough is enough. Before you punch someone in the face or say something shitty, just know that we are all gonna pay for it."

Jon stood up. "I have been really lenient on you guys up 'til now. But it ends here, today. We have a lot to do. Work out your differences and man up. We are soldiers. Now, we have to be on our best behavior. Let's go."

Six
Men are so Stupid

The *Outcast* jumped into the Cypra System. The ship lurched forward and halted abruptly as it slipped from the piece of folded space that it had just ridden with. Traveling by way of wormholes was the only way possible for travel like this to have occurred. Somebody had figured out that folding space to shorten distances was easier than fighting with the impossibility of each ship getting to light speed or faster. There were risks though and consequences that were worse than childhood nightmares.

Each crewman went through his checklist to ensure a safe entrance into the system. Jon and Leroy found that their things checked out fine pretty quickly. Soon after, Rabbit reported no problems. The men continued working until finally, Jon asked for Harry's status. There was no reply from the engine room. Jon tried a second time, but again, there was no reply.

Rabbit spoke into the com, "Jon, I'll see what's up."

Rabbit dashed to the engine room and found Harry lying on the floor. Harry's eyes were open, but not moving. He showed no visible signs of injury, but who could tell what was wrong through clothing? No blood or bruises only confused the matter. An obvious wound might have given a clear indication as to the type of injury that may have been sustained. For all intents and purposes, he seemed unconscious.

Rabbit rolled him onto his side to avoid choking from possible regurgitation. He didn't even know why Harry was unconscious, but for some reason everybody was taught to put an unconscious person on their side. Rabbit did, although it was with some reluctance. What if Harry had been thrown from his chair and received a significant head or spinal injury? Rabbit grabbed the com and reported, "Harry is down."

Jon was worried. "What happened? Can you tell?"

Rabbit replied, "I'm checking him out now. No visual injuries. His eyes are open, but he's out, Jon. I'm a little off on his pulse count while I'm talking with you, but it seems okay; maybe a little slow."

"Okay? What do you make of it?"

"I don't know. He might be in a seizure. Maybe it was from the argument about the news thing and the pictures. He was pretty upset. The things he said and the way he said them wasn't like him."

"I know. I'll be right there."

By that time, Jon and Leroy put the ship on a course to the small weigh station that orbited the planet of Cypra. There were no ships in the area and no other objects that they would collide with. Autopilot gave them the opportunity to check on their crewmate and friend.

Leroy was first in the engine room. "What do you think?"

Rabbit affirmed what he had already suspected and reported. As Jon entered the engine room, Rabbit summed up the situation. "His vitals are good. His heart rate is fluctuating though."

Jon cut in, "How much?"

"Not bad; it's just erratic. Seems a little unusual compared to the other times that he's zoned out, like…maybe, he's dreaming?"

Like the others, Jon was puzzled. He began, "Strange. You guys haven't seen this before?"

Leroy responded, "No. I'm probably with him more than you guys and I have never had his heart rate go up *and* down. If anything, it usually drops a bit…as far as I know."

Rabbit concurred, "Yeah, same here."

Jon continued his earlier thought. "Okay, but maybe it happened, and we weren't aware of it. Do we know if he took his meds?"

Leroy answered, "No clue."

Rabbit added, "Yeah, I don't know either."

Jon made a decision. "Alright, let's get him to the medical area just to be sure. Rabbit, run through his checklist; then, check the video to see if we can tell what happened. Me and Leroy will take him and get him set up."

While Rabbit got to work, Jon and Leroy got Harry into a bed and hooked him up to a diagnostic unit. They placed a few electrodes, ran some wires, and got oxygen ready, just in case. Instantly, Harry's vitals and levels showed as fairly normal.

Rabbit reached Jon on the com. "Hey, Jon, I think we have something."

Jon replied, "What is it?"

"I don't know; something, though."

"Do you need me to come down there?"

"No. I'll give it to you the best way I can explain it."

"Okay, go ahead."

"First, the checklist failed in several areas. As soon as we made the jump, the oxygen in here disappeared. The camera showed immediate static. It only went fuzzy for a few seconds, but when it cleared up Harry keeled over. Then, the system showed a complete failure, but only for that same few seconds. When it came on, it showed numbers that I don't understand."

Jon was listening. He was evaluating what he was hearing until Rabbit stopped talking. "Did I lose you, Rabbit?"

"No. I'm trying to make sense of what I'm reading, but..."

"But what, Rabbit?"

"Jon, I don't know. The system was running. It checked itself. The thing is...the mainframe lost it during that same time."

"Okay? And?"

"Well, during that same time that the oxygen was lost...the mainframe is saying that the ship was much lighter."

Jon scratched his head. "What do you mean, lighter?"

"I mean...I'm guessing, but it's like we lost the engine room and part of the back of the ship for a few seconds."

"Well, obviously we didn't. It's there now."

Rabbit tried to reason with Jon. He wasn't even sure what he was saying. The information that he was processing wasn't logical. "It's like...for that short time...I don't know...Maybe we phased out of our fabric of space and partially transitioned into the void."

Jon and Leroy stared at each other. Jon gave a long, vocalized denial by cause of improbability only. His word carried out for four full seconds. "No."

Rabbit wasn't so sure. "Okay, if you say so."

"I mean...We are talking about the void here. Check the numbers that our ship got compared to the actuator that sent us."

Rabbit pulled up the numbers. "They look good. No, wait."

"Wait? Wait for what?"

"They are off. I have to carry out the numbers to um...seventeen digits, but they aren't the same."

"Rabbit, is that enough of a difference to cause phase?"

"I don't know, I really don't. Maybe. Figuring this out...You might have an easier time pulling me out of a hat."

Jon couldn't draw a conclusion from what Rabbit was telling him. The void theory was preposterous. Nobody ever knew of someone that had phased into the void. As far as he knew, they were just stories that dated back to hundreds of years before the newest actuator technology all but eliminated such threats. Regardless, he went to the bridge to investigate the prospect of missing an engine room for three seconds. Maybe he could find something that Rabbit didn't. He was doubtful of that, though. That damn Rabbit was good at everything.

***

Ucktock growled as he was forced out of his cell. Most days were the same thing; the stupid humans electrocuted him into submission, shackled him, and led him out of his cell. He was strapped to a hand-truck and carted down the same dreary corridor, his uneasiness pumping his heart faster.

Turning the first corner hastened his blood flow as anticipation of the inevitable was running through his troubled brain. His body began to produce adrenaline and endorphins that enhanced his body's reactions. Orcs weren't supposed to feel fear, but if that was the case, what he was experiencing was the closest thing to it.

He was brought to another area where he was hosed down to alleviate the foul stench that permeated every particle of air around him. This wasn't done for his benefit; no, his skin was painfully pressure washed with chemicals, so the warden could tolerate his stink. His initial growls turned to screams while his body took a beating from the scalding hot, high-pressured shower.

When the warden was ready, he summoned for the orc prisoner to be brought. Inevitably, questions about Ucktock's home-world, his senior officers, troop types and numbers, and orcs' overall intentions toward humans were asked.

The answers seldom changed. Usually, more electricity was used to elicit information that was thought to be withheld. This enraged Ucktock, further inhibiting his ability to communicate while angry, and simply feeding the viscous cycle of torture, for the more enraged he was, the harder it was for him to calm down and speak effectively.

The warden and his staff didn't care. Their job was to house the animal and obtain whatever information they could extract by whatever means deemed necessary. Four hours were spent almost every day over the last year and a half to help Humania through this method. As brutal and cruel as it was, it was something the warden needed to do so he could report to his colonel with some lifesaving knowledge.

Very little information of substance was forced from the tortured beast. On the contrary; the more the orc fought back and stopped communicating, the more the warden punished him. Ucktock just wasn't fully intelligent enough to realize this cycle of torture, not that he had anything to offer, especially under these most painful conditions.

Ucktock said nothing when it came to Rabbit Harrison other than, "Him be my friend."

No ties were ever linked to the man who killed millions, nothing ever surrendered, but still the interrogations continued. They continued as if somehow, under the same conditions that resulted in nothing hundreds of times before, the orc might give something up.

Eventually, Ucktock would succumb to the physical strain he had to endure and finally slip into unconsciousness. He would be carted back to his same cramped cell, somewhat cleaner than when he left as janitorial staff wiped down the walls and floors during his four-hour vacation.

Most of the time Ucktock was locked up, he envisioned being free, and when he awoke, he thought about it again. He thought about his squishy human friend and their good times while trying to escape. He figured Rabbit must have escaped if the warden was trying so hard to find out anything he could about him. He was glad.

He went over their failed escape attempts in his head; he tried to reason out what worked and what failed. Furthermore, he used his time being brought to interrogation to count the guards, determine the length of the corridors, and most importantly, to learn where the warden stayed. Additionally, he kept a mental note of where his ship was and the layout outside the prison buildings.

His next escape would be just that; not an attempt. He laid back and closed his runny eyes as he went over a plan to get out. He ignored the involuntary twitches the electricity caused in his muscles and nerves. Soon, his tired brain and weakened body fell asleep.

***

"But why?" The feminine voice was sexy, yet firm.

The young cadet fought against his male urge to give this vivacious woman everything that he could. In fact, he wanted to give her every inch, but his training simply wouldn't allow it. No, he had to turn her away. It didn't matter that it probably extinguished any outside chance that he might have had to hook up with her. "I'm sorry, Ma'am."

"Do I look like a Ma'am?"

"No Ma'am. I mean, yes Ma'am. I don't know Ma'am. I'm just doing my job here."

Evelyn continued to plead, "But you let that Zen guy through. Please." She batted her eye lashes.

"But Ma'am, he is on a top-secret mission. He is military and unless you are cleared, I can't let you into Cypra."

"Young man, I am military. I can show you my credentials. May I put my stuff on your counter?"

He was ever so inviting with, "Sure."

Evelyn put her leather file case on the counter as she smiled at the young, innocent man before her. This freed up her hands, so she could furnish the cadet with her identification. She said, "I should be on the log as cleared for Cypra."

The cadet smiled wide. "Well, why didn't you say so?"

Evelyn smiled in kind. She leaned on the counter, so she could spy on the cadet's computer monitor. She played with her hair and giggled. She made soft slurping and sucking noises while her tongue fondled the chewing gum in her mouth.

The cadet didn't even notice her attempt to view the information on his monitor. He had a hard time focusing as he saw her breasts pushed up atop his counter. Between that and the sounds of Evelyn's mouth, his imagination ran wild. The thought of one of her breasts popping out wasn't completely out of the realm of possibility at this point. They were squeezed so tight that they were being forced out of her slinky, silky, low-cut top. Once he pulled up the ship logs, his sweaty body was startled.

Evelyn pushed her briefcase over the counter in an act of innocence and stupidity. She exclaimed, "Oh, my. Silly old me. You have me so flustered young man that I can hardly contain myself." Papers and items found their way into every nook and cranny that they could fit. While the cadet was more than happy to aid this beautiful woman by retrieving her lost assortment of belongings, she went to work.

Evelyn's hidden camera captured page after page of ship logs in and out of Cypra. She managed to get everything over the last eighteen months. Even the most top-secret journeys were in the logs. They were hers for the taking. However, before she could return the monitor to the last page the cadet had called up, he popped his head up from behind the counter. He proudly plopped Evelyn's briefcase on the counter with unrivaled enthusiasm. He didn't notice the monitor.

Evelyn thought quickly. She grabbed the briefcase and hid her right hand as it pulled a breast from concealment. She saw the cadet's eyes light up when she put the briefcase on the floor next to her. Then she looked down at her exposed breast in an act of shock. "Turn around, young man!"

The cadet faced in the opposite direction, totally unaware that he was being played. It only took a few seconds for her to fix her breast, his monitor, and her clearance to travel to Cypra. When she allowed him to turn back around, he did so.

Evelyn smiled as she playfully said, "I'm so embarrassed."

"No, Ma'am. You have nothing to be embarrassed about. Truth be told, you made my day."

"No! You're just saying that. Oh, and call me Evelyn."

The cadet was happy to hear that. All potential suspicions were wiped away. He went to his monitor and pulled up her name. "Okay. See that? Evelyn Dulsey, you *are* cleared for Cypra."

"Thank you, Cadet."

"Oh, please call me Jeremy."

"Let's keep it at cadet for now." Evelyn smiled as she turned on her heals and walked away. She was sure to wiggle her ass as she played with the cadet right up until her departure. She had him on a string; wrapped around her finger; waiting with baited breath; hoping she would throw him a bone.

Before she left the room and headed for her ship, she turned. She blew a kiss and said, "Thank you, Jeremy. I'll be thinking about you."

Thirty minutes later, Evelyn would be sent to Cypra. Until that time, she wondered how many stupid men fell for such things at the hands of deceitful women. How many lives were compromised by unsuspecting fools? How many millions were jeopardized by all the Jeremys in the star cluster? She giggled, "Men are so stupid."

***

Strange rumors began about a small world called Libel. The population of just a couple million humans was considered odd to begin with for they told stories, usually embellished about the military abusing their citizens. These were most often discounted as "take it from where it came" fallacies constructed by a rebellious, disenchanted, and eccentric people. Anti-military sentiment further spurred backlash that labeled these people as troublemakers as well.

This made it hard to discern between the fables of dwarves and the recent attacks by giant spider-like creatures that regularly came from this strange world. Recent tales spoke of Spidanoids that had come in enormous ships, numbering in the thousands. A mass invasion all but decimated the people of Libel, but the military swooped in quickly and saved half a million lives.

Now, anyone who knew the military also knew that it didn't move very quickly, especially across star systems to save a world that was suspiciously rebellious and throwing accusations its way. Questions arose as to the validity of such claims because the military would need weeks to mobilize a force to counter such an invasion.

Rumors about insecticides being used on such a massive scale on enormous bugs as an argument against military intervention seemed ridiculous too. Neither the military, nor a stockpile of chemicals that would work on a highly improbable invasion could be mobilized so quickly.

When all communication in and out of Libel stopped, it was assumed that the planet had cut itself off from the rest of Humania as part of succession. The people obviously used the reason of mass solar ejections disrupting their communication as an excuse to mask their true intentions-succession.

Eventually the military did reach Libel in force and refuted any knowledge of a Spidanoid invasion. In fact, it again accused Libel as being conspirators to defection and quickly rounded up its leaders. Any and all traitors were tried, found guilty, and sentenced to death.

Furthermore, all traffic to and from the star system was restricted to military only. Local government officials and citizens weren't permitted to travel in space at all. All contact with the world was all but shut down so the military could control the situation.

Solar flares were still questioned as the cause for communication breakdown. Libel was accused of destroying its own satellites due to claims of solar damage, an excuse to throw off the military.

Very few first-hand accounts from the population ever reached the other worlds of Humania. Ultimately, this would hurt the validity of what those living on Libel were trying to tell. Many people outside of Libel didn't recognize the legitimate argument about trying to speak out about an invasion while losing communication abilities, all the while being accused of treason.

News would report the Spidanoid invasion as being the biggest hoax in modern times. Even detailed videos that surfaced were cast off as rigged or fixed, further perpetuating the feeling of disgust toward the people of Libel. People believed what they were told, and once told, the snowball affect took hold, causing a virtual truth through mass media.

Once again, men are so stupid!

Seven
Cypra's Hauntings Continue

The *Outcast* had been sitting in the Cypra system for nearly forty-eight hours. While stationary, all essential controls were forwarded to the medical area. It was here that the crew attended to Harry and kept an eye on the space that eerily blanketed them just outside the ship's walls. The smallest movement of a ship or satellite could be detected, and the crew would be made aware. The men were startled as something caused the rerouted proximity sensors to activate alarms on the nearest flight panel.

A military vessel jumped into the Cypra system. To Leroy, it appeared to be a runabout. It was larger than the *Outcast*, but not as big or heavily armed as a destroyer. Leroy scanned it quickly and found that he was correct. It was a weapons class vessel with six crewman and three attached fighter craft.

Leroy reported his findings to Jon and Rabbit, who were just a few feet away. Then, he put their minds at ease when he indicated that the ship continued toward one of the moons without incident.

Jon was relieved, and he said so with a simple, "Good."

Rabbit was equally pleased. "All we need is trouble now. Like there isn't *enough* going on."

Harry was unconscious and hadn't responded to stimuli. His crewmates ran tests and checked his vitals every hour or so. They were pretty sure that his condition was due to the jump into this system from errant numbers loaded into the actuator's computer. But they just weren't sure how that could have happened. Simple jumps like this were almost always preprogrammed with zero chance of error. It was surmised that somebody must have physically put in the wrong numbers. But who loaded the wrong numbers and why?

The crew discussed their options to somehow get Harry back to himself. The truth was that they didn't know what to do. After spending the last two days exhausting all medical options, they came to the realization that something else needed to be done.

Rabbit asked Jon, "What if we went back through the wormhole? Maybe we would get him back by sheer luck?"

Jon replied with a question, "What are the odds of it working?"

Rabbit answered regrettably, "Almost none. But what if we loaded numbers that were off in the seventeenth digit like the ones that got us here? Theoretically if we reverse the pattern it would have the opposite effect...theoretically."

"But it might do to us what it did to Harry," Jon cautioned.

Rabbit admitted, "Yeah, it might. Do you have any better ideas?"

"No, but we can't afford to take all of us through at such a risk." Jon didn't even want to *think* about jumping back with such unknowns tempting his own fate. He certainly didn't want to endanger other members of his crew.

Leroy chimed in. "What are your thoughts, Jon?"

Jon suggested, "Well, maybe you two should stay at the actuator on this side. I'll make the jump with Harry. I have no idea how this is supposed to work, though."

Rabbit tried to assure his leader, "I think if we put Harry back in the engine room and change that last digit by the same amount in the opposite direction, it may work. You should be fine, Jon. I believe the tail end of the ship was caught. Hopefully, and this is just hopefully, the out-of-phase shift will revert Harry back to a current time and position in space."

Leroy looked at Rabbit with doubt. "How much do you know about this stuff, Rabbit?"

"Unfortunately, I know about the same as I knew about igniting an atmosphere, so not much. But, I'm fully aware this time and have had a couple days to think this through. This is our best hope."

Jon was sold. He didn't trust anyone in the star cluster like he did Rabbit. Even in matters that Rabbit wasn't an expert, his opinions would hold more water than an expert he didn't know. "Let's do it, guys."

Leroy shouted, "Wait!"

Jon did just that. He waited twenty seconds before asking, "Wait for what?"

"It disappeared. Jon that ship just disappeared."

"No, it didn't. How could a ship that size just disappear?"

Leroy asked as he raised his hands and shrugged his shoulders, "Okay, where is it, then?"

Jon leaned around Rabbit and viewed the screen and readouts. The ship that had been there just seconds before was, indeed, gone. "That's a good question. It couldn't have gotten to one of the moons that quickly, right?"

"Right," Rabbit surmised.

Jon read the readouts, but asked for confirmation, just in case he missed something earlier, "Did it dock with the actuator?"

"No. I double checked, too."

"Hmm. Well, it didn't fire on us. Let's move quickly. I was uneasy enough with this jump before a weapons ship showed up and vanished. By the way, is there a mystic here at this actuator to send us back? I didn't see one before the last jump."

Leroy had a thought and he found himself communicating it aloud. "First of all, do you think this other ship got stuck in the void? Maybe the actuators are messed up or something. Maybe that's why we didn't see a mystic to send us here, too."

"We're gonna find out soon enough."

Rabbit blurted out what his comrades all felt, "Cypra's hauntings continue."

Harry was carried to the engine room and setup where the video showed him to be as the *Outcast* made the jump. Then the *Outcast* docked with the actuator. Rabbit and Leroy went to work there as they prepared the *Outcast* for its jump. Rabbit calculated and recalculated. He couldn't leave anything to chance. The whole idea of manipulating time and space was beyond him. Furthermore, Jon and Harry meant so much to him. They were the closest thing to family that he had.

Finally, Jon hastened, "Sometime today, Rabbit."

Leroy interjected, "Jon, there is no mystic here. I need to get help from the last place we jumped. Give me a few minutes while Rabbit goes over the numbers."

While Rabbit ran numbers again and again, Leroy reached the actuator that had sent the Troublemakers to this system just two days before. He had gotten permission from the same Jeremy that oversaw that jump and he confirmed that a mystic was ready on one of the Humania outposts to ensure safety for this jump. The mystic would accomplish this feat remotely.

Leroy told Rabbit, "Okay, we have a go to jump."

Rabbit nervously smiled and typed in some figures one last time. "Jon, we have a go. Whenever you're ready."

Leroy added, "Good luck, Jon. See you back here in less than an hour."

Jon felt a little better by willing himself to safety with, "Damn straight."

The *Outcast* glowed just before it shot forward and disappeared into the darkness of space that lay before it.

***

Zen Furer sat in his command chair while being surrounded by two of his crewmen. His slightly elevated throne accentuated his dominance over his subordinates and he would have it no other way.

Whereas some victims of torture and experiments on Cypra later suffered from seizures, headaches, or depression, a few like Zen were overtaken by episodes of psychosis. Most succumbed to death through multiple attempts of suicide, whereas others became institutionalized. However, none of them were ever mentioned publicly. They simply faded into obscurity by means of being classified and hidden in files.

Zen had a different fate in store for him; he was promoted. In fact, he was given a crew of similarly gifted men. Also, he was given top security clearance about all files related to Cypra. He would use this clearance to call on the most sensitive information relating to the star system, the Troublemakers, and anything or anyone that would help him in his mission.

Zen's ship, the *Paragon*, had jumped into the Cypra system just fifteen minutes earlier. It passed the *Outcast* as it scanned the drifting ship and headed toward one of Cypra's moons.

The information that one of the *Paragon* crewman read to Zen was perplexing. Zen was told that there were three men aboard the *Outcast*. Zen was sure that four had been aboard when the *Outcast* jumped. He had followed her into the system. He, himself, checked the log at the actuator just minutes after the *Outcast* jumped, yet, two days later and the *Outcast* hadn't moved since its jump and it was down a crewman.

Something occurred to Zen. Maybe the missing crewman had somehow been dropped off at the Cypra actuator. He ordered the actuator to be scanned for other life forms, but it turned up empty. While he pondered what had happened to one of the *Outcast's* crewmen, he decided to hide his ship by engaging the *Paragon's* cloaking device.

The *Paragon* hid in the space around it. She was still a dangerous ship and still vulnerable like any other ship, but she was, for all intents and purposes, invisible.

While hidden by way of cloak, Zen ordered the *Outcast* to be scanned again. This time he was informed that there were four crewmen. The number changed to three and then, back to four. His imagination began to get away from him. He envisioned all sorts of possibilities as to where a crewman might go in deep space and return so abruptly. His mind saw a man that transformed into energy. He thought about a man with cyborg technology that might confuse his sensors. However, even his psychotic brain deduced these outlandish thoughts to just that. Still, he scratched his head when his final sensor scan revealed two men aboard the *Outcast*, then one, and then again two as it jumped back from where it had come two days before.

The *Paragon* waited a few more minutes before uncloaking. Once it revealed itself, it lined up with the actuator and jumped back to find the *Outcast*.

***

Evelyn was getting impatient. She had been sitting in the cockpit of her ship for almost an hour. She wasn't sure why there was such a long delay, but she knew something was wrong. She used the sexiest voice she could and spoke into her communication link, "Jeremy? Jeremy, can you hear me?"

"Yes, Evelyn Dulsey. I hear you."

"Oh, good. What is the delay?"

"Well, I'm not sure. There is a security lock in the actuator's system."

Evelyn questioned, "What does that mean exactly?"

"I don't know. It could mean somebody tried to access something illegally or it could just mean that the actuator's calibration is off. Although, personally, I have never seen that before."

"How long will it take for me to jump?"

"Oh, I just don't know. I have contacted security. They will come and check things out. If it's just a calibration thing, I'm guessing that a Mystic will have to come out, too."

Evelyn was disappointed, but she was also cautious. She didn't want security to find her sitting in her ship, waiting to jump illegally. She decided to go and to go quickly. "Okay, Jeremy. Thanks. I'll be back in a couple days to try again."

"Okay, Evelyn. I'll see you soon."

Evelyn piloted her ship to a small outpost on the moon of Remoir. She hoped to evade detection by security as long as she could by hiding on this little, backwoods world. She couldn't fathom how long she might have to hide though. Even if she ducked security indefinitely, she would have to use the local actuator to go toward Cypra or to go back from where she came. If she tried to travel at all, she would be discovered. All access points would be alerted; certainly, all between Cypra and her home back on Dextra.

Upon landing on Remoir, a small landing strip led Evelyn to a connected hotel. She didn't think it qualified as a hotel, but having a bed in a room that was rented for a minimum of one night made it so. It lacked the comfort and quality of hotels she had grown accustomed to. It didn't sport lavish columns outside that led one's eyes into a grand hall. There were no lush carpets, ornate stonework, or opulent structures lined in gold trim that she associated with hotels.

Instead, Evelyn's eyes were led by several boarded-up windows to a few crates in a dusty room that was heavily decorated in cobwebs. The smell of mildew was accompanied by the lingering waft of regurgitated alcohol and the soup of the day. The soup of the day was typically made several days before and stored at room temperature.

Evelyn signed in with a fictitious name and was shown to her room by a man with one arm. He wore dirty clothes and a shirt with a sleeve that simply hung over its lost appendage. He had a decidedly unshaven mug with multiple scars that made him appear older than his true thirty-five years would argue. However, he did look better than the individual who was laying on the walkway that they needed to step over.

Evelyn kicked herself for never having bought a bigger ship with sleeping quarters onboard. There were times like these that she yearned for being stuck on her ship a little longer. But long-distance travel meant stocking up on other necessities. That typically left little or no room for creature comforts. Actually, that reminded her to see just how comfortable the creature was that she saw in her bathtub. She poked it several times with a clothes hanger before concluding that it wasn't comfortable at all. It had probably died from the soup of the day.

With the door locked behind her, Evelyn sighed, "I guess this will have to do." With that, she went to the window, made sure it was closed and locked, and pulled the long, orange, wool drapes across the dank air unit that sat beneath the window. She turned and sat down on the bed. She was reluctant to allow her back to fall into the crevice in the mattress that had formed over the years because of unlucky patrons like herself, but she was tired, so tired. Traveling so far had taken its toll.

Eventually she leaned backward, never slipping her shoes off or turning the light off. She remained vigilant to defend herself at a moment's notice. As she defiantly drifted toward sleep she mumbled, "How do I get myself into these situations?"

She dreamed about Rabbit.

***

Leroy was still talking about the *Paragon*. From the actuator, he could view information that was up-linked from the last actuator that sent the ship. He saw the ship's description, her travel logs, and her crew. None of that meant anything to him; at least he didn't know it at the time. He was more concerned about the ship's brief disappearance. It still boggled his mind.

He thought for a moment that he had seen the ship again before it jumped back toward the actuator above Remoir. He poked Rabbit in the shoulder. "Did you see that?"

"See what?" Rabbit answered,

"I think that ship reappeared and then, jumped back through the wormhole."

Rabbit was distracted by other thoughts as he answered, "No, I didn't see anything. I did notice that there are no other ships here though."

That fact caught Leroy's attention. Why were there no other ships in the system? He responded slowly and quietly as he tried to reason out possibilities as to why this could be. "It is a restricted area, so maybe everyone is staying away like they are supposed to?"

Rabbit looked at the computer monitor then, the large window into space. "No. No way. We should have jumped into a few ships at least here. For a restricted area there should be military vessels to ensure that the quarantine is enforced. We would have felt a strong military presence."

Leroy agreed, "I know. I'm just trying to figure out why that isn't the case. Why is there no operator at this actuator?"

"Something isn't right here. I hate just being in this system so close to where we were all tested on. Well, you know."

"Yeah, I do. I hate the fact that we..."

Leroy's words were cut off by an incoming transmission from the *Outcast*. He tightened the frequency and responded to his commander, "Jon, I hear you."

"We made it to the other side and Harry is doing pretty well. He's back."

Rabbit added, "That's great, Jon. Then, it worked."

"Well, yes and no."

"What do you mean?"

"I don't know what I mean. The computer is having a hard time recognizing him as being completely him."

Rabbit thought for a second or two before responding, "Maybe he is still a little out of phase?"

Jon wasn't so sure. "I don't think so, at least not completely. It says that he has a Noid35 chromosome. What do you make of that?"

Rabbit leaned forward in his chair as he wanted to make sure that he had heard Jon correctly as he asked, "Noid35?"

Jon reaffirmed what he had already said. "Yeah, Noid35. Does that mean anything?"

"Yes, it does. Leroy had the same thing come up last year during his annual checkup. It was discounted as the thirty-fifth chromosome being confused with the thirty-sixth chromosome or something like that. Apparently, it happens at times."

Jon was relieved for the moment. "Okay."

Rabbit's voice had a sound of uncertainty as he spoke this time. "No, Jon, it's not okay. Only people that have been bitten by Spidanoids have had false positives, and those were less than one thousandth of one percent. Toxins from Spidanoids shouldn't even affect anything at a molecular level. The whole idea is odd. Anyway, Harry has never been bitten. The odds of this Noid35 chromosome being found at all is unlikely, to the degree of maybe one hundred billion to one, maybe more. Now, factor in that Leroy tested false positive, too. I'm baffled."

"Well, this is something we will have to look into, but for now, he seems alright. We are gonna come back to Cypra once we are cleared."

"Sounds good, Jon. See ya then."

Leroy was ecstatic about Harry's apparent well-being, but he couldn't help the thoughts that kept creeping into his head; The *Paragon* still bothered him. He decided to pull up recent ship logs, attempting to ease his worrisome mind.

At first there wasn't much that jumped out at him. Just as he suspected, there were mostly military vessels that had passed on their way to or from Plenna. Others Jumped to or from Cypra and were probably part of standard defense for the forbidden system. This lessened his concerns momentarily.

However, there were other ships that had traveled to and from Cypra that weren't military. The majority of these were barges and transports while the others were science vessels. Leroy investigated further.

What he found was that a steady stream of science vessels belonged to Crystal Technologies. Leroy guessed that the ships were under government contract to evaluate Cypra's atmosphere after Rabbit's incendiary accident. Crystal was an enormous enterprise, and if any company would be considered for hire, Leroy assumed there would be none better. He tucked Crystal's involvement into the far reaches of the memory area deep inside his brain before looking up the *Paragon* once again.

Eight
Destiny

Space, a perceptive vacuum, seemingly without the same properties that governed life and otherwise, as experienced by individuals from the comforts of gravity and breathable air, has always been considered more than perilous. Full of hazards and devoid of consolation, it has remained an endless sea of perturbation, regardless of attempts by intelligent races to control its affects.

Its unfathomable reaches and effects on time have unquestionably denied the psyche of the reliability of quick, safe passages across its vast expanse. The invention of actuators, gravity inducers, and hibernation chambers have assisted in reducing its affects to some degree. However, many travelers have passed time by sleeping to avoid the insanity that so often accompanies seclusion amongst the stars; others slept to prevent boredom, at the very least.

Rabbit was tirelessly searching for answers to Cypra and Plenna, or so he thought. Eminent fatigue and boredom from constantly working within the carboncrete and steel structure that provided life support for him and his accompanying mates had taken a toll. He found himself in a deep slumber that his body sought, but his mind rejected.

***

Rabbit was back on Alstar, a small planet on the rim of Humania that had rebelled against being absorbed into the corrupt Human empire. Humanity had been expanding its influence throughout Hyades by repairing and reactivating many of its actuators this far out in space, thereby allowing easier access to previously remote systems. Earlier settlements were currently able to be reunited with their people, unimpeded by distances that separated them before now.

Standing before the justice of the peace, Rabbit and his new bride took vows, signed paperwork, and kissed before a small gathering of family and close friends. A party ensued before the newlyweds scampered off for a quick honeymoon in a villa by the local lake.

Rabbit looked into her eyes, lifted her sexy frame from the terrace, and carried her into the master suite beyond the opened door. He exclaimed his love for, and devotion to her, promising loyalty for all time. She, in turn, did the same and followed with kisses to his face and neck as he carried her.

Soon, they were on the bed, kissing passionately. Rabbit had been with women before, but had never felt love like this for any of them. They were simply sexual encounters; women that he liked a great deal, but never had lasting relationships with. No, he had been with this woman, his new bride for almost three years; never cheating or even hinting at such a horrific act of infidelity. He didn't care to think of anyone else, not even himself.

Events were not to unfold so easily for the loving couple, though. The room was rocked by nearby explosions as glass blew inward on them; the support beams cracked, and plaster dropped from the walls and ceiling.

As they jumped to their feet, another blast separated them and threw all contents in the room, scrambling them chaotically. Smoke and debris littered down upon them.

Rabbit lost consciousness, only to awake in a hospital several days later. As he came to, the first thing he cried out was, "Where's my wife? Where's Evelyn?"

Leroy coaxed Rabbit into reality. "Hey, dude, it's okay. You had a nightmare."

Rabbit sighed and rubbed his eyes. "How long did I sleep?"

"Maybe a few hours."

Rabbit heard something in Leroy's voice; it was disconcerting in its tone. Furthermore, Leroy's facial expression showed concern. He was obviously upset by something, but what?

Harry, who came in while Rabbit was thrashing around in his sleep remarked, "Rabbit, you yelled, 'Where's my wife? Where's Evelyn?'"

Rabbit questioned, "Did I?"

Leroy softened a bit with, "He wouldn't have said it otherwise."

Rabbit offered, "You two worry too much. It was a dream."

Harry, like Leroy, wasn't satisfied with Rabbit's sweeping the comments away so easily, so he pushed further. "Well, it wasn't a dream. It was more like a nightmare. Was it because you saw Evelyn recently?"

"Probably," Rabbit muttered as he looked away.

Leroy saw that Harry wasn't getting anywhere. He was able to tell that Rabbit was withholding something; *his* tone and facial expressions indicated so. So, he cut to the chase. "Are you married to Evelyn?"

There was a pause of ten seconds as Rabbit considered how to respond. He wasn't the type of individual who elaborated on his feelings toward women, especially after his personal losses had added up over the last couple years. He was guarded, and rightfully so in his estimation. But, these were his mates; his battle brothers; friends that offered their lives for his, just as he had done for them. They were all he had now, so he reluctantly opened up. He kept his head down as he began to speak, finally making eye contact as he further explained, "I married Evelyn on Alstar. *Am* I married to Evelyn? Yes and no. Humania doesn't recognize the marriages on settlements like Alstar until the settlements renounce independence and remit collateral as retribution. Even though Alstar is under Humania control, it still rejects Humania as its legitimate government and considers itself an independent world that has been invaded."

Harry interjected, "Why didn't you just marry Evelyn legally?"

Rabbit explained, "I was going to; I was. I even joined Humania's military after they saved Alstar from pirates. I don't know...Evelyn and I drifted apart. My going into the military put a distance between us that was hard to overcome. She went into counterintelligence, too. She wasn't always available even when I was. She halfheartedly agreed that we should see other people. In hindsight, I know she didn't really mean it. She certainly wasn't pleased to find me in bed with a couple of her friends. Anyway, guys, I don't know about you, but for me, I planned my life out and things happened along the way that just changed it; that changed me. I don't like to talk about Cypra, or my marriage, or a number of other failures that cost me my destiny."

"Your destiny?" Leroy scoffed. "Dude, I don't think we are destined for anything. We just live our lives the best we can with the hand we are dealt. I was a white man before Cypra. Now, I'm black. Am I destined to be a black man? Is that why I protected those on Cypra, only for them to turn around and torture me, eventually screwing with whatever they did to cause my DNA, or whatever, to change my pigmentation? I guess, somewhere up the line, one of my past relatives was black. I don't care about any of it, except that I can't shake the vision of my mother flipping out when she saw me like this for the first time. I sense an uneasiness when I speak with my brothers. What is my destiny?"

Harry agreed, "Or mine?"

Jon, who had hung in the corridor outside, heard most of what was said by his crewmen. "I can tell you what your immediate destinies are. You are going to carry out this mission and put all of this behind you." He picked now to poke his head through the bulkhead opening so his men could see and hear him clearly.

He went on, "Rabbit, I'm sorry about your marriage. I'm also sorry about all the other stuff you have gone through and are dealing with and for teasing you when I met her. I didn't know your situation and wrongly assumed she was another fling. Forgive me. Your destiny is still unsure."

Jon continued with, "Leroy, I'm sorry for your pigmentation issues and you having to cope with looking different. You *are* the same man, regardless of your appearance. You are a good officer, a great friend, and a hell of an asset to Humania. You will get command of a ship again down the road, no question."

Then, he turned to his engineer and weapons officer. "Harry, you are an unknown quantity. The sky is the limit for you once you fully realize your potential. I am floored by some of the work you have done and am convinced your destiny includes greatness."

Finally, Jon stated, "I believe we are living our destinies right now. Who's to say that we won't expose Cypra or Plenna for more than what they appear? We are on a mission, gentlemen, and not a mission that anyone can handle. We are the best of the best and I'm damn proud of each of you; proud of your accomplishments, proud of your abilities, and proud of who you are and having you under my command. I know my destiny includes you three."

Rabbit, upon waiting for Jon to finish kidded, "Awe, that's so sweet. Group hug."

Leroy added, "Well, Jon, that's why you have command of a ship and I don't. I'm honored to serve under you."

Harry ribbed Leroy, physically and figuratively, "Not the last time you will serve a man while being beneath him."

Leroy retorted, "Dude, I like to be on top."

Rabbit jumped in after the group laughed for a few seconds. "Speaking of being on top; I have been thinking about the genetic changes we have gone through. We have been mixed with orcs. We are still human, but we have the strength, power, and other positive orc attributes that make us almost super-human."

Jon asked in an respectful way, "So?"

Rabbit said, "Well, I believe we now have denser, stronger muscle, bone, and connective tissues; not to mention our organs' capacities to withstand damage they wouldn't have been able to withstand before. Our blood is more coagulative now, our endurance is greater, and we can breathe air that is more toxic."

Jon tried again. "We know most of this, but why are you telling us the details?"

"Because, although we know that we were supposed to be engineered to be stronger, faster, or whatever, why cross our DNA with orcs? Why only orcs?" Rabbit asked.

Jon was starting to see the bigger picture, but still needed to explain the obvious to his genius underlings. "The first, and most simple, answer is the number of human cells containing two sets of twenty-three chromosomes, one set inherited from each parent, or forty-six in total."

Rabbit agreed, "No, no; I got you. But, humans have one fewer chromosome than apes, with ape chromosomes two and four being fused together, known as chromosomal polymorphism, right?"

Jon was following and nodded so. "Right."

"Well, my point is that we share so much more with apes than orcs. We could gain most of the same attributes from them much easier than from orcs which we share very little code with and have different strand lengths and number of chromosomes. So, why orcs if we could get the same thing from gorillas?"

Leroy chimed in, "Like you said, we can breathe toxic air that humans and apes can't."

Harry called on his genetic knowledge. "No, Rabbit's right. It isn't just the ability to breathe under hazardous conditions. We could use prosthetic lungs or other apparatus for that. There's more to it."

Leroy found himself agreeing. If two of his highly intelligent counterparts agreed, there was some substance to it. Then, he remembered, "Okay, what about the Spidanoid chromosome that Harry and I tested positive for?"

While Jon had listened to the conversation, his mind took him back to Cypra. It searched for answers, scanning his long-term memory for images of his surroundings while he was forcibly experimented upon. The vagueness of his understanding during that time and the ambiguity that left him doubt caused him to ask the other Troublemakers to recall what they could.

The men struggled to remember anything that might help them with their plight. Not only were the procedures torture, a form of punishment not even acceptable for violent crimes, their minds were altered by induced comas and experimentation while on Cypra; massive quantities of drugs didn't help. All four men shared moments of clarity with much more time in confusion.

"Wait," Harry ordered. "I remember someone talking about an invasion. Was it us invading orcs or them invading us? Damn, I can't remember. No, there was talk about Spidanoids. Spidanoids invading orcs."

Rabbit had to ask for clarification, "How the hell would we be involved in Spidanoids invading orcs?"

Harry concurred, "I know; it doesn't make sense. But, I heard it and I know we have something to do with it."

Leroy added, "We probably have some Spidanoid in us, too. Two false positives out of two of us tested; you do the math."

Jon wrapped things up, so they could get on with the business of running scans, maintenance, and the like. "Yeah, one hundred percent positive with a one in a billion chance? Not likely. Okay, guys, keep on it. Let's get our stuff done and try to figure this out as we work."

***

Adolph Gruber wasn't accustomed to waiting for things to get done. His position as Crystal Technology's lead scientist not only guaranteed virtually everything he wanted at a moment's notice, but things that were illegal across the galaxy. His self-adoring image as a god gave him a feeling of indifference to all living beings beneath him. This also gave him the gods given right to indulge in all manners of painful, life threatening experiments he and his underlings conducted regularly with impunity.

A small cage was brought to him and uncovered, revealing an orc of minuscule proportions. The orc had tubes that were inserted in holes, cut haphazardly into the tiny being without regard for its existence or probable lack thereof in a relatively short time. Gruber didn't care in the least. He was pushing the boundaries of discovery to promote humanity throughout the Hyades Star Cluster and beyond, for gods' sake. He would be damned if an infant orc's suffering would halt that progress. Besides, the orc was helpless to speak so Gruber began carving into its chest as it screamed.

The baby was succumbing to its wounds. Gruber was outraged. Surely, these barbaric animals could endure more than he was subjecting them to. In disgust, he grabbed the useless non-human entity, viciously ripped tubes from its body, and tossed it in a bucket while it gasped. He covered the bucket with a lid to conceal the unwanted cries.

The walk down the corridor only took a minute or so, but a lifetime to Gruber's subject. Gruber swiped a security card that hung around his neck through a machine that opened a door for the scientific god-genius. He entered after stopping to rub one of his eyes as it itched. This took longer than his leisurely stroll up until now. When he was good and ready to enter the next phase of brutality, he walked into a long room with windows that lined each side.

"Another one, sir?" came from a Gruber subordinate.

Gruber laughed as he shook the bucket in hand. "Orcs aren't so special."

The subordinate agreed to a point. However, he had been working for several months providing Gruber with fresh subjects. He was aware of the unusual amounts of punishment orcs were able to be subjected to.

Each window looked into a virtual mirror like the one adjacent to it on either side. Every room had a female orc chained by wrists to the ceiling and ankles with legs spread apart connected to the floor. This made mass production of infants easy. Procreate by use of test tubes, inseminate fetuses for best resulting pregnancies, take milk as needed, and repeat the process. Every female was carrying up to ten lives, or subjects as they were so fondly referred to. Very few females expired, giving birth to dozens of subjects, the few exceptions being those who died during multiple c sections. No anesthesia was ever wasted on orcs.

Gruber traversed the long room, not showing any sign of compassion to the mothers and children that were suffering all around him. He pushed through a door at the end of the room, put the bucket down, and opened it. He grinned as a large spidanoid flew across its cage toward him. He acknowledged the hunger of one of his most prized possessions, "Okay big guy, its coming."

The screaming infant was pulled from the container by a leg and tossed into the Spidanoid's cage by way of a small opening where the giant insectoid fed quite frequently this way. The Spidanoid ripped the food apart within seconds.

Somewhere in the adjoining room a mommy cried.

Nine
Plenna

The *Outcast* made its final jump into the Plenna System. Jon and Leroy began running through their checklist. Harry and Rabbit reported from their stations that everything was good. The jump was successful.

But, an alarm sounded. To the Troublemakers' surprise, the jump brought them dangerously close to a number of ships that they didn't expect. The alarm was a proximity alert, a standard in most ships that made sure ship commanders were conscious of possible collisions with vessels in these very types of situations. They understood that space was vast with such a minor chance of such collisions. However, many ships had been lost to assuming great distances between themselves and planets, only to fall victim to colliding with another man-made object.

Jon looked up at the bright, glittering star field as it danced across his entire horizon. His eyes settled on a dozen or more dots that grew in size as they got closer to his ship. He requested answers from his copilot. "Leroy?"

"I'm on it, Jon."

"Make it quick," Jon ordered.

Leroy fired answers in rapid succession, "Fourteen vessels at seventeen kilometers and closing fast...unknown make and type. Jon, they are short distance fighters of some sort. I just don't know."

Jon's voice was loud and emphasized urgency in its tone. "Shit! They're not ours or the computer would recognize them. Get to your fighter!" He got on the comm and shouted, "Rabbit, get to your fighter. Harry, you have copilot."

As Jon turned the ship to put some distance between the *Outcast* and the incoming fighters, the crew scrambled to their stations. Within seconds, Harry pushed past Rabbit and Leroy, who were getting dressed in the corridor outside the bridge. A snap here and a tug there were the finishing touches on their preparation. Rabbit and Leroy exchanged good luck gestures, and then gave a sacred, "For Humania!" They punched fists and backed up against the hydraulic lifts that brought them up through the bottoms of their fighters.

Rabbit sat in his pilot's chair that was provided seemingly by magic. His cockpit came down around him and strapped him in as things automatically moved into position. He fired up his engines and ran through a silent checklist in his head. He did this with amazing speed as the situation warranted such expedition. Red bursts of fire exploded around him as his orientation righted itself. He looked across the outside of the *Outcast* where his eyes met Leroy's. He had matched Rabbit, button for button in his own fighter, and gave a thumb's up sign to indicate his readiness to lift off from the *Outcast*. The two men were pushed back in their seats as they soared into battle.

A barrage of fire raked the *Outcast*, over and over, from the fighters that were sweeping by. Harry adjusted the strength and location of the shields in an attempt to better protect the ship from the onslaught of high velocity laser bullets that skipped across her hull. He hadn't even finished sitting down yet. He was shaken by the violent rolls that Jon brought the *Outcast* in to avoid as much damage as possible. He fell into the copilot's seat and balanced the ship's power to cover shields, computers, and weapons systems the best he could.

Leroy called out, "Anyone know who we are fighting?"

Rabbit made light of the situation. "Yeah, the guys shooting at us." Truth be told, he didn't worry much about the outcome of ship battles that he partook in. He had been in quite a few, and to this date, had come through with flying colors. He even felt this way after weighing the odds. Fourteen enemy ships against his three wasn't that bad. If Leroy stayed close and covered his wing, he figured he would plow through the enemy. Leroy would probably take out a fair number because he was an exceptional pilot. The *Outcast* was a tough ship, too. Her survivability level was pretty good. That combined with Jon and Harry running her…it was a no-brainer.

Rabbit swung around to his port side and took out two enemy ships within fifteen seconds. He snapped, "Leroy, take low."

"Got it." Leroy dropped his ship below Rabbits and destroyed an enemy ship with two bursts. "That's one for me."

Rabbit targeted and destroyed two more from his elevated plain. "Two more here, buddy."

Jon now fought to protect his larger ship which appeared to be the enemy's primary target. The trick was to do so and keep within range of Rabbit's and Leroy's fighters. With some effort, he adjusted his path here and there to do both, but the *Outcast* was taking some hard hits and minor systems were beginning to fail. Jon made the decision to handle all operations of his ship even while he piloted and sent Harry to the Gatling gun. The automatic weapons systems just weren't cutting it.

Leroy's peripheral vision picked up two enemy fighters approaching at five o'clock low. They had Rabbit's ship in their sights. Leroy directed, "Rabbit, quick. Bank left!"

Rabbit threw his ship into a deep left turn. Red lights flashed to his right. He craned his neck, so he could see what Leroy had. Sure enough, he saw the two fighters that struggled to follow his sharp turn. Leroy cut to the right and dropped in behind them. He could only take out one enemy as his adjustments put him too far behind the lead fighter. Rabbit addressed Leroy, "Two kills for you."

"Great, but I can't get this one. He's on you, Rabbit."

Rabbit piloted his ship, so he always remained just out of the line of enemy fire, but this would only last for so long. He was closing in on the *Outcast* which was trailing a handful of enemy ships. Room to shift and roll was going to stop abruptly. Rabbit hailed Harry, not even knowing that he was operating the Gatling gun. "*Outcast*, coming in fast with one on my tail."

Harry instructed, "Rabbit, come straight over the top of us."

"Sure thing." Rabbit threw his ship hard to the right and shot over the topside of the *Outcast*.

Harry targeted the enemy fighter that was following him. A few quick bursts from his Gatling gun and the enemy foe was a thing of the past. Harry yelled in excitement, "I got him, Rabbit!"

Rabbit didn't answer. He found himself in an unintentional game of chicken with five ships. They came together so quickly that he never decided which way he would swing to avoid all of them. His intuition and reflexes caused him to swing and roll between them without thought. Several ships were missed by mere inches by his rapid contortions. How he managed to do so was nothing short of a miracle, even without firing a shot. They did though. Still, he passed them, somehow unscathed.

Leroy wasn't as lucky. As he came over the top of the *Outcast*, he fired some shots and hit one enemy. That ship blew into pieces just behind Rabbit's ship. Its remnants exploded against the surface of the *Outcast* and ricocheted up toward Leroy's ship. Leroy leaned hard on his stick and rolled to the left, barely scraping the surface of the *Outcast*. However, he took damage along his ship's starboard side, including one of the engines. "I'm hit."

The remaining four opened fire as they sped from the opposite direction. Meanwhile, Leroy fired his guns into the incoming ships on the left side. As skillful as Rabbit was, he couldn't fire quickly enough to take out any ships as he fought his way past the enemy squall line. In desperation, a little luck put an enemy fighter in the way of Leroy's errant shot. He racked up his fourth kill. But he was hit again. "Damn...Just damaged my other engine. Not good! I'm losing fuel."

Jon called out, "Fire! We have a fire on the starboard side in the engine room." The ship that exploded against her hull had sent shards into the *Outcast's* body. An oxygen tank erupted in flames.

Two more enemy ships had come around behind Leroy. They were eager for a kill and they saw their prey take several hits. They, too, came up over the top of the *Outcast*, and one of them got so close as it turned that Jon made out its pilot. They were gaining on Leroy's damaged ship as it slowed from its substantial loss of power.

Jon shouted out, "They're orcs. These are orcs we are fighting."

Harry fired in their direction as he snarled, "Not for long they aren't." The first ship passed, untouched. The second didn't though as a multitude of powerful golden spurts from the Gatling gun ripped into its fuel system and engines. Another brilliant explosion sent shards into the *Outcast*. Things were getting dicey.

There were four enemy fighters that remained, but more trouble was on the horizon. Jon's voice incited disgust. "We are in real trouble guys. We lost our shields and there are more ships coming in; big ships. No weapons here either." The automatic weapons systems were knocked out, too.

Rabbit said, "Hang in a little longer, Jon." Then, he instructed Leroy to bank right, so he did. Instantly, Rabbit fired into the ship that had set its sight on Leroy. This ship exploded, but had passed the *Outcast* as it did so. There was no damage taken on any Troublemaker ships this time.

Leroy was grateful. "Thanks, man." He wiped a bead of sweat that was gathering on his forehead before it ran into his eye.

Harry cried out, "Fire, fire! I can't gun any more. Jon, this fire is spreading too fast."

"Okay, get on it. Dammit! The *Outcast* is defenseless. I repeat, the *Outcast* is defenseless."

Leroy admitted, "I can't do much either, Jon. I can't hook up with you. My ship is too damaged near my bottom hatch."

Rabbit talked while he targeted the three enemy fighters that were swarming around the *Outcast*. "Leroy, can you make it to the planet?"

"Yeah. I'm pretty sure I can."

"Go ahead down there. I'll cover the *Outcast*," Rabbit exclaimed.

Leroy didn't hesitate to answer, "Already on my way."

Rabbit eliminated an enemy fighter. "Only two left."

Harry was being overwhelmed by several small fires in the upper bowels of the *Outcast*. He was knocked off his feet again and again due to enemy fire, but the hull held. Jon managed to keep any more damage from being too severe. Harry worked his way toward the engine room, but in the end, Jon called him off. Instead, Jon sealed the hatches from the main console in the bridge. Then he sucked the oxygen from the engine room. The main fire was out, making Harry's job a little easier now.

Jon was reluctant to do this though. Killing the oxygen in the engine room compromised his starboard engine, just as he feared it might. Now, he had a ship with no weapons and shields, small fires burning, and working with half power. He gave Rabbit the order, "Rabbit, after you get rid of these bastards, get down to the planet with Leroy. I'm heading to the planet, too. We have to make repairs."

Rabbit replied, "I hear you."

More red bursts spit across the *Outcast's* hull. However, they bounced off without any significant damage. This happened over the next few minutes until Rabbit finally destroyed the last two fighters.

Leroy's voice was heard. It was faint, and it cut out, but his message came across. "I'm on the surface. My ship is da…"

Jon tried to hail Leroy. "Leroy, come again." There was no response. "Leroy, can you read me?"

Harry called out, "I got the fires under control."

Rabbit also spoke. "Jon, those are huge ships coming. They have big batteries. I'm not sure, but they might be heavy cruisers or maybe battleships."

Jon tried Leroy one more time. "Leroy, can you hear me? Leroy?" After getting no response, he replied to Rabbit, although he was speaking generally, "I can't raise Leroy. I'm not getting his signal. I don't know if it's his ship or my system here. I can't make out what those ships are either. I have no idea what they are. But, yeah…they are big. I didn't know orcs had ships like that."

***

Leroy wasn't getting any signal. His engines were completely dead. He didn't realize just how lucky he was until he exited the cockpit and examined the damage on the exterior of his ship. His eyes took in the twisted metal and holes that ran down the starboard side. The engine panels were blown off, exposing hanging wires that were frayed or melted. The engines actually looked okay, as far as he could tell. He was thankful that the second engine didn't quit until he landed. He probably wasn't going to fly the ship again, at least, not any time soon.

He was able to set down in a clearing near a tree line that sat along a small mountain range. He had passed over a lake that was probably a mile behind him. If he was stuck without help for a while he could at least get water. He thought he saw smoke in the distance. However, he was busy trying to control his ship that was losing power and altitude quickly. Who knew what he saw as he barreled toward the ground in the dark?

Plenna Four was hot and wet. The lush vegetation was soft beneath Leroy's feet. He heard masses of insects and animal life; the amount of noise was staggering. He wiped the sweat that accumulated on his forehead in the few short minutes that he stood outside. He began to explore his surroundings and hoped to find the other Troublemakers, that is, if they survived the battle in space and made their way to the planet's surface, too.

He walked cautiously, carefully pushing through tall grass as his eyes surveyed every corner in the dark. To his surprise, he could see fairly well, even with the green hues that seemed to blanket everything. Not only was the night pretty clear and fairly well-lit from the huge moon that hung above, but his night vision had improved since the experiments on Cypra. He thought to himself, "Maybe there were some benefits to Cypra." He saw a ship fly overhead and dip down beyond the line of trees to his immediate northwest. He hoped it was the other Troublemakers. He would make his way up there shortly, but first he had some things to do.

Soon, Leroy found the Lake that he had passed over to the south. To his disappointment, it smelled putrid. It had a strong chemical smell that reminded him of something he couldn't put his finger on. Maybe it was some kind of outdated petroleum smell, like diesel or kerosene. Either way, it wasn't drinkable. He decided to backtrack to his ship. He did so by first heading east and then turning north. It would take a little longer, but maybe he could find some food or another source of water.

He didn't travel very far before he heard voices. He crouched as he moved among the tall growth of grasses and ferns that hid him well. He moved in a general direction toward the voices, adjusting which way he went. He accounted for the thought that as the voices became louder, he was "getting warmer".

Leroy poked his head out from a heavy tuft of vegetation. He saw a huge clearing with a fenced enclosure to his far right. He squinted to see who was talking. There were humans sitting and lying about within the fenced area. They weren't saying anything of substance, just chatter really. Leroy worked his way along the perimeter, staying hidden behind the tall grass as he moved.

Upon getting as close as possible to the other humans without being seen, he whispered to them, "Hey. Hey, over there."

Two men stood up and looked around to try and figure out who was talking. They looked left and right, but generally followed the direction of the voice, just like Leroy had done to find them. They saw Leroy. One spoke softly, "Hey."

Leroy needed to know the situation. "What is all of this?"

The long/short was, "Orcs captured us in a fight earlier today. We were defending a mining area southwest of here. There is only a dozen or so orcs in the area right now, but probably thousands west of here."

"We can travel from the way I came. It's clear, but orcs can see pretty well at night."

"Well, we have two advantages. We know the area better than they do and its almost morning. They won't have a sight advantage then."

Leroy wasn't convinced. "Yeah, but they have weapons and we will try to hide in broad daylight. Okay, here." With that, he threw a pair of metal cutters that landed at the foot of the fence. One of the men sat by the fence, picked up the cutters, and went to work. The other got his men to make a distraction. They got in a circle while two began to fight.

A few orcs ran over to the fence. At first, they were going to open the gate that held the humans inside, but then they decided to watch the spectacle. One said, "Dems fight lika gurls." They were all laughing. Another jeered, "Maybe you coulda kiss him to death." More orcs came together as the entertainment continued.

The captain of the captured troops broke up the fight and separated the men. "That's enough, you two. Save it for the damn orcs!" He looked at the orcs and snarled. Then, he spit on the ground.

Several orcs growled. One of the orcs yelled, "Not if you all fight lika dat!" The others laughed as boisterously as they could, trying to drive home humiliation into the little, squishy humans. Soon, they disbanded and went back to take up the positions that they had come from.

Ten minutes passed. Things had settled down and the orcs were visibly complacent. The captain sent his men to the opening in the fence. They began escaping in pairs. After three groups made it to Leroy, the orcs realized that the escape was underway.

Leroy gave a laser rifle to one of the men that made it over to him. He tossed a handgun to one that was on his way. He yelled to the men within the enclosure, "Let's go! Hurry!" He ran into plain sight and threw a smoke grenade to the far side of the enclosure.

Orcs were shooting blindly through the smoke. The humans began returning fire from the cover of the foliage. The guy with the handgun stopped shooting, though; his shots weren't accurate at this distance.

Two orcs had made it over to the area where the humans were escaping from. Leroy met them face to face. Several things happened that were key in the humans' attempt to escape. The first was that Leroy instructed all the men to get to cover and provide whatever covering fire they could. The second, and strangest, was this:

The two orcs stopped in their tracks and looked at Leroy. They didn't know what to make of the dark-skinned human. They had never seen one before. He was different than the little, squishy ones. He was bulkier and kind of scary looking. His dark complexion gave him an air of danger; he was dark like them. Plus, he confronted them without hesitation. Surely, he was a human to be reckoned with.

Leroy punched the one that was closest to his left with his right hand. The orc dropped to his knees. Leroy's momentum had swung him to the left. Now, he swung his left arm with the weight of his body to the right. His left fist caught the second orc under his chin, sending him into the air, and throwing him back ten feet to the ground. Then, Leroy kicked the orc that had dropped to his knees in the face to finish him off. The two orcs were momentarily stunned and nothing more. They would be up fairly quickly.

The guy with the rifle had taken a couple orcs out of the fight as well, but he couldn't see the ones that were emerging from the smoke until it was too late.

An orc had tackled Leroy and brought him to the ground. Another was standing over him in an instant. The guy with the handgun jumped from cover to get closer to the action. He fired several shots at the orc whom was standing. One of his bullets cut through the orc's shoulder. The orc stepped back. This was just enough for Leroy to kick out his knee, sending him to the ground. Leroy threw a right elbow into the nose of the orc that was holding him on the ground. As soon as the orc released him, Leroy turned and smashed his forehead with a devastating forearm. Then he turned and finished the orc that had been shot by crushing his airway with an open-handed chop to the throat.

Leroy was fighting his way back to the cover of foliage that hid the other men. He flipped an orc, he punched another. He found himself on the ground several times as he fought off one orc after another. He couldn't stop them all though, so even though orcs weren't terribly accurate with guns, enough of them firing could do damage, simply by odds of probability. This was the case as several men had been shot. And those that were shot didn't survive. Orc bullets were almost as big as shlogger cans. This was because orcs could wield huge weapons due to their great strength.

Leroy made it to the brush and led the men out of the area. Upon backtracking to his ship, he made attempts to reach the other Troublemakers, but he still couldn't reach them. He turned to the security force captain and asked for his help. "I think I have other ships in the area. You think we can split up and try to locate them?"

The captain seemed skeptical. "Without weapons?"

"Just stay off the paths," Leroy suggested. He cracked the knuckles on his right hand that found one of the orc's jaws. He grimaced, "Do you have supplies anywhere around here?"

One of the other men spoke. "Hey, Cap. What about the cave on the south ridge?"

The captain replied to his subordinate, "Yeah. If we can make it, we can resupply there." Then, he replied to Leroy's earlier question with, "Maybe we can find your friends as we head north along the mountain range."

Leroy was thankful. "Awesome, Captain. I'll head through that mountain pass to the west."

"What? I wouldn't do that."

"Why not?"

The captain reminded, "Remember? Thousands of orcs over there?"

"Yeah, I remember, but I have to find the other Troublemakers and I gotta see what the orcs are doing, too," Leroy stated.

The captain gave a look of revulsion. "Are you kidding me? Did you say Troublemakers?" He looked around at the other men and spit on the ground.

"Yeah. Why? What's wrong with the Troublemakers?"

The captain said sarcastically, "Nothing, if you don't mind a million of your people dying at their hands." He spat again.

Leroy was pissed. Who the hell did this guy think he was? "I saved your ass, didn't I? We aren't bad guys."

"Yeah, well, we will see about that. It isn't over, yet. The orcs will send out patrols and we are defenseless. You might have just gotten us killed, too," the captain said with disdain.

Leroy grabbed some stuff from his ship and growled, "I'll tell you what. You do your thing and I'll do mine. I put my life on the line for you, you ungrateful bastard!"

The captain threw Leroy's rifle back at him. "Here. Take your fucking handgun, too. Good luck, asshole!" He gathered his men and they headed north. They grumbled and cursed as they left, more spitting and head shaking in Leroy's direction.

Leroy was beginning to wonder if all humans were getting as indignant as the security captain. He was pretty sure that all Marines seemed to be that way. For all of humanity's capacity, even with all their technology, they seemed to be getting worse. Maybe, it was a sense of entitlement. Maybe, it was greed. Maybe, it was more prevalent in the military. Maybe, *he* should have given the captain a break. The captain had been in deadly skirmishes that cost his men their lives.

Leroy found himself thinking about his own qualities. Was he a bad guy after all? He had a hot temper. He admitted to himself that he walked around with a chip on his shoulder most of the time. Maybe, it *was* him. Maybe that was why he was able to stand off against those orcs in hand-to-hand combat without blinking an eye. He mumbled to himself, "Maybe, I have as much of a death wish as Rabbit."

He directed his attention to Rabbit. He had to locate him and the other Troublemakers. Well, he wasn't going to head north with the captain and his men. It looked like he would travel west, instead. He set off to a small pass that divided the mountains a few miles in that direction. He checked a few things and set out.

Ten
A Meeting of the Minds

Rabbit had landed less than ten minutes after Leroy did, although he ended up in a clearing, maybe a dozen miles away. He removed his helmet and stepped down from his virtually undamaged craft, took note of his surroundings, grabbed some supplies, and headed southwest.

After walking for a half hour, he heard gunfire south of him. The melee was muted which indicated some distance between Rabbit and the gunfire. However, he had a difficult time discerning between it and the heavy sounds of life that flourished on this tropical world. He decided to generally head south, but keep a pace just to the west, working his way around potential trouble, but being close enough to engage the enemy on his terms.

Gunfire erupted again, but this time it was much louder and closer. Rabbit dashed behind trees just off the trail he was following. In the distance, he saw humans running toward him, but not making it to his location. Several dropped as their bodies went limp, blood covering them. Others scattered into the trees with orcs close behind, their shrill screams an indication of their finality.

Rabbit wanted to help, but he just didn't know the situation. He was lucky that he didn't reveal himself because a group of twenty or so orcs came out of hiding within a stone's throw of him. He was shocked that these orcs moved so quietly. They were disciplined and cunning!

As the last few humans panicked north on the trail, they were met by these noteworthy orcs. The human leader of the group, a captain as best as Rabbit could ascertain, pled for his men's lives.

He was met by a large, brooding orc, dressed in a navy-blue uniform, with leather boots and gloves. The orc holstered his gun and unsheathed a long, heavy sword as he intimidated his prey. He calmly said, "I let you a men live if you tell me wer da big, brown man goed."

The captain, scrambling to save his men and himself at this point never hesitated. Besides, the damn Troublemaker had caused more of his men to die. It was in a way, payback. He begged, "Please, let us live. The brown man went west toward the mountains."

The orc growled, "On da trail?"

The captain shook his head violently "no" as he cried now, "No, he went through the jungle just south of here."

The orc swung his sword, severing the man's head from his neck. The other humans met the same fate at the hands of other orcs standing nearby. The brooding orc let out, "I want dat brown human!"

Rabbit observed the orcs head southwest into the jungle, gauged his chances to survive against these monsters, and estimated his odds of getting to Leroy first. He hoped Leroy was the brown man that was mentioned. After seeing the orcs travel safely out of view, and deciding to risk his life for his friend, Rabbit ran south along the trail.

He ducked into cover again as he tried to reach the *Outcast*, but like Leroy before him, his attempts failed. He didn't know if the planet's magnetic field was causing interference or if it was due to the thick, wet, and heavy vegetation that acted like a blanket, covering communication in a surface of disturbance. Perhaps all communication was being jammed. Regardless, Rabbit, Leroy, and the *Outcast* were going to have to rely on themselves for a while.

Morning light crept up in the east, casting long, low shadows that stretched the landscape beneath the turbulent, green skies. Thunder could be heard as gathering clouds grew in the ever-increasing heat and humidity.

Rabbit ran at nearly full speed for an hour, finding the trail that cut west and pierced through the mountains. However, he was unsuccessful in finding Leroy. Heavy rain mixed with hail and frequent lightning that resulted in endless sounds of thunder pelted his senses, hiding the very things he sought. What he did find was a series of caves that cut beneath the towering peaks above. He left some small rocks in chosen patterns every couple hundred feet to help him find his way back out the way he entered. He didn't want to risk getting lost so close to the orcs that he had begun to hear.

Startled, Rabbit drew his gun and fired repeatedly at the two orc guards that surprised him. They came upon him totally unaware of his presence. It was just a case of being in the wrong place at the wrong time and it cost them their lives. Rabbit thought for a moment that it may have cost him his life, too. He scurried around to his left with his back facing the cave wall, so he would easily see anything that came upon him. Based on the elevated commotion, easily heard as orcs alarmed each other and their sturdy, rugged frames pounded their weight upon the rock beneath them, Rabbit knew he was in trouble.

He pulled out his sword, and just in time, too. The close quarters in the caves gave little distance or time to shoot at every enemy. Rabbit found himself engaged in hand-to-hand combat with three orcs, all the while shooting at other targets that he could keep at bay. A slice here, a parry there, and an occasional strike kept him alive. He was an expert at self-defense and offense, too. Were it not for his years of training and his new-found strengths, he may have succumbed earlier to the overwhelming odds that fought against him. He would engage dozens of green brutes before fighting his way to an expansive opening, each large, intelligent orc pushing his skills to the limit.

The hallway of sorts had led him to an enormous room, carved out of the stone that was the mountain itself. With more orcs closing in behind him, he fired furiously into the room, using his gun like a scalpel. Bullets ripped through a half dozen orcs, each targeting hearts and lungs as skill and precision made their mark. Two bullets that ricocheted off the hard walls of the cave felled nearby enemies. Return fire met Rabbit as well. One bullet grazed his arm as another tore through his right thigh, causing his legs to buckle.

Rabbit aimed his gun at several silver, metallic tanks that lined the wall to his left, a hundred feet away. He fired, causing each to erupt in fireballs that ejected shards of metal in every direction. Most of the shrapnel pierced some of the spacecraft that were parked in the cavernous reaches of the hollowed-out room while a small amount entered orcs bodies that had entered the area. Fires now began to engulf several spacecraft, drawing attention away from him, but further endangering his well-being. Superheated fuel wasn't something he relished being within a hundred feet of.

Dozens had fallen, but more came into view. Things were becoming desperate.

***

Nuttybomb was awakened by the furious sound of battle. Even the colossal thunderstorms couldn't hide these sounds he had come to know. He rushed past an officer that began to explain how a human had passed security by using the caves to the east. Nutty surmised that there couldn't possibly be this much gunfire, explosions, and blood curdling screams because of one human. It just couldn't ring true.

He rushed to the largest cave in the area to ensure the safety of his sister, Pretty, who had just landed on the planet and was due to disembark from her spacecraft. Several officers, including Nuttybomb's brother, Booma, and several of his top guards followed closely.

Chaos reigned as debris rained down. The cave Nuttybomb and his orcs entered was littered with bloody orcs. Explosions had wrought havoc with his troops and his ships. Gunfire had erupted again and minor blasts from isolated pools of fuel caused more collateral damage. Nutty and his orcs hunkered down behind barrels, crates, and anything they could to avoid the incoming objects that were cutting through other orcs. They were seeking the company of the squishy human that was the antagonist of so much carnage. Their eyes darted from one object to the next, hoping to locate the bastard.

Just then, Booma received bullets that tore through his body, causing him to shriek as he slumped to the ground. He was temporarily out of commission, a consideration lost on Nuttybomb, for Nuttybomb didn't worry about outcomes. Even his brother would live or not when it came to battle, something Nutty knew all too well in fights like these. Still, he sought to stop the incoming gunfire and explosions to mitigate any further damage.

Nutty jumped to his feet in an attempt to help his brother. As his head turned quickly to his right, his eyes picked up movement in his periphery. He spotted the human! Instantly, he fired his gun and pulled his sword, barreling frantically in the direction his eyes led him.

He was raked with gunfire, as were his guards. Several of his most trusted orcs fell back to the ground, bullets ripping through their essential, life-giving organs.

Nuttybomb sprang forward, almost immune to the damage his body was taking as heightened adrenaline levels and endorphins poured throughout his body. In an instant, he was on the enemy, thanks to a fuel blast that knocked the human to his knees. His speed and agility were amazing, considering his monstrous size. He pulled his sword and engaged the squishy little bastard. It was time for this lucky human to die!

***

Leroy followed several strangely placed rocks within a series of caves. He immediately recognized the formations as being Rabbit's handiwork. Dead orcs strewn throughout the caves confirmed his suspicions; he was on Rabbit's trail.

The walls cracked, and dust filled the air as distant explosions rocked the caves that Leroy was traveling within. As he traversed from one to the next, closing the distance between him and his friend, the shock waves from the blasts became stronger. Pieces of rock fell from the ceilings, first pebble-sized, and then, dangerous boulders that began to block the passage behind him.

Leroy was becoming increasingly concerned. He recognized the luck that gave him the upper hand at the prison camp, something he hoped would continue, but surprise and the orcs' underestimating his strength helped in his earlier fights. Even if he reached Rabbit, the two might not be able to get back out the way they came in. Either way, he continued on, occasionally finding a way to eliminate each orc he came across. However, like the damage from blasts increasing as he got closer to the action, so too was the number of enemies he encountered. He began fighting several at a time.

***

Jon had put the *Outcast* down in a clearing somewhere near Rabbit's and Leroy's ships. All fires were extinguished, and any essential minor repairs were quickly made. The gravity inducers were never harmed, and the hull had only received minor damage. The shields and weapons were easily fixed as they only needed rewiring and patching in spots, as did the engines; some systems were bypassed or rerouted through the mainframe computer, saving hours of work.

Although Jon wanted to help his crewman, he knew that the *Outcast* needed to be operational for their survival. Years of Humania battle and leadership protocol dictated such. Unfortunately, the ship's well-being had to come first.

Within two hours, Jon and Harry were finally ready to look for their friends. Jon called out a checklist of ship functions as he ran tests. In return, Harry confirmed operational status for each as he readied the engine room and weapons systems. They lifted off.

Jon called to Harry through the *Outcast's* internal communication system, "Harry, you saw one of our fighters as we passed over before?"

"Yeah, Jon; a couple clicks south."

Jon ordered, "Okay, that's where we're headed first."

"What about this damn storm?" Harry asked.

Jon replied, "Unfortunately we have to go out in it, but yeah...it's a horrible storm."

Harry barked, "I've never seen lightning like this."

Jon tapped the radio in hopes of it giving him something it had refused to do so far. "Are you getting any signals or able to communicate on this gods forsaken planet?"

Harry despairingly answered, "No to both."

"What do you make of it? Why can't we communicate here?"

Harry rubbed his face in disappointment. "There are two things I can think of. It's not the storm because we would get intermittent static, not the steady crap we are getting. Plus, I don't think there is a power grid with transformers that a storm would knock out, so forget that. The first is just electrical interference caused by transmitters. However, this would have to be done on a massive scale to cut our communication like it has. The only other thing I can think of is maybe an electromagnetic pulse, similar to nuclear explosions detonated in the upper atmosphere. It would require immense amounts of energy to do that though."

"EMP, huh?" Jon wasn't so sure. The power to halt communication would have needed to be huge. He had a thought. "Harry, could it be done with nuclear reactors on the ground, or maybe even underground?"

"That's a good question. Factors would include energy yield, gamma ray output, and interaction with the planet's magnetic field. Altitude is key though, so I'm just not sure."

Jon paused as he thought, but eventually continued, "What about amplification into the atmosphere from a ground source?"

"That would be more plausible related to electrical interference; more likely. But who would be causing it? Isn't Plenna devoid of humans, other than small colonies?"

"That's what we are here to find out. I don't think orcs would know how to use technology like that, even as simple as it is. I guess we'll see." Jon's attention was diverted to one of his fighters that he spotted on the surface. "I have a visual on one of our fighters below. I'm taking us down. Get ready to go outside."

Within minutes, Jon and Harry had examined and determined the fighter to be Leroy's. Its damage was significant, an obvious giveaway that it was his fighter, rather than Rabbit's. In fact, it was too damaged to reunite with the *Outcast*. In the end, Jon decided to leave it on the planet and continue the search for his men. He took Harry back into the sky to accomplish this task. But, before he did, he had Harry detonate Leroy's ship, so it didn't fall into enemy hands.

***

Rabbit threw himself onto his rear and swung his legs up and backward to send the huge beast sailing over him. The weight of the hulking creature wasn't what he calculated in the split second that he conducted this instinctual move of self-defense. The orc was *heavy!*

Just as Rabbit jumped to his feet, so did the menacing orc. The two stared at each other momentarily, sizing up the other to determine what to do next. Rabbit's eyes darted from left to right, trying to locate his gun that was knocked out of his hand from the explosion that sent him to his knees. Then, he noticed that the orc before him didn't carry a firearm either. If there was one saving grace for the squishy human, it was the fact that the enormous orc couldn't shoot him either.

However, fear gripped Rabbit like he had never felt before as he evaluated his enemy's capabilities. He was shocked at what he witnessed; his brain was struggling to comprehend what his eyes strained not to see.

Standing ten feet away was a massive, green creature, around seven feet tall and easily weighing over five hundred pounds, maybe even six or seven hundred pounds. The orc had tree trunks for legs, a barrel chest, and cannons for arms. Its skin tightly wrapped all five hundred plus pounds of bulging muscle, fighting to contain the immense power contained within from bursting out through the veins that rippled its surface. The gnarled face that it wore tried to contain its dangerous teeth and powerful jaws.

The orc growled, "You a bit of a handful fo' my troops, but not fo' me. You wer lucky to flip me. I thought you would be a lil more squishy. I will not maka dat mistake again."

If the orc was seeking a response, he didn't get one, at least not intentionally. Rabbit was too horrified to formulate words, a first for him. He simply shrugged his shoulders as if to say, "Okay?" The word stuttered out on its own.

Nuttybomb walked toward Rabbit as he angrily spoke. "Who are you, human?"

Rabbit stepped around to Nutty's left, like a boxer in a ring. He positioned himself as he had earlier; his back facing the wall near the area he entered. He back-peddled as best he could to cover his hindquarters.

The defensive act was noted by Nuttybomb as he circled around his prey and closed to within six feet. He also took note of the location of his troops, ships, and items nearby. His mind carefully calculated distances, formulated contingencies, and eventually, his plan to remove the squishy human from a living existence.

Rabbit needed to buy time and he needed that time to think. Time, the most important commodity in a life, seldom thought about, but so essential to any existence, and perhaps, the barometer of life itself, was moving quickly.

As terrified as Rabbit was just moments before, he was floored by the revelation of what occurred next.

Nuttybomb briefly discontinued his pursuit of Rabbit, tipped his head to the right, somehow extrapolated, and began, "Time a funny ting. It precious. Yes, very precious. Time to tink? You don't need time to tink. It time fo' you to die."

Rabbit ducked beneath Nuttybomb's blade, stepped left, and parried another near-death blow. Sparks danced as blade met blade and the sharp contact of metal on metal rang out. Rabbit struggled to anticipate Nuttybomb's movements, and knew that it was he, his movements that were being anticipated. What he couldn't believe was that Nuttybomb had somehow entered his mind; no, invaded his mind and read his thoughts. He didn't know how that could have been possible, but Nuttybomb's words confirmed the violation that Rabbit felt in the deepest reaches of his soul.

Nuttybomb used all his abilities to their fullest potential. Unlike his interrogation of human prisoners, he used his telepathic capabilities to defeat Rabbit. He was bigger and stronger than his foe, he wasn't inferior to anyone in close combat with his sword either, and he had a decided advantage in being able to foresee Rabbit's movements.

Rabbit barely managed to deflect attack after attack; each heavy blow precipitating painful shock waves through his arms that were caused by the orc's powerful strikes. He was desperately trying to clear his mind, yet somehow think about a way to defeat the highly intelligent and gifted individual he was being victimized by. His heart was in his throat, his legs were shaky. But he eventually yielded to something he had learned time and time again. He began to respond to Nuttybomb's thrusts without thought. He put his fears aside and didn't worry about the outcome.

As Nuttybomb swung downward, Rabbit dodged and deflected, slipping down and to the right. Intuitively, he returned a thrust with his own weapon, slicing his previously invincible enemy. This occurred, not once, but three times over the next two minutes, leaving Nuttybomb marked on both upper arms, his left hand, and a deep gash in his abdomen. Nuttybomb managed a deep cut in Rabbit's left forearm. None of these wounds inhibited the pair from ending though.

Rabbit, a bit more confident in his abilities to injure his opponent spoke between clashes. "Who are you, orc?"

Nuttybomb returned dialogue as he fought. "I am Nuttybomb, Warchief of Hotta, Angra, Lilst, and Plenna. You bein' here anda attackin' my troops is an act of war fro' da humans to orcs. Tortuin' orcs and killin's dem is not permitted!"

Rabbit kept pace with his larger foe, "I attacked your orcs because you attacked us in space and shot down one of our fighters. Where is my friend who landed here before me?"

"You a friend not a here."

Rabbit barked, "Your orcs viciously killed so many unarmed humans on the trail. I'm supposed to believe you?"

Nuttybomb upped his attack, but with every strike came a counter. The fluidity of movements was breathtaking; sword against sword, sometimes two hundred swings and counters per minute as the two performed a fine art under the direst circumstances.

Nuttybomb was reminded of the engagement he witnessed back on his home world of Hotta between two of his top guards, Gunza and Headhunta. Headhunta had gone rogue, joining the enemy, changing his allegiance to protect his criminal son. Gunza and he were locked in a display of strength, speed, and agility, matched only by their skills as they fought to decimate the other. Nutty thought how close this fight was to that one. Both he and the human were highly skilled warriors. Nuttybomb was no longer a clumsy child. No, he was a grizzled veteran, having felled twenty top warriors over the last two years.

Finally, a response of, "I don't care what you believe," was returned. With that, Nutty inconspicuously altered his angle of attack and caught Rabbit off guard. His blade found its way under Rabbit's left armpit and buried itself between two of his ribs, comfortably cutting through skin, muscle, and lung. It was just the stroke of luck Nuttybomb had hoped for. He lulled his enemy into a pattern of attacks and counters, only to spring an unsuspected trap.

Rabbit was shocked. He grabbed Nuttybomb's forearms as he stared wildly into his predator's eyes, pulling himself off the sword that he slightly hung from. It took all his strength with both hands to pry himself from Nutty's deadly intentions. He staggered backward as he kicked out one of Nuttybomb's knees, causing Nutty to lose enough balance to let Rabbit slither free. Rabbit gasped as blood came up from his damaged organ and filled his mouth. He choked and spat dark red liquid away from his air passage that was so vital to his existence.

Nutty pressed, "Squishy humans no survive a sword through da lung. You a finished now."

Rabbit struggled to gather himself, each cough nearly bending him over as pain caused involuntary reactions. "No, Nuttybomb, I'm not quite finished, yet." He inhaled a deep breath and stood up straight, took up a defensive posture, and stated, "I'm not finished with you."

Nuttybomb wasn't so persuaded by Rabbit's words of denial. Nutty questioned his own brother's chances of possibly being shot through his lung and maybe his heart too...and he was an orc!!! Orcs' bodies were able to absorb unusually large amounts of damage; damage that would kill other, squishy species.

A human surviving such a life-threatening wound was hardly possible. Still, he wondered how this human could resist such a blow and even stand up. "Who are you, Human?"

Rabbit thought it might cause fear or maybe just a mental lapse in Nuttybomb to allow his name, a name that was famous and infamous to be revealed. After all, hadn't he killed fourteen million orcs? Didn't he just kill or seriously wound dozens more single-handedly? He sought to expose any weakness in Nuttybomb, so he agreed to give his name and figured he would probably have to elaborate about his connection to all the orcs' deaths on Cypra. What would an orc know about him, anyway? "I am Captain Rabbit Harrison. I have dealt with orcs before. You have no idea why I am here and what my intentions are, but killing fellow humans is a mistake you will pay for."

Stunned by Rabbit's words, Nuttybomb lowered his sword as he comprehended just how unlikely his encounter with the very human he wanted dead was occurring. The hair on the back of his neck stood up and his muscles automatically tensed, the veins in his neck and temples throbbed. As his anger grew to a boil, he bobbed forward and back, growling under his breath, spitting through his teeth. "Rabbit Harrison, tortura of millions, murdera of my brudders...what do you have to say before you die?"

Rabbit smiled. "Well, I don't want you upset. You seem like a nice guy and all, but we are all gonna die...even you, Warchief Nuttybomb. I'm not just some ordinary, squishy human you can kill so easily, though.

I don't feel like dying today." Rabbit paused as he observed Nutty's reactions. He was amazed by the orc's composure considering the facts he had just learned. Why wasn't he attacking in a mad frenzy? How did this Nuttybomb exude such self-control? How did he continue to listen so carefully, even with his posture revealing his undeniable anger and hate?

Most orcs had left the maelstrom that was ripping their comrades apart. However, a few watched the encounter between their Warchief and the squishy human from the protection of random objects that sat about, ravaged at times by uncontrolled fires and explosions that continued to rip everything apart. Ignoring the carnage around him, and only focusing on Rabbit, Nuttybomb spoke in a deliberately controlled manner as more explosions rocked the huge cavern, sending rocks and dust onto everyone below. "It ok if I upset or not. It not ok fo' you to live anda hurt more orcs, tho."

While Nuttybomb spoke, Rabbit spotted a female orc who was trying to escape a spacecraft that was parked in the cavernous hangar. Fires had engulfed it and smoke poured from its hatches, an indication that being aboard the ship was risky at best. Rabbit dashed toward her, seeking to outrun Nuttybomb, ultimately hoping to take her as a hostage to save his own life.

Nuttybomb pursued his smaller adversary as he yelled to his sister, "Pretty, go back in da ship!" He was faster than Rabbit, at this point; Rabbit had a damaged lung and a bullet wound that had severed muscle and nerves in one of his legs. Nutty's own wounds, although severe to other orcs, were moderate to him. Rabbit turned just as Nutty's sword surely would have finished him. Swords met again.

Rabbit had slowed considerably, and he realized it. Blood loss was further weakening him by the second, too. It wasn't very difficult at this point to lose his sword to the much stronger Nuttybomb and that is just what happened. But as Rabbit was disarmed, he finagled his way to Nutty's right, using leverage to his advantage, and quickly pulled his back up against the orc's chest. As his body blocked Nutty's left arm from the sword he held in his right, Rabbit used both hands to work on disarming Nutty. However, the immense strength of the orc made that feat impossible.

Options were slim, and Rabbit was being denied his life. On a whim based on the quickest of calculations, he took a risk. He actually grabbed Nuttybomb's blade with both hands, using force and balance to minimize the chance of being cut, and began to exert all the remaining strength he had to bend Nutty's sword.

Nutty gasped at the display of power of his tiny foe. His sword was being bent into the shape of a horseshoe, a deed he hadn't seen performed by any orc. Who was this Rabbit Harrison and how could he do such a thing? As it turned out, Nutty was just stunned enough to be smashed in the face as Rabbit, after rendering the sword useless, further exploited him through leverage, and brought both hands around in a coupled fist.

Following a jaw-breaking strike was a takedown move that flipped Nuttybomb over Rabbit's shoulder and threw him hard to the ground. In an instant, Rabbit had a choke hold on the powerful orc, an act that was as unlikely as the unbendable sword being bent.

But, Nutty was so strong, too strong, in fact, for Rabbit to keep him on the ground. He forced his left hand between them and reached into Rabbit's chest where his severed lung sent a pool of blood onto the ground. Rabbit screamed in agony, pushing away from Nuttybomb, releasing his hold and squirming at the end of Nutty's hand. He somehow freed himself.

As Rabbit staggered backward, he again saw Pretty, Nuttybomb's sister trying to escape the burning ship. He wearily made his way toward her in a last attempt to use her as a shield.

As stars stopped dancing before his eyes and his lungs were full of air, Nutty arose to gauge Rabbit's progress toward Pretty. He rationalized Rabbit's attempt as a meager opportunity to deny him of his kill and not a very good one at that. But the human was getting too close to Pretty for his comfort.

Nuttybomb pursued Rabbit across the western side of the hangar when he noticed Rabbit drop to his knees, just ten feet in front of Pretty's ship. He upped his pace once he realized Rabbit had picked up his gun, lost earlier to the shock wave from an explosion.

Rabbit tiredly stood up and turned his weapon to cut down his opponent, but he couldn't aim fast enough. He was tackled and thrown twenty feet as the momentum from Nuttybomb's onrush smashed his back against the cave wall, causing the gun to fire involuntarily; one that fired upon contact and the other as Rabbit was molded into the wall. Both bullets did damage, although the effects weren't immediate.

The immense power and weight of Nuttybomb shattered Rabbit's ribs and crushed several of his vertebrae. A handful of Rabbit's organs were cut or smashed by the impact as his body was readying itself to shut down. The back of his skull fractured, brain and soft tissue swelling occurred almost immediately.

Nuttybomb wasn't right either. He felt his heart pounding in his chest, and upon looking down, saw blood spurting from holes above his left nipple. Rabbit had somehow fired off two miraculous shots that tore through his heart. He was incensed at the thought that he might die at the hands of this Rabbit Harrison. He roared as he brought his left hand around Rabbit's throat. He leaned down and gathered a piece of hot metal that had been thrown from a combustible tank. He lifted Rabbit off the ground with one hand while he spoke, "Now, you will die."

The knife-like apparatus that was coming toward Rabbit's chest was deflected. Rabbit used both hands and whatever strength he could muster to grab Nutty's hand that held it and tried to force it away. Ultimately, Nuttybomb was too strong to be completely stopped, but enough force was used to keep the weapon from reaching its intended target.

Instead, Nutty's slow thrust was diverted away from Rabbit's trunk. It was simple math really; for every inch the cutting utensil moved forward, it was equally pushed to the side. Nutty leaned hard against Rabbit. This accomplished two things; the first was it broke Rabbit's grip from two hands to one while hastening his demise through internal bleeding; the second was that it dislocated his arm from his shoulder, keeping Rabbit a single-handed fighter if the battle would continue. Nuttybomb added insult to injury as he forced the makeshift blade through Rabbit's limp wrist, fastening him to the wall.

Rabbit cried out. Even with his throat being crushed while his body clumsily dangled, his pathetic screeches were audible. He was dying. But he didn't want to die here at the hands of this ruthless monster. Something inside him clung to mortality. He summoned the strength to kick his feet back against the wall he was stuck to. This engaged five-inch blades in the front of his boots. He kicked wildly, severing everything he could to Nuttybomb's thighs and groin.

Nuttybomb released Rabbit as he, himself dropped to his haunches holding whatever he had left in his groin from spilling out. He helplessly watched as Rabbit wriggled free and pulled the metal sheath that had confined him from his wrist.

The fight was over. Neither opponent had the strength to finish the other. Both fought to get to Pretty first, but in the end and against all odds, it was Rabbit who did.

As Rabbit approached Pretty's ship, Leroy dashed into the cave, guns ablaze and sword swinging. He held enough orcs at bay, so he was able to reach Rabbit and grab Pretty.

Pretty wasn't the grabbing type however, and she let Leroy have it. Her teeth clung to his throat as he attempted to manhandle her into submission. The human who stumbled upon her was taken aback by how strong and wild she was.

It was an odd scene; the three were locked together; Leroy was holding Rabbit, so he didn't fall over, Rabbit held Pretty in a choke hold, and she held Leroy's throat in her mouth. It took the combination of Leroy's strength and Rabbit's skill to force her release of Leroy. All the while Leroy tried to maneuver them back through the caves as he took potshots at any orcs that got too close.

Pretty screamed, "I da Warchief's sista. You gonna pay!"

As the three left the hangar, words emphatically left Nuttybomb's lips, "Rabbit Harrison!"

Eleven
More Incoming

"Incoming!" Harry alerted his crewmates. The *Outcast* dodged blasts from the huge ships that tracked it from Plenna Four's surface into space.

Jon instructed, "Evasive maneuvers. Get us to the actuator as quickly as possible. Hopefully, we can outrun them."

A nearby explosion shook the *Outcast* to her core, the gravity inducers shuddered enough to cause each man onboard to be lifted from his seat.

Harry gulped, "Damn, that was close, Jon."

Jon agreed, but before he spoke he was cut short by a transmission he and Harry picked up. "Dis is Warchief Nuttybomb. Do not letta da human ship leave da area. Anyone who fails will deal wit' me. Dat is all."

Harry questioned, "Isn't that the orc Rabbit fought?"

"Yeah, so?"

Harry explained, "So, his transmission was clear. Maybe he's in space now as well, but if he isn't, how could his transmission be so clear while being sent from Plenna?"

Jon looked at Harry in a bit of disbelief. "Hmm, that's a good point. Did you see any ships leave the surface after us?"

"Nope."

Jon reasoned, "So, it seems that our orc friends have the ability to cut communication from down on the planet."

Harry agreed, "It sure seems that way." Then, he addressed the crew, "Guys, more incoming."

The *Outcast* shook violently as two more blasts rocked her. Leroy screamed from the medical area, "Dammit guys, I'm losing him! Can you please keep the ship from falling apart?"

Jon made an observation that made him shudder. His vessel was being overtaken by the massive orc ships. He ordered Harry to, "Line up with the actuator at top speed and get us through."

Harry shouted, "At top speed? Without time for calculations? This isn't gonna go well."

"Yeah, they're gaining on us and that last one was too close."

Harry started pleading, "Jon..."

Jon hastened, "I know, but we have no chance of saving Rabbit if we don't make the jump and we just don't have the luxury of time to line up properly to run calculations. Use the same ones that got us here from Cypra."

Harry barked out orders that were somehow acceptable to his superiors under the circumstances, "Leroy, strap down Rabbit and put away all loose objects. Do it now! Give him 3CCs of Hyperstatic Glycine. Then, you guys better strap in, too. This is gonna hurt."

Thirty seconds later Leroy hectically replied, "Done." After a few seconds he added, "Wait, the orc girl..." He unstrapped himself and flew through a bulkhead, opening a hatch that had locked Pretty behind it.

Pretty growled at Leroy and started toward him to finish tearing his throat out. He cautioned, "Whoa, Sister. I need to strap you down, so you don't get hurt when we punch through the wormhole."

Pretty's growl softened to more concern as he approached. "Why I get hurt?"

Leroy looked into her eyes as he explained, "The ship is liable to be thrown around pretty hard. You would be tossed like a toy. We wouldn't want that."

Pretty asked another question, one that left her currently puzzled, "Why you care if I get hurt?"

Leroy instructed, "Here, sit down and give me your arm. Make it quick." Then, he laughed and continued, "Why would I want to hurt you? Besides, isn't your brother the Warchief? You getting hurt would only kill our chances of diplomacy later."

Pretty obliged, "I know dis duplomicy word. Duplomicy tween orcs and humans? Ok." Then, she asked about Rabbit. "What 'bout yer friend who is really hurted bad?"

"I don't know. He's not doing well. That's why we have to jump through the wormhole so quickly. I think the plan is to save him, break one of your orcs out of prison, and get you guys back to Plenna."

"You gonna bring me home?"

Leroy said, "Maybe. Now, shut up and sit still. I'll come back and let you free after the jump."

"Human, maybe I can helpa you friend. I workid wit' doctors back home. But, you promise you taka me home?"

Leroy regrettably stated, "I'm not in charge here, so I can't promise anything, but I'll see what I can do. You save my friend and I can almost guarantee your safe return to Plenna."

"Plenna?" The confused orc asked.

"Yeah, the planet you just came from." Leroy battened down the hatch and secured himself.

Just as he finished he was asked, "Leroy, we good? Gotta jump right now!"

Leroy replied, "I'm good. Punch it."

No sooner had Leroy finished talking when the *Outcast* stopped in her tracks and lurched forward, propelled by the invisible forces of the actuator. There were no calculations, nor was there a mystic to channel energies and help the transition from calm, uneventful space to that of breakneck chaos.

The violent maelstrom put unimaginable pressure on the *Outcast* and her crew, but the ship and passengers survived. And as soon as the *Outcast* was flung somewhere beyond, the opening to the wormhole closed, leaving the frustrated orc ships to halt their pursuit of the phantom ship that disappeared before them.

Like clockwork, Jon ordered his men to run through their checklists, and like clockwork they did just that, each a wheel in the cog. Miraculously, the jump was successful. The crew and the prisoner were shaken, but handled the topsy-turvydom fairly well.

Leroy scrambled to release Pretty and urged her to help Rabbit in any way she knew how. For being an orc, she seemed eager to do so; an unexpected surprise. Leroy chalked up her willingness as payment, or good intentions, or karma, or anything that would help her to get back home. He didn't care as long as Rabbit lived.

Pretty went right to work and began to evaluate Rabbit's condition and the severity of his wounds. She turned to Leroy and asked, "You have adrenaline stuff like we orcs use?"

Leroy's eyes shot daggers at her. "Adrenaline? Yeah, but it would kill him. No way!"

"Ok, just dat it work on orcs. Dat's all."

Jon had just raced down from the bridge when he heard the discussion. "It works on orcs, huh? What else can you do without adrenaline?"

Pretty didn't want this Rabbit to die; saving him might very well mean her ticket home. But he wasn't doing well, so she stated, "I dunno human medicine. I don't. If I gets him stable, I can start a fix stuff."

Jon pried, "Leroy?"

"Damn, Jon, I have no idea. I'm not a doctor. I do know that if we are wrong here, he'll die." Leroy's hands went to his hips.

Jon encouraged, "Yeah, but it works on orcs... See where I'm going with this?"

Leroy understood. Maybe Rabbit was enough orc now that adrenaline, which would kill a human in his condition, might somehow work against all odds. He didn't like to agree with Jon because it meant the inevitable task of signing off on one of his best friend's lives. He reluctantly threw up his hands and said, "You're the boss, Jon. It's you're call."

Jon pleaded with Pretty, "Please, give this to him in small doses. I don't know how he will react."

Pretty was on a mission to get home. Like the concerned humans, she didn't want Rabbit to die either. "Ok," came from her lips as she began injecting limited amounts of adrenaline into his failing body. Four injections later and she was satisfied. She had to rely on the crew's knowledge of their species' anatomy to gauge Rabbit's ongoing health, but she was starting to stabilize his condition.

Both Jon and Leroy sighed relief as Rabbit's vitals began to normalize. He wasn't out of the woods yet, but just a couple minutes into a long process and the first signs were positive.

Jon's words were of concern to Pretty, whether they were true or not. Six days to get to the next wormhole and four more days to any world with a real hospital seemed very long indeed for such a desperate situation. Rabbit's struggle to survive was firmly in Pretty's hands now. She simply had to do the best she could.

"Jon," Harry's voice cut through the internal system.

Jon replied, "Yeah, Harry, what is it?"

"The *Paragon* has scanned us and now hailed us," Harry explained.

"We don't have enough going on right now. Harry, I'll talk to them from down here."

Harry obliged, "Routing the link to you now."

"This is Zen Furer of the *Paragon*. Jonathon Valor?"

Jon responded, "Yeah, I'm here."

"Do you have an orc onboard your vessel?"

Jon smiled, "If you are asking, then you already know."

Zen commanded, "Hand it over to me. You aren't permitted to have any orcs onboard."

"Well, about that...First, *it* is a she and *she* is attending to one of my men that is wounded. I can't hand her over." Jon watched Pretty's reactions to his conversation with Zen. He had no idea the conversation was going to be about her when he agreed to have the conversation in her presence.

"I'm sorry to hear that your man is wounded, but it's the law, Jon," Zen clarified.

"Hey, nobody is more of a law-abiding guy than me, but the orc stays here."

An agitated Zen forcefully spoke from a position of power. "Don't make me fire on you. I outgun you three to one. Give me the orc."

Calmly, Jon rebutted, "The last time I checked, I outrank you, Captain. Go about your business or I'll have you court-marshaled."

Zen was relentless. "My mission outranks you, Jon. For the last time, give me the orc!"

"Tell me your mission, Zen. You know it's the only way we can skirt chain of command."

There was silence.

Jon pressed, "And who gave you orders to fire on my vessel?"

"Okay, Jon, I'll do this by the book. By bringing an alien from another star system, you have jeopardized the security of Humania. This is just the sort of thing Colonels Parker and Taggart feared. My orders are to stop you from causing harm to Humania by any and all means necessary. It is in my judgment that you are to be considered a threat to humanity. Now, give me the orc. Any other act will be considered hostile."

Leroy whispered, "How do we know he won't fire on us after we hand her over?"

Jon continued to speak on the open channel while he nodded at Leroy. "Harry, this guy says anything I do will be considered a hostile act, so I have to give him the orc. End this communication and have Zen meet us at the next actuator so we can do so."

Harry responded, "Got it, Jon."

Upon the transmission ending, Jon reassured Pretty, "Don't worry. I'm not handing you over to this guy. He's a maniac. Besides, I need you to help Rabbit."

After several minutes, Harry spoke through the intercom again, "Man, this Zen guy is an ass! Anyway, he bought it, Jon, but we need to stay on a direct course to the actuator or he will fire on us."

"Thanks, Harry. You think you can do anything to Rabbit's fighter to give us a fighting chance against the *Paragon*?"

"I don't know. Maybe? But it's gonna be kind of hard for Rabbit to fly it."

Jon addressed Harry's concerns with, "Obviously. Leroy will fly Rabbit's fighter."

"Jon, there's more. The *Paragon* disappeared again."

Leroy boasted, "I knew it...They cloaked."

Jon reasoned with himself aloud, "I'm pretty sure they can't fire while cloaked."

"Can they raise shields?" Leroy questioned.

Jon thought for a few seconds. He recalled what he learned from the Harem when it came to cloaking abilities. "Damn," he thought as he realized that he was the one who brought Harem cloaking technology to Humania. It was only fitting that it would come back to bite him in the ass! "I don't think they can do much of anything without uncloaking first."

"Yeah, but the problem is we can't fire on them first."

Jon stated, "Realistically, we can't fire on them at all."

Pretty chimed in, "Cloakin' maka dems invisible?"

Jon and Leroy quietly looked at each other, not allowing information about human held technologies to fall into an orc's hands.

She understood and pressed, "Can you only hit der cloakin' machine?"

The two men smiled. The orc understood what a cloaking device was, that the *Outcast* couldn't fire upon the *Paragon*, and a way to take out the device without compromising peace, as fragile as it was. She was intelligent, regardless of a limited vocabulary that seemed to hinder her ability to understand - a perception that simply wasn't true.

Jon spoke openly at this point. "I think I'll talk to Harry about taking out their cloaking device without attacking them. If there's a way, he'll figure it out...and without a cloaking device we can track the *Paragon*. We still can't attack her, but we won't be surprised."

***

Zen was second guessing his decision not to eliminate Jon and his Troublemakers. Two days had passed, and it was forcing his crazed mind to reconsider what actions he should take. Clearly, eliminating the *Outcast* and her crew would propel him to greater things; greener grasses and unimaginable prosperity were his for the taking, albeit probably while continuing part of his career in this gods forsaken star system. He could get rid of his adversary and be credited with taking out the hated Rabbit Harrison. The glory and recognition would be unmatched.

He had already decided it was Rabbit who was injured. His psychotic mind guessed correctly, although by strictly wishful thinking. The bastard would die one way or another by his hand.

Besides, he had already committed to meeting Jon at the Cypra actuator; a risky endeavor, but one he was ready for. He was actually looking forward to the confrontation. He would take the orc prisoner, stripping Jonathon Valor of his prize and further jeopardizing Rabbit Harrison's chances for survival. He could push the confrontation into a fight, one he was sure he and his Electus would win.

For now, he poured over Troublemaker files, hoping to find a chink in their armor...and a chink he found. Rabbit Harrison and Evelyn Dulsey were seriously involved. *Perhaps*, he thought, *If I could locate her, I can use her to get Rabbit Harrison...if he somehow survives.*

A devilish grin ensued as he began studying travel reports from all Humania actuators. It wasn't long before he discovered Evelyn being halted from entering Cypra from the Hydra System due to a security shutdown. He further found that her small ship left the actuator, but not the system. She was on or near Remoir, just waiting for him to use her, unbeknownst of his psychotic cognition.

***

Harry was feverishly working on a way to knock out the *Paragon's* most effective defensive capability, its cloaking device. An essential problem to this was not knowing anything about the very device he was targeting, or for that matter, how to target it when it couldn't be seen. He asked Jon over and over about the technology, but vague responses made it nearly impossible to figure out without having blueprints or first-hand knowledge about how it worked.

It was Pretty who thought of a way to target the device. She advised Jon to conduct a weapons check among others, potentially drawing the *Paragon* out of cloak. Then, the ship could be scanned, and its location confirmed. Maybe a difference in some unknown reading would indicate what the cloaking device actually was, and its unique signature might be revealed. Leroy agreed, "They would show us their hand."

Jon joked, "Yeah, but we aren't holding anything higher than twos."

Leroy exclaimed, "Dude, I'll take four twos every day of the week!"

Harry added, "With odds of about one in four thousand? Yeah, me too."

Jon wrapped up, "Okay, let's pull the *Paragon* out of darkness in one hour."

A frantic hour passed, and it was time. Jon barked orders, "Leroy, you're in Rabbit's fighter. Don't take off until I give the order, or we start taking fire. Harry already set up small nuclear-type charges in two of the warheads. Just fire aft, targeting five hundred meters for detonation, unless of course you have visual, then fire as close to the ship as possible without impacting it directly. We calculated the *Paragon's* distance based on her pattern of shadowing us before cloaking. Our flank will be shielded from it, specifically geared for EMP. Harry and I worked it all out. I'll be on primary weapons and scanners. You've got the engine room and secondaries. Be prepared to tighten up any of my scans, though, or be ready to make adjustments. Are we good?"

Harry asked, "What about Rabbit?"

Jon laughed. "Didn't the guy do enough? He isn't able to take up his post."

"No, how is he?"

Jon's smile left his face. "He's a little more stable, but not good...just a little better. His wounds are severe.

I hope to gods we don't end up in an all-out fight with the *Paragon*."

***

His eyes couldn't be shielded from the bright lights as he tried to focus, and it was much the same every time he was transported for whatever procedure he was undergoing. He tightened his eyelids; trying to wash away the burning sensation with tears that had welled up beneath the lids that fought to comfort the soft whites beneath.

He turned his head to the right, enabling him to squint, his eyes adjusting to the corridor without the blinding, unfiltered light's direct interaction. His focus tightened as he was swung into a room he recognized. It was here that the gods awful procedures took place, always painful, and always inevitable, regardless of his pleas for them to stop. His body began to shake involuntarily, anticipating the suffering it would be forced to endure once again.

Red and black with yellow spots, the Spidanoid displayed colors like many other poisonous species; a warning to others that it was not to be messed with, but the humans who had captured or bred it didn't seem to fear its potential destructive power. Instead, they subdued it and strapped it down just like Rabbit now lying next to it, trying to control it like they had done with the human. It occasionally hissed and strained to escape, so it could inject its lethal venom and ingest the body adjacent to it.

Rabbit's mind was still foggy. He drifted in and out of consciousness as he was hooked by wires to monitors that showed his vitals, and tubes that supplied blood-like fluid from the huge insect. He fought to tell those that seemed to hover in the room around him about his concerns and his discomfort, but in the end, he succumbed to the drugs and potent liquids that were pumped into him from the Spidanoid.

Before he plummeted into a deep unconscious state, his ears heard faint dialogue that wouldn't make sense until a short time later.

"Doctor Gruber, do you need anything else?"

"No, nurse. He seems to be adjusting fairly well."

Rabbit fought to wake up. He didn't want to be joined with the wretched creature that was running through his body. He didn't want any more pain, nor did he want to be in the Cypra system anymore. He screamed with every ounce of energy he could muster, relentlessly crying out, praying that someone, anyone might help him to awake and escape.

His eyes opened, his mind slowly processing the screams he heard. His pain was intense, and his mind still numb, desperately searching for comfort that couldn't come soon enough. When he realized he was awake and the screams were coming from his own mouth he lessened their intensity, although pain enveloped him and caused intermittent howls.

Pretty rubbed his forehead as she spoke softly, wanting to calm him. "It ok, Rabbit. You on you a ship wit' you a friends. Try not a move too much."

Rabbit clenched his teeth and his hands into fists. His breathing was labored, forced oxygen pumped into his damaged lungs, each expansion causing a pained expression on his face. "Got anything for pain?"

"I check fo' you." Pretty called Jon down and discussed Rabbit's condition. An amount of medication was agreed to and subsequently administered. Furthermore, Rabbit was brought up to speed about the *Paragon* and the attempt to disable her in the next few minutes.

Jon ordered Rabbit to, "Hang in there." Then, he went back to the bridge.

A quick shot of morphine and Rabbit went back to sleep.

Leroy prepared for disabling the *Paragon*. He suited up, complete with helmet, and was lifted into Rabbit's cockpit seat. He waited to turn the engines and power systems on until the last second for fear that these might be recognized as the threat that they were. He sent one "ping" to inform Jon of his readiness."

Harry was able to speak directly to Jon through the internal intercom system. When he was ready to raise shields that were EMP specific, he gave them, "All ready."

Just as Jon stated in an open channel, "This is a weapons test," Leroy powered up and launched. Within three seconds Harry raised shields and Leroy fired one of the missiles to the *Outcast's* aft, detonating it almost instantly.

The *Paragon* came into view, blue electricity silhouetting her hull. She was thrown backward from the blast, small fires igniting from electronic overloads from most of her systems. Her crew, shaken but not injured, began to extinguish flames that plagued their ability to scan the *Outcast*.

Thirty seconds after the explosion, Zen Furer hailed the *Outcast*. "Jon, what the hell do you think you are doing?"

Jon knew exactly what he was doing, but he tried to fool Zen and any future court martials by being coy, evasive, and recording all communications as he lied. "Zen, are you alright? We conducted a weapons test and I think you guys got pretty close to it."

Zen snapped furiously, "That was no weapons test. You fired on my ship and you will pay!"

"Well, I'm not sure what I'll pay for, but rest assured, I didn't fire on your ship. I didn't even see it there. Where did you come from? I thought you had gone to the actuator like we agreed to. One second, Zen."

"Leroy, don't fire anymore. I repeat, do not fire anymore. I am canceling the weapons test. We have a friendly fire. Reconnect with the *Outcast* immediately."

Jon returned to Zen, "Zen, do you and your crew need assistance? I'm going to run scans and see if there is any way I can help you."

Zen didn't respond. Instead, he hurried his men to repair the *Paragon's* damage, so he could take Jon's head.

Jon stopped recording the transmissions sent to and received from the *Paragon* after his next statement. "I'm going to assume you have lost communications, and because scans show that your vital systems are intact, I'm going to get you help."

Harry deciphered energy fluctuations while compensating for disturbance and energy caused by the blast. He now had a signature that was unquestionably that of the cloaking device. He altered the shields to a conventional format and gave Jon his findings.

Leroy reconnected Rabbit's fighter with the *Outcast* and powered down. Soon he was on the bridge with Jon.

Twelve
Orcs aren't Just Orcs

Rabbit was making strides; he was a little more stable each day, and being composed of alien DNA as well, his organs began to repair themselves. His broken bones began to fuse together, and his torn ligaments and tendons began to reconnect.

However, he was still in need of multiple surgeries to repair his lung, heart, and spleen. He would still need a week or more for his body to heal itself before he would be able to withstand the trauma of being opened up and having his ribs spread. For now, he hung in there, somewhat safe aboard the *Outcast*.

The Troublemakers lined up their ship with the vacant actuator and contacted Jeremy at the Remoir actuator to assist in their jump out of the Cypra system. After he responded, "Clear for jump," the *Outcast* passed through the wormhole without incident. They were one step closer to safety.

Jon requested assistance for the *Paragon* from the *Outcast's* bridge to cover his ass. Then, he met Pretty in the medical area as she observed Rabbit around the clock. He was grateful to her for her modest medical knowledge that kept Rabbit alive as well as her quick thinking that kept the *Paragon* at bay; not that any of his men wouldn't have considered it. He thought that it would be a good time to talk with her.

"Pretty, first of all, thank you for helping Rabbit. He wouldn't have survived without your help."

"It ok."

Jon tried to relate to his new captive. Whether by design or simply out of sympathy, he said, "Well, we forced you into a bad situation and you have done really well, all things considered."

Pretty explained, "I don't wanna be here. I didn't wanna help Rabbit, but I wanna go home and dis will help, right? Plus, I seed him fight, and I dunno...I curious 'bout him."

"Curious? What do you mean?"

Pretty explained, "I tought humans were all squishy, but hims fight like a orc warrior." She searched for the correct words and continued, "Hims so strong and tough. I try to figures out how when I helps him get betta."

Jon admitted, "Yeah, he's not so squishy. So, what can you tell me about your brother, Nuttybomb?"

"Not much a tell, really. Hims a great warrior, too."

"Why did he come to Plenna?" Jon pried.

Pretty stated firmly, "To stop humans fro' killin's and tortuin's orcs."

Jon decided to let Pretty in on top secret information in hopes of it reaching Nuttybomb and getting information in return. He acknowledged, "Humans tortured and killed other humans, too, not just orcs. Rabbit stopped them by destroying their facility. My whole team was tortured."

"Dat bad."

Jon went on, "It was bad, but I believe no more torturing is going on now."

Pretty didn't know if Jon was lying to her or if he didn't have all the facts. She blurted out, "But mo' orcs were found dead on Plenna. Dems wus tortued, too."

Jon was baffled. "Are you sure?"

"Yes, Nuttybomb told me. Anda mens dat wus captured said dat it happened, too."

"When were those orcs tortured and when did they die?"

"It still happenin'. Orcs bein takens to Cypra."

Jon assured Pretty, "Then, we might have to go back to Cypra and put a stop to it after we fix Rabbit and get an orc out of prison."

"Good."

Jon still pried for more information. "So, Nuttybomb is the leader of several worlds?"

"Yup."

"He must have a big army then, huh?"

"Yup, millions," Pretty gloated.

An intrigued Jon pushed further. "And big ships, too?"

"Yup, all kinda ships."

"How does he get these ships so far...um...from star system to star system without using the actuators that open space for us?"

"Him uses dems, I tink. Him so smart and uses his brain to tell da machines to get da ships fro' one place to da udder."

Jon mumbled under his breath, "He's a mystic."

"A mystic? What dat?" Pretty clumsily asked.

Jon explained, "Oh, a Mystic is what humans call someone who can use their brains to send ships through wormholes. Some have other special powers they can use, too, but most only work our actuators. Hey, does Nuttybomb have special powers?"

Proudly, Pretty stated, "Yup. Him know what you tink fo' one. Anda two, him can just look at sumptin' and figure out how it work to make more a dems. Lika da ships. Hims took enemy ships and made more just by learnin' how dems work. Really hard stuff, too, but not to him. Anda three, he can use his brain to move stuff anda make fires. It really crazy! My brudder is so cool."

"Wow! You must be so proud of him."

"Yup," Pretty exclaimed.

Jon kept questioning, "Can other orcs do that kind of stuff?"

"Yup. Well, some can do some a it. But hims can do it *all*."

Jon remembered what Leroy said about orcs on Plenna being the big, smart ones. Apparently, there were orcs from other worlds that were just as impressive or more so. He also reasoned the more humans spread out and met orcs, the greater the chances of conflicts arising. He knew Nuttybomb was determined to stop the human advance, not just in distance, but in technological advances at the orcs' expense...and Nuttybomb was capable of bringing a fight to Humania.

Orcs could no longer be depicted as dumb brutes that won battles by swarming their enemies and overrunning them through sheer numbers, regardless of their own losses. Now, they were to be reckoned with as being equal to humans, although much stronger, and probably just as ruthless, if not more so.

After reading Rabbit's vitals, Jon thanked Pretty again and returned to the bridge. He left his friend and crewman's life in her capable hands.

Pretty rubbed Rabbit's forehead with a cool rag to continue bringing down his temperature. She changed the ice packs that were inserted under his armpits and in his groin as well. Also, although he didn't show signs of infection, he was somewhat jaundiced, a sign of liver damage. She balanced his medications and worked to flush the contaminants from his system.

Rabbit began to stir; at first, he fidgeted, then took a deep breath and opened his eyes. He felt the cool, comforting washcloth that Pretty wiped across his head and face. He looked into her eyes, trying to gauge his odds of living.

Pretty smiled, her warm reddish-brown eyes looking back into his, "How you feelin's, Rabbit?"

Rabbit moaned. "Like I've been hit by a truck."

Pretty chuckled. "Nuttybomb is big lika truck. Dat fo' sure."

"Yeah, well I don't want to tangle with him again."

"Hims ok once you get to knows him."

Rabbit proceeded to ask about his condition; his vitals, what organs were damaged, what broken bones, and his overall prognosis. His basic knowledge of anatomy and his intelligence gave him the conclusion that he barely survived his encounter with Nuttybomb, but his chances of getting better were good. He felt comfortable enough with his current medical attention and the plans for future surgeries. He thanked the gods that he was part orc.

***

Vance Parker wasn't happy to hear that Zen Furer and the Electus failed to halt Jon and the Troublemakers from escaping the Cypra system. He had trusted Zen to eradicate the problematic team aboard the *Outcast*, but of course, Jon found a way to thwart any military orders as usual. Vance made an uncomfortable call. "Gary, Vance here."

"Ah, Vance, I trust our problem has been taken care of?"

Parker said, "No, our problem just got bigger. ZF dropped the ball."

"I'm disappointed. I tried to keep this as quiet as possible, but maybe we need to use other means."

Parker questioned, "Other means?"

"Let's just say that I'll handle it from here. ZF will report to me from now on. General Amadas had plans that need to be carried out and these Troublemakers of yours need to stop interfering."

"Gary, I don't understand. First of all, you were all for the Troublemakers getting themselves into trouble. I told you they were a handful. Secondly, General Amadas and the whole project was killed. We were friends. What plans did he have that I don't know about?"

"Vance, maybe you two weren't as close as you would like to think."

Once Colonel Vance Parker spoke, he realized the call had ended; His voice was met with silence.

**

Leroy asked, "So, how do we get through all of the actuators while we have an orc on board? Surely the *Paragon* alerted everyone."

Jon disagreed. "I don't think so. My guess is that Zen and his lackeys are top secret watch dogs meant to stop us. They could have fired on us, but they may have been exposed and linked to something more. If there is testing going on in Cypra or Plenna, then my thought is that the whole thing needs to be kept quiet. We have top clearance, so we should be able to get through without a problem."

"No offense, Jon, but that is a huge assumption. If you're wrong..."

"If I'm wrong, we have bigger problems than one orc and us going to prison. We may be looking at a full-scale war against super orcs while the government we defend is corrupt, the whole time using us as pawns."

"Or scapegoats."

Jon concurred with, "Colonel Parker does want us to fail. By the way, we'll skirt around Dupree and head toward the Rim, just in case we are wanted men."

Leroy asked, "Dude, no offense, but are you crazy? The Rim?"

"I know what you're thinking..."

Leroy asked, "Do you? You're talking about Pirate Alley, a war zone, and every derelict fugitive on the run there."

Jon smiled, "Well, then, we'll fit right in." He conveyed his thoughts as best he could to ease Leroy's concerns with, "It's better than facing the Humania fleet. We can hide the orc and get Rabbit help while we head home and alert Command of the situation. Plus, Rabbit knows his way around there. It'll be fine."

Leroy sighed, "Okay, who can we trust at Command?"

"I don't know. I just don't know how high this thing goes up and who knows what. Get Evelyn to meet us so we can compare notes."

***

Evelyn greeted, "Hi, Jon. What's the word?"

Jon prepared Evelyn as he led her up the catwalk to the *Outcast* belly from below. "Evelyn, we have had run-ins with Humania special forces and orcs. This thing is obviously bigger than I originally thought. What's more, Rabbit has been seriously wounded."

Evelyn's right hand inadvertently covered her mouth as she gasped and said, "Oh my gods."

Jon assured, "He's okay; he's okay. We have him stable enough to get him to the Rim."

Evelyn pushed passed Jon and ran up the catwalk, looked right, then turned left and followed her instinct toward the direction she believed the medical area would be. She raced to, and entered, it bewildered at what her eyes took in.

Before her was a female orc, leaning over Rabbit, doing something to him while he was unconscious. Evelyn's immediate reaction was to distance the orc from her husband before any more harm was done to him. She yelled, "Get away from him!" and lunged at the green invader.

Pretty turned to see a human female coming toward her, the first she had ever witnessed. Her surprise was short lived as her instinctual sense to defend herself met Evelyn's offensive thrust.

While Evelyn was highly skilled in martial arts, she lacked the power and raw angst that was genetically built into a warlike species like orcs. Thankfully, Jon intervened before either drew blood. He held them apart as Evelyn cursed and Pretty growled, both trying to rip the other apart. Finally, Jon hollered, "Enough. Evelyn, the orc is helping Rabbit."

It took a few seconds for her to calm down after Jon's words registered, but Evelyn did stop pulling free. Pretty took a bit longer. She didn't know why she was being attacked, but she was more than ready to put the pale-skinned bitch in her place. Eventually, she came to rest.

Evelyn asked Jon, "What happened?"

"He decided to tangle with Pretty's brother, a warchief."

Evelyn shook her head as she replied, "Yeah, that about sounds like something Rabbit would do."

Pretty chimed in, "He lucky he not dead. Nuttybomb da greatest warrior in da star cluster."

Evelyn retorted, "Maybe for an orc." She found herself hating orcs now, the damned barbarians!

Pretty asked, "What dat supposed to mean?"

"It means Nuttybongo or whatever the hell his name is, is lucky. That's what it means."

Pretty understood where Evelyn was coming from. "Oh, I see. You lika Rabbit. You jealous a me."

"J...Jealous? Of an orc? You really are a stupid species."

Pretty crossed her arms and tapped her foot. "Maybe too stupid to keeps him alive? Who da stupid one, squishy human?"

Jon's voice cut through the air, "Evelyn, shut up! She's here to help. He wouldn't be alive if it wasn't for her. And, Pretty, you let him die and I will kill you myself. Both of you, stop!"

The two women sized up each other, Pretty smiling as she turned away to commence administering medications to Rabbit. Evelyn gritted her teeth as she read Rabbit's medical evaluation chart. Then, she cried out, "Adrenaline? She gave him adrenaline? He's lucky to be alive, because she's trying to kill him."

Jon simply laughed and stated firmly, "It's okay."

"It's okay? No, it isn't okay. He should have gone into cardiac arrest."

"That wasn't going to happen."

Evelyn pressed, "How do you know, Jon? What wealth of medical knowledge do you have that allows you to do the one thing that should have killed him, yet somehow didn't?"

"You just have to trust me. Not only was it the best option at the time, it was the only thing we could have done based on facts I can't share with you right now." Jon winked and glanced toward Pretty in an attempt to steer the conversation away from the orc's ears.

"Well, he seems stable enough." Evelyn thought it best to help his chances by showing appreciation. "Thank you for helping him, Pretty. I'm sorry for assuming you were hurting him."

Pretty smiled. "It ok."

***

Jon and Evelyn met Leroy and Harry beneath the ship. It was here that the four began to figure out the best course of action.

Leroy began with, "Sorry, Evelyn. I know Rabbit looks bad, but he'll be okay."

Evelyn agreed, "Thanks. I think so, too, but Jon mentioned going to the Rim?"

Leroy rolled his eyes and shrugged his shoulders. Harry quietly hung his head.

Jon explained, "We need to lay low for a bit. That means going in and out of low security areas. We will get Rabbit help and hide Pretty out there, too. Anyway, let's talk about what we know. Evelyn, ship logs and actuator reports?"

Evelyn's professionalism kicked into high gear. "Yes. This here shows minimal activity from Cypra to Plenna and back. It's mostly Crystal Technologies ships."

Leroy interjected, "Probably doing atmospheric studies after Rabbit nuked Cypra."

He was corrected. "That's what I thought, too, but most of the ships are prison barges."

Leroy questioned, "Prison barges?"

Jon concluded, "They are bringing orcs back to Cypra for testing."

Evelyn agreed, "That could be when you consider empty barges going to Plenna and coming back to Cypra full."

Harry added, "Hey, Rabbit said something about Crystal Technologies developing new actuator and mind controls that would allow for jumps that I think could be undetectable. You guys think there's any correlation?"

Jon surmised, "That would hide their prisoners in the future."

Leroy added, "Or now. Seems odd to me that we have made a number of jumps without a mystic now."

Evelyn was torn. On one hand, she disliked orcs and thought them to be stupid, barbaric creatures. On the other hand, she had compassion for all life and didn't agree with suffering forced on lesser species. "What are they testing for?"

Jon cautioned, "Evelyn, you being an intelligence officer, you understand the sensitivity of classified information and that you would have to take it to your grave?"

"Of course."

Jon revealed, "We were tested on, too. We have a bit of orc DNA in us; Leroy, Harry, and I. Rabbit, too. That's why the adrenaline worked, opposite of what you would expect in a human."

"So, they are cross breeding?" Evelyn asked.

Jon replied, "In a sense, yeah. Or at least, they were. I thought Rabbit put a stop to it."

Evelyn shook her head in disbelief. "I can't believe you guys are part orc."

Harry burst out, "Maybe part Spidanoid, too."

"What do you mean, Spidanoid?"

Jon said, "These two had false positives. Might be nothing. Why do you look strange? It hasn't changed us."

Harry chuckled, "Yeah, I don't go out to eat little kids at night or anything."

Evelyn mentioned, "It's just odd that I have had a number of orc and Spidanoid things come up in the last few months."

Jon asked, "Like what?"

"Like Spidanoid contact on Libel. It was a possible invasion that was refuted after Crystal Technologies developed a chemical to kill the bugs. Funny thing is, after they fumigated, there was complete denial by all parties involved about the Spidanoids even invading. If a colleague of mine hadn't died on the planet, I wouldn't have ever known."

"What about the population? Somebody would have spilled their guts, even by accident."

"No, not with a secret quarantine. No one has been allowed to leave Libel. Communications are supposed to be down, a matter of convenience, I think. My colleague said that people were being taken from the planet, too. I don't know to where, but lack of communication would hide that fact as well. It's another Crystal Technologies cover up, aided by the military."

Leroy questioned, "Jon?"

Jon responded, "Are you thinking Cypra?"

"I am."

Evelyn pointed out that prison barges brought nearly three hundred thousand lifeforms to Cypra before they emptied their cargo and left for Plenna.

Jon had been wondering about the same information he had retrieved from the disc that Rabbit had provided him from the fake prison break.

The four turned abruptly as they heard Rabbit say, "They aren't just taking the population of Libel to Cypra. They are taking the Spidanoids, too."

Jon screamed, "Rabbit, what the hell are you doing out here?"

A visibly hobbled Rabbit waived to Evelyn as he staggered. "Hi, Hon." Then, he continued, "They breed Spidanoids while they continue to build a super army. Then, they unleash the Spidanoids on the orc "uprising" and exterminate the Spidanoids with Crystal Technology's newest anti-bug chemical. It keeps everything clean. If we get caught in the cross hairs, that's just icing because if we have Spidanoid DNA we succumb to the chemical, too. If either orcs or bugs survive, just send in the super army. Ultimately, they can deny everything unless they have to claim it was an uprising. They can achieve all their goals with several contingency plans to get out. It's genius, really."

Leroy and Harry rushed to grab Rabbit before he collapsed. As they carried him inside to the medical area Jon questioned, "But who are they?"

Thirteen
Exposed

Nuttybomb was healing nicely; his organs were on the mend and his male parts were patched together well enough to work in time. He had a dozen or so bullets still in his body from battles over the last two years, but this didn't impede him in his quest to unite and protect his species. His various broken bones were surgically repaired, or if simply cracked, miraculously fused on their own.

To his troops, his immortality was becoming legend. They had seen him receive death blows that would have killed any other orc, yet he survived them again and again. They didn't know how his powers as a shaman worked, but work they did, and not just on others, but on himself as well. Furthermore, his other mind powers were amazing and his skills in using them were breathtaking. He had killed hundreds, maybe thousands of foes single-handedly with his sword or the greatest weapon he used between his ears.

He now sat with Arc, his young aspiring wizard. Arc had an unusual ability to harness and release energy in the form of electrical discharge. Unlike Arc, Nuttybomb wasn't able to devote enough time to control his own ability to do the same. Instead, the minuscule time he spent in trance was used to gather information from beyond and cleanse his own mind and soul. He sought guidance from a central hub, perhaps in a realm on a different plane. Either way, it gave him solace and the confidence from having an intergalactic knowledge that he was acting according to the laws of his gods.

Conversely, Arc wasn't as mindful of such things. He lacked the discipline to seek knowledge as it was tedious and boring. No, he sought to become as powerful as he could, so he could destroy any enemy laid before him. He didn't care very much about learning how to use his mind to heal. The glory of orc fanfare was his calling; he wanted to be revered as a feared warrior. This was fine with Nuttybomb for the time being. He didn't fear his disciple and the kid's abilities complimented his own.

The two smoked from a long, ancient pipe crafted somewhere in the Eastern Continent of their home world, called Hotta. After passing it back and forth several times, they became silent, each taking a path beyond that led them in very different directions.

The mind-altering opiates gave each a vision. Nuttybomb heard a familiar voice that was leading him on a path to the gods. He was carried to a distant world, pulled through a hole in space, eventually granting him a seat over the planets he currently governed. From this perspective he saw his orcs below, he heard their wishes, and he felt their pain. He knew the cries were from those being tortured by humans before he even looked upon Plenna and Cypra. Visions of Pretty and Rabbit Harrison drifted by, although hazy. Ucktock was in a Humania prison. The voice told him things that transcended sound. He could envision specific details about places in vibrant colors that he had never seen. Mathematical formulas and scientific inventions were revealed to him. Then, the voice, knowing the limits of Nuttybomb's capabilities to learn and remember, returned him to his pipe.

Arc waited intensely for his Warchief to open his eyes. Just as Nuttybomb returned to reality, Arc pounced. "What did you a learn?"

"Much dat I already knew. But, now we can travel farther. I have da way. It time to save our brudders fro' da grips of da bastid humans." He paused, then continued, "anda Rabbit Harrison will comes to me."

***

Evelyn went into hiding while moving along a different route than the Troublemakers as she proceeded to acquire as much information as she could through back channels. She avoided Zen and the Electus by searching for the *Paragon's* cloaking signature. It wasn't perfect, but she knew they were on the move and it was the best way to track them. Moreover, she skirted major population centers and military installations to further avert possible entanglements with the powers that be.

Coming into view was a small reddish colored world with yellow and orange clouds that marked its atmosphere. Evelyn ran some scans and prepared to descend toward its surface; not an easy endeavor under the best of conditions; and now, considerably more difficult considering the shift in the planet's axis. Changes in climate due to the repositioning of the world in relation to its mother star caused monstrous winds that distributed heat from newly affected areas. Additionally, a polar shift repositioned the magnetic field and gravitational forces were in flux until a final point of position was settled.

All of this meant little to Evelyn, though. Her mind was on the mission at hand and the conditions below were dangerous, but it was something she merely had to contend with; for it was here on this forgotten world that Crystal Technologies housed its mainframe. A myriad of information was hers for the taking if she accessed it correctly.

She ran through her checklist and began to descend. A golden hue enveloped her view as her ship entered the atmosphere and began to encounter friction that burned around her. She was tossed about, rather mildly compared to her ship that didn't have the luxury of a harness to restrict its violent throws. After a minute of turbulence, she was able to control the steering of the ship and began to look at areas to put down.

The onboard navigational map showed a valley to the northeast where she decided she would be a safe distance from Crystal's compound. It was here that she brought her ship to a safe stop. She spoke to herself in reassurance, "Okay, I'm here...all in one piece. Now, it's time to see what Crystal has to show me."

She worked her way along a high barbed wire fence with guard towers every hundred meters, a fact that seemed very strange for a private company to have. She spotted a few guards at the main entrance dressed in standard marine uniforms and more atop the buildings beyond. Again, this was very strange, even for a huge conglomerate like Crystal Technologies.

It was obviously being protected by government. The howling winds blocked all sound.

Evelyn backtracked and followed her instinct to a place she found through her intelligence gathering. She forced open a locked door to a utility shed that accessed corridors beneath the main buildings and went through the dimly-lit labyrinth.

Along the way, she turned a corner and stumbled upon a guard. Before he could pull and fire his weapon, she closed the distance to him, knocked the gun away, and subdued him by using a headlock to restrict his carotid arteries from supplying blood to his brain. He fell unconscious for the time being.

She worked fast, pulling him into a closet and tying him up; a considerable feat, considering her size compared to his. Then, she went back to work and broke into a computer room. She used hijacked fingerprints, eye scans, and passwords to finally retrieve the information she sought.

She was struck by how many government contracts were actually granted to Crystal, their scope and unimaginable magnitude, and undeniable leverage that the company had as it stole from the common people. Not only that, it used that same leverage to destroy its competition, usually by attaining government endorsements to do so. Moreover, when looked at closely, it had overt ties to General Amadas and several other high ranking military officers and government officials.

All this information was obtained and briefly scanned. Now, she needed to get the hell out from the belly of the beast and report her findings to Jon. It would be up to him to determine what else was important and how to handle things.

Evelyn retreated to her ship and immediately sent the information to Jon as a locked file through a coded message. After a few minutes, he replied that the transmission was received successfully.

"Success," she blurted out happily.

"Success?" Zen Furer asked angrily as he grabbed her throat and put his hand around her gun's grip, his massive strength allowing just enough air to fight its way to her brain. Two of his men each grabbed one of her arms and held them behind her back. She was helpless.

An unnatural rasp came from Evelyn's throat. "What do you want?"

Zen playfully growled and moaned as he licked her face, the stench of his breath overwhelming her senses. "You'll find out, sweetheart."

Evelyn fought the grip of Zen's hand around her throat and the vile smell of his breath to speak in the sexiest voice she could. "I'll do anything you want," was all she could muster to save herself.

Zen concurred after licking his lips and taking in the scent of her perfume, "Oh, you will."

***

Almost a week had passed since the Troublemakers and Evelyn went separate ways. Jon and his men landed on a forgotten moon, just within the Barnacle Belt, a decidedly useless rock that existed amongst other useless rocks. But for its small population of criminals, anti-Humania unsocial types and pirates, it was a haven for safety and a chance to live without law.

Jon shook the hand of Doctor Dippel. He felt the doctor's cold, clammy, scrawny fingers crumple within his own; an uncomfortable feeling that came with an accompanying reluctance. Not only did he want to withdraw his handshake from the ghastly man's meager grip, but he also shuddered to think that he would be entrusting the life of Rabbit to this same sawbones.

Leroy, questioning the same, asked, "You *are* a doctor, right?"

Doctor Dippel hastened, "Shhhhhhh," looked around wildly, and continued in a loud whisper, "Not so loud. Where is the man that I am to work with?"

Jon clarified, "You mean work on?"

Again, "Shhhhhhh. One more comment that links me in any way to being what I am, and I'm done helping."

Jon whispered, "But, you can help?"

The thin, wrinkled, unshaven doctor replied with a wink, "Oh, I think I can."

The room wasn't well-lit. Garbage littered the corners – everything from empty bottles to used cigars cluttered the crevices. The tables were old and scratched. Tablecloths were discarded or lost eons ago, their discolored material eaten through by bullets and bugs. Now, the exposed wood had little stain left at all.

Two ancient chandeliers swayed precariously as the rocking from intimate, yet violent, encounters occurred upstairs. The few bulbs with any light left, shined through a generation of cobwebs. The dim light danced across long, drawn faces.

A rowdy group at another table in the watering hole became more raucous. An offhanded comment led to an insult, and finally gunfire that left a man bleeding out. A scantily dressed woman ran to the wounded man and screamed out, "Can anyone help him? Please!" She looked around the room, her eyes pleading with any others that met hers.

Jon turned to Doctor Dippel. "Can you help him?"

The doctor growled under his breath, "I wouldn't dare." His eyes darted around the room, communicating an uneasiness that was part of his everyday life on this junk world. He hung his head in shame and defiance, a deliberate act so he wouldn't make eye contact with the desperate woman.

The dank room began to clear as most patrons feared for their own lives. The few that remained were unconscious or too inebriated to turn and even notice what had happened. Only a drunk, uncaring barkeep remained semi-aware.

After Leroy watched three men drag the crying woman upstairs he stated, "I care." He stood and began to head past the dying man several tables away.

The doctor pleaded as loudly as he could without drawing attention to himself, "I wouldn't. Not with them. They're trouble."

Leroy looked to his leader. "Jon?"

Jon was conflicted. He didn't want more trouble or even exposure that might jeopardize Rabbit's health or risk the mission's chances of success. Still, he wasn't one to let murder and rape go unchecked, so he looked around for listening ears, and upon feeling satisfied that he wouldn't be heard by others, calmly stated, "Leroy, take Harry with you. You do this, and they can't ever trace this back to us. Clear?"

"Oh, I'm clear," came without hesitation as Leroy rose from his chair and made his way to the wounded man. Upon arriving, he knelt and checked for a pulse. It was apparent to him and others by his negative head nodding that the man had passed. Anger welled up inside him, a raged animal that needed to be tamed, a justice that needed to be administered. Judge and judgment were coming!

Harry sighed after seeing Leroy's enraged eyes. He followed his determined friend upstairs.

The door was kicked in, its splintered shards of wood flying across the room. Leroy entered quickly and disarmed one of the men who was jeering and egging on the other two in a cruel and violent sexual act. The man's forearm was snapped into an ungodly shape that defied any normal sense of what an arm should look like. As the man screamed and fell to the floor, his neck was broken in an instant.

The other two men made attempts to stand, but were quickly taken out of the fight as Leroy's eight-inch knife removed their exposed members. Harry pulled the woman away from the two suffering men and took her just outside the room. He watched Leroy enact revenge. He watched with a feeling of nausea.

Leroy quietly cursed the two men. His penned-up anger was being released, his demons revealed, his skeletons coming out. He removed their weapons, so they were no longer a threat and stood over the two as they bled out like the poor fool downstairs. When they finally died, he turned to Harry and unemotionally said, "Let's go."

***

Rabbit and Pretty were concealed safely in a dungeon somewhere beneath the doctor's hovel. Secret passages and hidden doors made it virtually impossible for thieves, thugs, or other undesirables to locate them. The area was sanitary enough and the doctor had a somewhat modern medical facility. He didn't lack any necessary medicines or equipment to help Rabbit. His sanity was questionable, however.

Regardless, the other Troublemakers left The Rock and headed back toward Humania space. Jon had decided to confront Colonel Parker to determine his true position on Cypra and Plenna. He didn't know if the colonel was privy to knowledge pertinent to the mission or if he might even be part of the possible ongoing development of a super army and torture. Jon just didn't know how to report to his superior officer and how much to trust him, but he felt that he had to.

Then, the question arose as to how he would contact the colonel. Subspace transmissions weren't wise as they would probably be monitored. The *Outcast's* Strenus were changed ever so slightly to give a different engine signature to hopefully fool sensor detection and certain actuators were also used to slip through Humania's ever watchful eyes.

It was during Killball day that Colonel Parker paced in his den, watching some plays and keeping up on scores, but mostly contemplating how to handle the

217

Troublemakers, the Electus, and his own career. His old friend, Gary Taggart, seemed to have the pulse of the military and would probably assume command in General Amadas' absence. Taggart was becoming more of an issue than a friend these days.

Parker took his usual seven paces in one direction, turned and began to take the next seven when he was startled. Jonathon Valor was standing a few feet in front of him, just staring, waiting in his house; Parker's personal space had been invaded. He pulled his firearm and aimed at Jon's head. "What the hell are you doing here?"

Jon didn't flinch, and he showed no sign of threat. He was calm, and his arms were at his sides. He was unarmed. "Sir, I had to sneak in undetected to see you."

"You broke into my house, soldier. I could kill you right here, right now."

"Yes, sir, you could. It's a chance I had to take," Jon calmly replied.

Parker squinted, Jon's trust further jeopardized by his decision to show up unannounced. "What is so damn important that you should break into my home, risk being killed, and at the very least, court martialed?"

"First of all, I'm sorry, sir. There are things going on that I need to report to you." Jon took an approach of being submissive to his colonel, an act that wasn't threatening, like his posture. He stood at attention and waited to be spoken to.

"Go on," Parker cautiously commanded.

Jon explained, "There is a war brewing on Plenna and Cypra."

"A war? I think if there was a war coming, I would know, soldier," Parker scoffed.

"Yes, sir, I would agree. But there is a large orc force on and around Plenna."

"There's no secret that there are orcs on Plenna, Jon, but there aren't enough of them for us to worry about a war. What do you mean when you say around Plenna?" Parker slowly lowered his weapon.

Jon elaborated, "These orcs aren't indigenous to Plenna, sir. They're from another world and they came in large ships, heavily armored and fast. They have a well-equipped army and technology similar to our own."

"And you deem them to be enough of a threat to move a bulk of Humania's forces away from the Rim to deal with them?"

Jon carefully replied, "I wouldn't assume to know, sir. That isn't my job to assess how we should respond. I'm just reporting what I found."

Parker asked skeptically, "How many troops are we looking at and how many ships?"

Jon surmised, "Two to three million troops and I counted fourteen capital ships."

Parker's eyes widened. "Are you sure?"

"Yes, sir," Jon confidently stated.

Parker mumbled to himself as he digested the information given to him, "Probably took them years to travel from their home world. That would give us an advantage; they wouldn't have reinforcements."

Jon corrected, "Sir, they use actuators like we do. They could move extra troops as quickly as we could."

"How? We don't have any that far out. And how could they power them?" the doubtful colonel questioned.

Jon explained, "Yes, sir. We do as part of the advanced exploration program two hundred years ago. Many actuators were abandoned and forgotten about. Also, some of these orcs have abilities like our Mystics"

"Okay, Jon. I've heard enough. Orcs are orcs. Every study ever conducted proved their limited potential. They are never going to be anything more than dogs with thumbs." Parker chuckled, "Should I court martial you now?"

Jon answered, "One of these *dogs* used mind control over one of my men. These are a dangerous breed, sir. I can't stress that enough. They aren't like orcs we have seen so far. A court martial is your decision, but I do have more information."

Parker was visibly annoyed. "More information? What could be more amusing than dumb orcs perceived as the next coming? I'm to put my career on the line with this?"

"Again, it's not up to me how this is handled, sir. I am standing before you, risking everything as part of my job and dedication to service."

"Okay, I'll hear you out," Parker said.

Jon still didn't know Parker's level of involvement in the situation at hand. He hoped to relieve some of the tension between the two men, so he might endear himself to his superior and avoid a court martial. Jon chuckled, "I think this may be forward of me, but after breaking into your home, it doesn't seem so shocking. May we sit, sir? There is a lot to discuss."

Colonel Parker considered Jon's request. He knew Jon could kill him easily if he intended to do so and he wasn't sure if his sidearm would make any difference. Standing six feet apart or sitting the same distance didn't seem to matter either. Jon didn't seem to be a physical danger, so the colonel played along. "Sure, Jon. Have a seat and tell me what you know."

"Yes, sir. Thank you. I have to say a few things that relate to us. You are my leader, so not only do I report to you, I confide in you. Also, our personal lives shouldn't affect our abilities to do our jobs."

Parker halted Jon. "How do you mean?"

"Well, I apologize for anything my men may have done to you or your family and I am deeply sorry for your loss of General Amadas."

"It isn't just my loss, Jon. Humania lost a great leader."

"I agree, sir. He was my general, too. I continued to serve, as did my men, even though we were tortured. Our allegiance is to Humania and we serve under you."

Parker questioned, "Why are you telling me this now, and how would any of this affect our jobs? You are insinuating that I still have an ax to grind?"

Jon said, "Because bluntly, the Troublemakers have been a pain in the ass to you, sir, but not by design. There has been friction between us. You need to know we are with you; we follow you. I don't allow myself or my team to be affected by things that affect us personally, even if it is potentially harmful to us as individuals. I broke into your home, didn't I?" He half-smiled.

Parker thought for a minute or so and the silence became somewhat uncomfortable. "It isn't the orcs that really worry you is it, Jon?"

"Partially, sir. They are formidable."

"Then, what is bothering you?" Parker quizzed.

Jon found himself using his hands to convey how important his words were, certain words coinciding with greater gestures. "I believe the explosion on Cypra only delayed the production of a super army, sir. I have reason to believe there are still operational facilities that have come under attack from orcs on Plenna as well. Here are ship logs and intel reports." This was the huge risk Jon was taking by revealing what he knew, or thought he knew. As he handed each printout, he discussed loaded prison ships, Crystal Technologies, Spidanoids, and everything else to prove his theory.

Parker scanned the papers and asked, "Do you feel a super army would somehow be detrimental to the overall success of Humania?"

Jon admitted, "In the wrong hands, yes, sir; I do. Either way, whatever is going on on those two planets, has brought orcs to defend their comrades. There are untold billions more beyond the Rim."

Parker pressed, "Whose hands do you worry about?"

"I'm not sure, sir. But these are the names linked to Crystal Technologies, Cypra, Plenna, and Libel. Please take notice to the political officials' and officers' home worlds. They are all farthest from the Rim."

"Meaning?"

Jon put his neck on the line even further. The information he was giving was damaging to all the men and women he was listing, as well as to himself and his team. Exposing a coupe wasn't something that happened every day, especially from a middle-ranking officer within its military. He continued, "Meaning a war with orcs would probably spare those worlds furthest away. Is it coincidental? I submit that these individuals can rise to power on those worlds while the rest of Humania struggles against orcs and Spidanoids. I believe Crystal Technologies has already perfected the use of actuators without mystics and they tested them between Remoir and Plenna. We made several jumps without a mystic. It all adds up."

Parker wasn't so sure. "This is a pretty big stretch, Jon. Hanging is all but inevitable for you now."

"I understand, sir, but only if I'm wrong. Sir, one more thing?"

"What?" Parker asked.

Then, came the test of tests. "Were you aware of Libel?"

Parker seemed annoyed again as his tone raised, "Now, you are questioning your superior officer's involvement?"

Jon explained, "No, sir. It's just that if you didn't have knowledge, you weren't in the loop. If you did, your involvement may even have been involuntary through chain of command. That would make me part of it, too."

"There are a lot of holes in all of this... this assumption... you do understand, Jon?" Parker warned his subordinate.

"I do, sir. It was hard coming to you after I found out you were willing to kill me and the Troublemakers at the hands of the Electus, too. I didn't think an old grudge warranted it, but I came anyway."

Parker stressed, "Wait, I never gave an order to kill you, Jon. You were to be watched, and if thought to be a threat, brought in. I figured I might have to bust your rank. Just so you know, the Electus hasn't reported to me in almost two weeks. They aren't operating under me."

"Well, they seemed awfully trigger happy and hung it on you."

Parker chewed on the side of his lip as he thought. "Yes, and another officer seemed more than happy to end my involvement when you survived."

"What do you think, Colonel?"

Parker stood up. "I think we are finished here. I am sending you back to Cypra, Jon. I have every confidence that you can confirm what you have presented. At this point, it is somewhat convincing, but a little thin."

Jon agreed that there was no hard evidence. He also understood that he was hanging by a thread. Somehow, he still found the courage to ask for assistance in breaking out Ucktock from the prison and getting to Cypra as safely as possible.

Parker smiled as he saluted. "I'll do what I can. Thank you for coming to me."

Jon reluctantly left Parker's home and was soon back in space. But on the way, he found himself using his peripheral vision to scan for marksmen that might finish his mission for him. He still didn't know Parker's involvement. Hell, maybe the gods didn't even know. Would he be hunted down by militia until he was caught or killed? Would the order come from Parker or someone Jon had exposed?

Fourteen
So Pretty

"Show me what you sent, bitch!" were the angry words from Zen Furer.

Evelyn tried to play dumb. "I sent this, but it is encoded. I can't open it."

Zen looked at the transmission and file type. He knew immediately there were original pieces of information that needed to be locked and coded before they were sent. "Give me the originals," he demanded.

It didn't matter if Evelyn handed over the information she had obtained from Crystal or not; she was probably dead, anyway. Actually, showing her hand might have hurt the Troublemakers, or worse, all Humania. She gritted her teeth as she defiantly spoke. "I sent stuff about orcs invading Cypra."

"Give it to me," Zen growled as he released her bruised throat. One of his men let her right arm free.

Evelyn picked up a disc from the console she had sent the transmission from and before she turned, Zen ripped it from her hands. He popped it in the computer drive and ran it, hoping to view a display of everything she had sent. But to his disappointment, the disc was blank.

Zen shouted as he rushed his powerful hand back around her throat, "There's nothing here, you lying bitch."

Evelyn gulped as she fought for air. She gasped as her legs trembled, lack of oxygen and blood flow was beginning to affect her. She quietly muttered, "I can't...I can't"

Max Dullus, Zen's first officer laughed as he finished her sentence for her, "Breathe?" Then, he addressed Zen. "Captain, I don't think she can breathe...kinda makes it hard to talk."

Zen released his grip and Evelyn fell to the floor. He ordered his men to rip the ship apart if necessary to find the information that was sent. Meanwhile, he threw water on Evelyn's face and slapped her around until she came to. He spat, "I'm not very patient. You are pushing me to a place that is very dangerous for you. For the last time, where is the information you sent?"

Evelyn, weak but coherent, cried, "I deleted it."

Zen was not happy, to say the least. Without physical evidence, he had no way to know what she or anyone else was aware of. He ground his teeth from side to side and asked, "You erased it?"

"Of course. You think I'm stupid enough to allow a disc that details an orc invasion to float around?" A fairly innocuous lie that she hoped wouldn't be proven false.

A devilish grin ran across Zen's face. "We'll see how stupid you are. You wouldn't have come here to poke around Crystal Tech without a reason."

Evelyn's hands and feet were tied. She was dragged and placed in a locked room within the bowels of the *Paragon*. One more offer was made for her to tell the truth in exchange for her life. She denied having obtained any more information than she had already disclosed.

Her route to and from her destination within Crystal was figured out right down to the missing guard and the computer she used to hijack content. However, no history of use on the computer, nor any information transferred was found as the hard drive had been wiped clean.

Evelyn was thorough to hide her tracks as best she could. If she had more time to finish her tasks, she would have destroyed the real disc and not the blank one she gave to Zen. The smoking gun was sitting in a second disc drive at her computer back on her ship. She prayed to her gods that it wasn't found.

Unbeknownst to Evelyn, Zen never found the disc. He ordered her ship to be destroyed and asked the maintenance crew to send the remains to a salvage yard where it would be compressed, and any remains lost forever; there were to be no records of these activities. The military and Crystal weren't to be linked. She never asked about the real disc, because it wasn't supposed to exist, and Zen never informed her about her ship as she was just a prisoner.

Over the next week Evelyn was only allowed to eat once per day and bathe before a Paragon crewman decided to use her for sexual exploits. Zen and seven crewmen each did so an average of twice per day for seven straight days. By day three, she endured agonizing pain from a dislocated hip and a broken wrist. Worse was that her fingernails were removed to convince her to reveal information to avoid more pain. Additionally, her neck, wrists, and ankles were bruised. Finally, she was dehydrated and very weak.

Every covert op considered the possibility they might be killed or tortured because of their dangerous career. But how many seriously considered it? How many could possibly imagine the unbearable pain of torture without going through it prior to their decision? How many truly accepted that as their day started, it might be their last? Evelyn didn't. She actually became so good at what she did, she thought she would go undetected forever. It was in this state that she finally accepted death, if it was offered.

***

Doctor Dippel performed three separate surgeries on Rabbit and was amazed at how well his patient responded. He was shocked at the condition and severity of the wounds that somehow didn't manage to end his life. All in all, Rabbit was doing much better than expected. The semi-insane doctor was a very good surgeon. Who would have thought?

Dippel left for the day as he did every day over the last three weeks. Pretty had been seeing to Rabbit's needs during the doctor's absence for much of that time until recently as Rabbit began to get up and about on his own and could take care of himself.

Rabbit was grateful to Pretty for keeping him alive, especially after he kidnapped her. He had no way of knowing she would save his life in two ways; the first as a shield for his escape and the other as an administer of the care he needed to get back to health. He had grown comfortable with her over the last month.

He stood up in the tub after he bathed and dried himself the best he could without moving too much. He still had significant pain and wasn't able to bend or turn easily. His fingers fumbled with some clips for bandages he needed to wear and began to cover his wounds.

Pretty saw Rabbit through the screen struggling to wrap bandages around his torso and back where he had a number of vertebrae surgically repaired. "You need some a help, Rabbit?"

Rabbit sighed, "Yes, please, if you don't mind."

Pretty was confused. "I have a mind. So, no help?"

Rabbit chuckled, "I'm sorry. I said it wrong. Yes, please, help me."

Assistance was given by Pretty; she took the loose bandage and asked him to hold it by his left rib while she began to wrap. She worked her whole body around his back and toward his sternum, pulling the wrap tight as she ducked beneath his armpits each time she went from side to side.

Rabbit giggled to himself as he thought it might have been easier for her to stand in one place and use her hands to extend around him while she worked, but he didn't mind. The last few days he had taken particular notice of her eyes as she looked up at him. He was aware of other things about her, too, things he hadn't thought he would find interesting in an orc.

Pretty's eyes were a warm reddish-brown, with colorful specks that caught the light in the room and sparkled. Her hair, slightly darker than her light green skin flowed down to the middle of her back and smelled of natural herbs and flowers. She tossed it slightly as she worked around him. Rabbit wondered if male orcs found this attractive.

She leaned her body against his as the end of the bandage was being applied so she could hold each clip and firmly attach them. Rabbit felt the warmth of her on his bare skin and smelled her perfume. This, combined with the cold room, gave him goosebumps and raised the hair on his arms. He shivered briefly.

Pretty put her hand on Rabbit's chest and asked in a concerned voice, "You ok? I hurt a you?" Her eyes blinked quickly as she looked into his, afraid that she had done something wrong and harmed him in some way.

Rabbit rubbed her arm in comfort and eased her mind with, "No, no. I'm fine. I was a little cold."

Pretty relaxed and smiled. "Ok, now you a leg to be fixed. Sit down."

As Rabbit backed up to the bed and sat, Pretty followed with some cloth and more bandages. She dragged a chair over and put it under Rabbit's leg. She knelt down in front of him and began to apply the cloth over several long cuts that were made by the doctor to save his leg. He was healing well, but the nerves were still hyper-sensitive as she worked. Rabbit grimaced each time she applied the slightest pressure on the inside of his thigh.

She showed concern again as she pointed to the area that she had just touched. "It hurt here?"

"Hell yeah, it does!" Rabbit added, "My back doesn't help. Also, I think the doc took some skin and tissue from that area." Rabbit pointed from the crease of his groin across and down most of his thigh.

"Want me to stop? I wait a minute, if you need."

Rabbit was a man and full of pride, but his leg was jumping as it spasmed, lightning bolts ripping through it from buttocks to toes. Orc females probably saw their male counterparts without limbs not complaining, but here he was with all his limbs acting like a big baby. He reasoned that the lack of a limb would leave one without pain throughout the wounded area, but his leg being attached left it damaged and it hurt like hell. He couldn't help it and moaned out loud.

Pretty responded by whispering, "Shhhhhhh," and massaged his thigh. She started under his butt and worked around the front, moving her hands to cover areas that were near the wounds. She tried to cover every area because she just didn't know which were the most sensitive and why.

Rabbit found himself laying down and then fighting to sit back up in an attempt to alleviate some of the pain. He grabbed her hand as she pressed too hard on an area that was particularly painful.

She jumped up and screamed, "I sorry, I sorry. I so sorry." She dashed across the room and prepared a pain killer mixed with a muscle relaxer and returned in what seemed like an hour, but was really only two minutes. She jammed the syringe into his left butt cheek, emptied it, tossed it onto a nearby table, and went back to massaging his leg.

Rabbit struggled with the pain for only another minute or so as the injection began to work. The sedative was also taking affect and caused some lightheadedness and drowsiness.

By this time, Pretty had worked her hands down toward Rabbit's knees and the back of his lower thigh. Her hair brushed back and forth against his groin, enough so that she noticed a change in his anatomy as she straightened up and her hands were back toward the crease in his groin. From her knees, she looked up, and stopped rubbing his leg.

Rabbit took her hands and rubbed them gently. He thanked her and directed her hands back to the cloths and bandages. He smiled and began wrapping his own leg.

Pretty half-smiled and understood to complete the task of wrapping his leg. She looked down as she worked, focusing on her job and seldom looking up at Rabbit's eyes. She thought that she was just an orc in his eyes, stupid and useless; green and ugly. Embarrassment and shame washed over her, especially when she had to unwrap her hair from around his exposed groin. She felt so stupid that she couldn't even think enough to not allow her hair to wander into the same area again.

Pretty knelt there, between Rabbit's legs with her head down in shame. She liked him, but now, thought she wasn't worthy of the same in turn. If he was an orc he would have forced his way on her, proving his attraction toward her, but Rabbit was a human. She just didn't know what to think or do. She leaned back as her butt rested on her calves, her head remaining down, and her toes wiggling nervously.

Rabbit rubbed the top of her head and thanked her again. When she looked up, he smiled and thanked her one more time. After her response of a nervous smile, Rabbit worked one of his hands down Pretty's face and caressed her neck and shoulders. He placed his other hand behind her head and lifted her toward him.

Now, *her* skin blossomed in goosebumps and *her* hair stood at attention as she raised to feel Rabbit's warm lips and tongue on her neck. She became aware of her increased breathing while his mouth worked upward and met hers. His five o'clock shadow was just long enough to tickle her when his face made contact with her skin.

Rabbit was lean and muscular, a bit of a departure from the bulky build of orcs Pretty was accustomed to. He moved slowly and deliberately, taking his time to not only please his partner, but to explore and satisfy every sense he had available. The orc in him wanted to throw Pretty around, and take what he wanted, but the other side of him relished this new experience.

Pretty had never felt the sensual sensations that were streaming through her. Any encounters with male orcs, and they were few, were in a way that could be described as rushed and uncaring. Maybe they were more brutal and territorial like one would thrust a flag into the ground after winning a battle. This was different; there was an intimacy that was totally unexpected.

Several hours of intimacy occurred with each partner exhibiting traits inherent to their species and each was exposed to a partner unlike any they had ever been with. Breaks were taken as Rabbit needed to stop due to pain, other times because the two laughed uncontrollably or were playful, sometimes just to kiss or chat.

In the end, they dressed and talked, finding out about the other's history over a hot meal.

Fifteen
The Break

"It's good to have you back," Harry exclaimed, grabbing Rabbit's hand and welcoming him with a back slap.

Rabbit obliged his friend's kind words and gestures with a returned, "It's good to be back."

Leroy went so far as to extend his open arms for a hug. "You look good, dude."

"I'm getting there. Dippel patched me up and Pretty took good care of me. I feel okay, I guess." Unbeknownst to Rabbit, Pretty smiled and looked away from the Troublemaker's eyes. The secret she held between her and Rabbit was safe for now.

Jon smiled, "Good to see you."

"Same here. I'm just as happy to see that you guys are still alive."

"Thanks for the vote of confidence. We managed. Hey, time for us to get your friend out of jail. I think you're the only one who can handle him. You up to it?"

Rabbit was pleased. "Yeah, I'm good. This time's for real?"

Jon joked, "There has to be something that smells worse than Harry that can cover his odor."

Harry asked, "Do I smell again?"

Leroy poked, "Again?"

Harry lifted his arm and sniffed his armpit, only to wrinkle his face in obvious discomfort. "Okay,

okay. I'm a little ripe. Now, that Rabbit's back I can get out of that red-hot engine room. But just remember...if I'm stuck in that heat on sixteen hour shifts again...you will all smell it."

Leroy retorted, "It's gonna take sixteen hours to kill the smell."

Jon added, "I promise; no more long hours in the engine room. We can't take it."

Everyone laughed.

Harry left for a shower. The rest of the crew dispersed to their respective areas of work, each performing important tasks that put them on course to the prison and kept them away from the watchful eyes of their enemies.

Once in the engine room, Rabbit was made aware of Harry's newest engine configurations and advised to change its unique signature every few hours. Also, he was brought up to speed about information that was received from Evelyn and reported to Colonel Parker. He understood the cautionary measures he and his mates were taking at this point.

Jon asked Pretty to run blood samples of the crew to confirm or eliminate concerns regarding Spidanoid DNA. He remembered that certain lizards passed their DNA through biting their prey and that maybe, just maybe, the Troublemakers had been exposed to Spidanoid venom and nothing more. Still, he needed to know how much DNA was mixed with human and orc DNA in the event that battle led to a possible enemy using chemical insecticides that would kill him and his crew.

Of course, Pretty wasn't made aware of what she was sampling. Even though she was trusted, who knew what would happen if she was allowed to know about their DNA having orc and possibly Spidanoid DNA? If Nuttybomb was as highly intelligent as The Troublemakers thought he was, he could very well use the information to better his own troops. Maybe he could find a weakness in the Troublemakers. No, Pretty wasn't allowed to know.

Jon piloted the ship and worked on a plan to save his and his crew's lives, his career, Humania, and a way to expose the torture and atrocities he thought were occurring behind a veil of secrecy, a plot of deception, and a grand design for treason. It was overwhelming, but what could he do? He accepted his responsibilities and thought.

Leroy adjusted the *Outcast's* path and monitored traffic and communications. He noted an increase in fleet activity near Remoir and passed it on to Jon.

This was disheartening to Jon. There was no discussion about an orc invasion; nothing in open channels, nor anything coded through back channels. So, why the military buildup and who had ordered it? Was Rabbit correct about the ideas of a rebellion, all but confirmed by Evelyn, and brought to Colonel Parker? Maybe Parker was in on the whole thing and felt it necessary to eliminate the Troublemakers far from civilization. The border of Cypra would certainly do that.

First thing was first. Jon contacted the prison and asked for a meeting with the warden. To his surprise and dismay, he was denied. His repeated requests to interrogate Ucktock were also denied, as were his pleas to acquire access to Ucktock's ship.

Leroy was concerned. "No go?"

Jon shook his head. "I can't even get them to allow us to land there."

"So now what?"

"So now I send a message to throw them off."

Leroy agreed, "Good, because if they know we are coming and have any ties to this whole mess, there may be a welcoming party waiting for us."

"That's my concern, too," Jon admitted. Then, he sent a message to whomever he had been communicating with that read, "Please send the warden my regards. I'll contact him in several weeks as I am headed to a location we discussed the last time we met. He should know the location I am referring to."

"Making him think we are headed to Cypra?" Leroy asked.

"Yeah, I just hope he bites."

***

Jon ordered, "Harry, change our engine signature again. We are getting close."

Harry replied, "You got it."

The *Outcast* made it's jump into the system where Ucktock was imprisoned. This time, unlike the last, there were immediate problems. A voice from the wormhole actuator they jumped from was onto them. "This is Actuator Nine. *Outcast*, do you read me?"

Jon responded, "This is the *Outcast*. Everything okay?" He glanced at Leroy nervously.

The voice sounded strange as it asked, "Do you have an orc on board your vessel?"

Leroy grumbled, "Shit!"

Jon lied, "No, no orcs here. Why?"

The voice cautioned, "An orc life sign showed up during your transfer. Bringing alien life forms from system to system is prohibited."

Jon figuratively danced around with, "Understood. No orcs here."

"Then, why am I seeing one on my scanner report?"

"I don't know. It's your scanner." Jon turned to Leroy with a stressful appearance. "This is not good."

The Actuator voice pushed, "Are you sure you don't have any orcs on board? This is very irregular."

Parts of Jon's brain were passing information to others. He needed to make an excuse as quickly as he could to avoid a military response from blocking his attempt to break Ucktock from prison. The planet of Delphi was pretty close, but potentially intervening forces would have enough time to stop the *Outcast* and her crew. Plus, this conversation with the actuator guy was on an open channel. Jon was betting that the warden knew the Troublemakers were nearby.

He tried something that might satisfy the actuator guy. "Listen, we are on a top-secret mission, ordered by President Orson Korgue himself...and you are speaking on an open channel. I am advising you to stop all communication on this channel."

The voice came back, "Sorry, Sir. I have no way of knowing your orders and you didn't specify them at the checkpoint here. You may come back here to fix this, or I will have to call the authorities."

Jon cursed, "Dammit. I really don't have time for this. It will take over an hour just to get to the next actuator to jump back."

"That's fine. I'll be waiting for you. In the meantime, I am alerting security in your sector as to your status, which is temporarily disallowed to jump anywhere but here."

"Understood. I figure I can be at Delphi Actuator in maybe an hour and a half. I'll check in with you then."

Leroy shot, "Jon, it will take almost twice that to get to the planet. By the time they figure out we aren't going to the actuator, they will hunt us down. We aren't going to the actuator, right?"

Jon nodded his head, "Right."

"Actuator Nine understands and will be waiting for contact from you."

Jon said, "Thank you, Actuator Nine. *Outcast* out." He snarled, and shadow punched his console without doing any damage.

Leroy joked, "Got anything else up your sleeve?"

Jon momentarily showed a look of disgust. "No. I don't know how many times we can come up with new ideas to get ourselves outta trouble. This is getting ridiculous."

Harry cut through on the comm, "I heard all of that. Should I change our engine signature again in case we get scanned again?"

241

Jon replied, "Actually, get in the habit of doing it every fifteen minutes or so until I tell you not to. Also, all power to the engines so we can make good time to Delphi."

"Will do."

Jon asked Leroy, "Have you heard from Evelyn?"

"No, I haven't been able to raise her."

"Maybe she's laying low like us." He shook his head and continued, "That was dumb. She's an intelligence operative. Of course, she's laying low."

Leroy looked puzzled as he questioned his superior officer, "Jon, you okay?"

A half-smile and reply of, "Yeah, I'm fine," was returned. "This whole thing has been a little more than stressful. You know as a commander, you are never supposed to show weakness to your men and all that crap, but you have had command of your own, so...you know."

"Yeah, I do. This has been more than any of us bargained for. I don't even know if there is a way to get even with those for Cypra or even if it's worth it, but I think about it a lot. Every day I think this is more than I bargained for. My stress levels have been through the roof at times. Doesn't mean I'm gonna let any of my mates down." Leroy reassured, "We'll get through this."

"I never said we wouldn't. I just admitted that it was stressful. That's all."

Leroy taunted, "It's okay if you're scared, Jon." He made an accentuated gulp sound and drove it home visually with a physical swallow.

Jon snapped, "Alright, alright. That's enough. I'll never confide in you again."

Leroy teased, "But we were becoming so close. I started having feelings for you."

"You think you can feel your way back to the med area and get me something for a headache?"

Leroy chuckled. "Sure." He got up and left the bridge to his worried commander.

Jon reached out to Evelyn again, but like Leroy before him, he heard no response back. He called Rabbit on the comm, "Hey, Rabbit. Are you awake?"

"I am now. What's up?"

"Have you had any contact with Evelyn recently?"

Rabbit sat up in his bunk. "No. Are you concerned?"

Jon semi-acknowledged, "Not exactly. She's probably in hiding or something. I was just curious."

"It's not like her not to respond though when business is concerned."

***

Zen was brutalizing Evelyn when he was interrupted by one of his men. He angrily wiped blood from his hands into a towel, left her, and answered the internal comm outside her cell. He stepped from the dank confines of her imprisonment into the well-lit and fairly clean passageway. "What is it?"

"Colonel Taggart wants to speak to you."

"Put him through." His tone changed dramatically when speaking to his superior officer, "Yes, sir?"

"Captain Furer, I've not heard anything from you for some time."

Zen submissively replied, "Sorry, sir. Nothing to report since the *Outcast* fired on us." He hid the fact that he held Evelyn Dulcey aboard his ship.

"Have I made a mistake choosing you for this mission?"

"No, sir. Actually, I have some leads I'm looking into. One should bring the Troublemakers to us for sure. But I'm not overlooking anything until then."

The colonel replied, "I may have found them for you. A warden friend of mine believes they are heading to Cypra, although they may be near Delphi now. Find them and do what you must."

Zen almost saluted as he answered, "Yes, sir." He disconnected the comm and shouted out loud, "That asshole colonel thinks he's big siht because his little warden told him where they might be? I'll show him!"

Zen punched his fist into the bulkhead where he stood. Sparks flew as his skin made contact with wiring in the wall. He was unphased, however. He went back into Evelyn's cell, even more twisted than minutes before.

Evelyn barely looked up at him through blackened eyes. Her face was bruised and her pupils strained to see through swollen eyelids.

Zen gave her a bit of a kick to fully get her attention. "I've had enough of your lies. It's time for you to tell me what information you sent, or I will kill Rabbit Harrison."

"You have him here?"

Zen laughed, "No, but I know where he is and when we get there, he's going to suffer because of you."

Evelyn knew Rabbit would be killed anyway. She had been in intelligence long enough to know that terrorists never released hostages after they got what they wanted. It would kill her to have Rabbit die because of her unwillingness to help him, but somehow, she knew his life or death was already determined, regardless of her giving information or not. Still, maybe she could offer something to Zen, not anything too incriminating, but something to possibly get the maniac to soften. It was worth a try. "I sent more than just information about an orc invasion."

Zen squatted close to her and turned his head. "I'm listening."

Evelyn was silent. Her pause was meant to show her resistance about telling him more, but she would finally reveal her secret to him to save hers and Rabbit's lives.

"Spit it out. I have your lover to kill."

"Okay, okay. But don't hurt him. He doesn't know any of this. He thinks his mission is to find out why production of something is down on Plenna."

Zen leaned his face against hers as he shook in anger. "Now!"

Evelyn sighed and began, "I think these orcs are special, like really smart or something like that. I had to warn Humania about the invasion, yes, but not because it was just an invasion of orcs. I had to warn Humania because these are different kinds of orcs."

"Go on."

Evelyn swallowed heavily. "That's it."

Zen leaned back on his haunches and probed in a sarcastic, baby voice, "Really, that's it?"

Evelyn immediately realized he wasn't buying it, but she was gonna do the best she could to sell it. "Yeah. I don't know why these orcs are different, but they are."

Zen's finger nails clicked the cold, dirty floor in a pattern from pinky to thumb, over and over. "So why were you at Crystal Technologies?"

"Oh, yeah. I only had Crystal Tech ship logs going in and out of Cypra...A couple to Plenna, too. I was hoping to see if there was a connection to the smart orcs, but I couldn't find one. I found that they were just testing the air after the big explosion." Evelyn stared into Zen's eyes to show sincerity.

"Anything else? This is your last chance."

Evelyn appeared to think. After a few seconds, she looked into his eyes again and responded, "No. That's all I know. Please, leave Rabbit alone."

Zen sneered, "That will depend on whether or not his story matches yours now." He half kicked her leg, turned and left, laughing the whole time to abuse her a bit more.

***

Jon asked, "Can you make out what type of ship?"

Leroy pushed some buttons to bring up information about a ship following the *Outcast*. "She's a frigate, Jon. Planetary defense."

"Fuck!" Jon exclaimed, "A frigate will eat us for dinner!"

"Well, we won't make it to the surface without a full company of troops to get through, too; if we get past this frigate, that is."

Rabbit's voice came over the speaker, "You guys seeing this?"

Jon answered hastily, "We see the frigate, if that's what you're asking."

"I had a thought. We probably won't get passed the ship, and even if we do, we will have a whole company to fight before getting to the prison."

Jon hammered, "Thank you for that, Captain Obvious!"

Rabbit explained, "Yeah, anyway...Let's jump to Actuator Nine, and then jump back in an hour. We can handle the actuator guys a hell of a lot easier than the frigate and her troops. Reset our jump status and jump back here with a different engine signature. By the time anyone figures out what's going on, we should be long gone. And, hopefully, we can better evade the frigate."

Jon asked Leroy, "Any chatter about the frigate making us?"

"Not yet."

Jon called down to the engine room, "Harry, I need you to get some small explosives ready, so we can disable scanners and communications at an actuator."

Harry spoke through a wide smile, "I have just the stuff."

Jon went on with, "Rabbit, get to your fighter. I calculate jumping in forty-six minutes. I need you to pull that frigate away from Delphi in the opposite direction as long as you can. We will jump and meet up with you at the prison."

Within a couple minutes, Rabbit launched his fighter and headed toward the frigate. He stayed just ahead of the few fighters that came from her launch bay. They remained on his tail over the next forty minutes while the *Outcast* contacted their destination.

"Actuator Nine, this is the *Outcast*. We are ready for jump."

"This is Actuator Nine. You are late, *Outcast*."

Jon reasoned, "Sorry about that. We took the time to rearrange our storage stuff and started figuring all our jump times to make up for the hours we are losing because we need to come back to you. It's only a couple hours, but that's huge with our workload."

"*Outcast*, prepare for jump in three, two, one, jump."

The Troublemakers quickly overran security and set small explosives, eliminating the actuator's ability to communicate or scan any ships. Security guards and technicians were tied up and locked away, all unharmed, save for their egos. Jump status was manipulated and fire-walled so the *Outcast* could jump anywhere going forward.

Within a few hours, they were putting down on Delphi where Rabbit already worked.

He knew the place like the back of his hand. Several fake jail breaks with Ucktock gave him all he needed to know about the number of guards, their locations, and how to get Ucktock out to their ships and into space. Yes, Rabbit knew this place all too well.

He moved from his ship toward the eastern wall. As he got close, he watched from behind shrubs and timed when to make for the wall that stood about thirty feet high. There was a clearing of fifty yards from the perimeter of the compound to anything with foliage to prevent such an attempt. Timing the guards' positions in the towers was critical so he could cross the opening between the bushes and the wall. As one turned away, another always seemed to face Rabbit.

It took fifteen minutes, but Rabbit finally ran to the wall. It was here that he planned to gain entrance to Ucktock's ship just beyond the huge carboncrete rampart. He opened a duffel bag and laid out what he needed along the edge of the wall to hide it from above. He grabbed what he needed and set a charge timed to detonate in five minutes. Then, he made his way around the north wall and began placing charges there, too. These were set to go off thirty seconds before those on the eastern side as a distraction. Next, he cut the power and fuel lines to the backup generators and the communications lines. This way, the prison couldn't send an alarm or call out.

Rabbit made his way back to the eastern side and readied his two stun grenades. As soon as the explosions went off on the northern side, Rabbit tossed one grenade into the northeast guard tower. He ran to the southeast tower and tossed the second grenade. Both detonated within ten seconds of each other, confusing the guards that manned the towers.

When the final explosion happened, Rabbit grabbed the duffel bag and entered the compound. He stayed low to be undetected as he made his way to

Ucktock's ship. On the way, he hurriedly grabbed a small amount of fuel and readied more explosives. "A lethal combination," he muttered to himself.

The sound of guards moving around the outside of the compound began. He fueled the ship and quickly moved from the cluttered yard to the building. More charges were set as distractions and actual entry points. The timing was perfect. How he anticipated guards' movements in response to the explosions was truly amazing. That and Harry's knowledge of explosives made trespassing a breeze. Getting Ucktock and getting out would be more difficult though. He hoped he left nothing to chance.

Rabbit entered the main prison building. Without hesitation, he knocked out the camera that probably watched him enter. Soon, he was in the ventilation system set in the ceiling, crawling above guards he spotted from time to time as they searched for him below. Their fairly large numbers validated his suspicion about being seen.

When he decided he would do maximum damage, he eased open the grate he entered and dropped a grenade. A loud bang disabled a dozen or so unsuspecting guards. There were over a hundred guarding the entire facility. He noted the math somewhere in his subconscious and moved on.

He marked the distance and direction he traveled in his mind by seeing his position through grates he crossed. When he arrived just short of Ucktock's cell, he saw another dozen guards that had taken up position. "Yup," he thought. "I've been seen for sure." Why else would Ucktock be guarded?

Now, Rabbit needed to figure out how to eliminate all the guards without harming Ucktock, free the orc, and move without being seen...or maybe not. He reasoned he could probably get Ucktock out and make it to the security room. Once there, he could kill all the cameras, making escape at least possible. There just wasn't time to go back to hit the security room first.

Guards flew in every direction. A well-placed grenade killed almost all the guards and left the others as good as dead while keeping Ucktock unharmed. Rabbit dropped from the ceiling and complimented, "You're looking good, old friend."

"Rabbit," the overzealous orc shouted.

"Pull these bars open with me. I think we can do it together."

Ucktock's and Rabbit's combined strength pulled the bars apart, but not far enough for the orc's massive frame to fit between.

Ucktock growled, "It not big enough."

Rabbit played, "If I had a dime for every time I heard that."

"Wut?"

"Never mind. Here." Rabbit grabbed guard bodies and shoved them between the leveraged opening. Ucktock was instructed to pile the bodies up and hide behind them. Then, an explosive was set against the carboncrete wall, just next to the nearest bar. Rabbit ran around the corner.

A thunderous blast blew the bars from the wall. Ucktock tossed bodies off himself and ran toward Rabbit. The two made it to the security room in seconds. Another charge was set, and soon, they entered the room.

Bullets danced around them. Ucktock dropped and rolled to the left. Rabbit instinctively dove to the right and gave covering fire for his big, green friend. Ucktock ripped apart the few guards near him while Rabbit, not only protected him, but took out a couple of his own. Soon, they were the only two in the room.

They busted into some lockers in an adjacent room and found Ucktock's seized handgun and ammunition. Rabbit hurried, "Okay, let's get out of here."

Ucktock refused, "I can't go yet."

"What? Why not?"

"I gots to break dis place befo' I go so no udder orcs get hurted lika me."

Rabbit pleaded, "But we might not escape if we stay longer. Your ship is just outside."

"You go, Rabbit. It ok."

"No way, Uck. Not without you. Lead the way."

Ucktock burst into the corridor and ran, his heavy, large body bounced off the walls as his feet pounded the floor with each deafening thud.

Rabbit half-shrugged and followed. Other than the other Troublemakers, he didn't have much to live for. He didn't want to die, certainly not knowingly, but he figured everyone did eventually. Besides, he was much more likely to survive a gunfight than a couple years earlier. He went along with his friend.

Ucktock fired his enormous weapon as needed, and when he failed to hit his target, he simply crushed it up against a wall. Several guards felt their bones snap between the mighty orc and the wall, ceiling, or floor. His chilling howls were heard throughout the complex as he downed victim after victim.

He was first to reach the room where he had been tortured every day. To his apparent dissatisfaction, there were no humans to kill here. He asked Rabbit to blow up the room though, again explaining, "So no udder orcs be tortured here." Rabbit obliged.

Rabbit got Ucktock's undivided attention with, "I think it's time to get the warden and end this thing."

Ucktock's eyes widened. "I wanna killa hims. You letta me killa him."

"Follow me, Big Guy."

Rabbit eliminated some more guards as he came upon the warden's office. He busted in the door and fired at anyone who wasn't the warden. Four prison personnel ceased and desisted from helping themselves or their superior officer.

The warden waved his arms screaming, "Now, hold on. Just hold on. Don't do anything you'll regret." His face became stricken and his eyes bulged upon seeing Ucktock push through the doorway.

Rabbit explained, "I think that's what should worry you, Warden."

The warden responded in a sheepish, "Wh... Wh... What? Worry, what?" He couldn't take his eyes off the intimidating orc.

"Well, the way I see it, there is only one outcome here I would remotely regret...and that's allowing you to remain here to do more harm."

Ucktock took an authoritative tone, "Ya, no stay here to hurt udder orcs."

The warden negotiated, "Right, right. I'll leave. I can find something else to do. I don't like things I have to do as a warden, anyway." His desperate attempt at separating his crimes from his duties was disgusting.

Ucktock stepped forward. The warden urinated himself without even noticing, but Ucktock did. The orc taunted, "Looka, Rabbit. Da big, bad warden peed himself."

Rabbit knew what was coming. He saluted and spat, "Sorry I won't be seeing you around, Warden." He stepped into the corridor, and just in time, too. He found himself in a gun fight with a few more guards.

Ucktock didn't care about the melee outside. He slid the thousand-pound desk to the side with one arm and got in the warden's face. "Tell ya wut, Warden. I might letta you live."

A panicked voice pleaded, "Anything, I'll do anything you want."

Ucktock remained visibly calm, something that was foreign to the warden from this less than human animal. "I letta you live if you head don't pop like a grape." His huge hands engulfed the sides of the warden's head, lifting him from the ground.

The warden's legs kicked, frantically, trying to feel some ground or something to free his head, anything to stop this last act from occurring. But he was just a squishy human, squishier than most, actually. In fact, many had claimed that his cold, cruel nature was his attempt to be more masculine. Maybe he never won an arm wrestling contest or knocked out an opponent in the ring. He probably shied away from confrontation unless he was in a position of power, something he was unable to do unless his adversary was employed beneath him or a prisoner at his facility, completely bound and defenseless. He definitely wasn't very masculine at the moment, especially as his bowel emptied itself down his legs and onto the floor below.

Ucktock calmly stated, "Oh, look. Now, he a pooed himself, too. Bad lil human warden. You bad. Stoppa cryin's. It all be ova soon. Justa say fo' me to end it."

The warden's nose spurted blood and his eyes were red and runny. His mouth resisted his attempts to vocalize. He still fought, his hands trying to pull Ucktock's from his head.

Ucktock played, "Say dat you wanna die. Dat all and it will a be ok."

The warden spat blood from his mouth, still fighting to survive. He knew he couldn't stop Ucktock, but he couldn't let this animal kill him this way. How long could he endure this, though? Surely his neck would break from the weight of his body hanging from his head. Thirty more seconds and he stopped fighting. His will to stop suffering outlasted his will to live. He half mumbled in a weakened cry, "I wanna die."

Ucktock smiled. "Ok." He pushed his hands together until they met. He breathed a sigh of relief and entered the fray.

Rabbit fired down the corridor as he kicked one guard and flipped another.

"Rabbit, you pretty good a fighta," Ucktock acknowledged.

Rabbit hollered, "Will you help me?"

"Ok." The orc threw bodies around and made his way down the corridor.

Unfortunately, he was a big target. Several bullets found his arms, torso, and a leg. He stumbled occasionally, but returned fire to stop his foes. Whereas the human bullets slowed him, his bullets removed chunks of their bodies the size of grapefruits. It was common to see a guard lose both arms or a head from the brute. Even shots that missed sent chunks of carboncrete as deadly shrapnel. He cleared the way while Rabbit set one explosive after the next.

The two were thrown to the floor as explosions started to rock the compound. Rabbit knew the damage wasn't from the charges he set. He assumed that guards must have been destroying the place to kill him and Ucktock, but that didn't add up.

"Rabbit, where are you?"

Rabbit jumped to his feet and dusted himself off. "Jon, I was wondering when you were gonna show."

"We are above you, taking out ground troops and guards outside. That damn frigate followed us down."

"On our way out." Rabbit raced for the door and flew down the steps. Ucktock, now free from the confines of the narrow corridors, did what he did best. He jumped from the stairs and rolled to one side. Then, he crawled a few feet, stood up, and rolled to the other.

Rabbit, who had already made it to Ucktock's ship, turned to see the spectacle. Even in a hurry not to be killed, he watched in bemusement as the orc ducked and rolled a handful of times, apparently avoiding nothing. "Will you hurry up?"

"I'm comin's."

"Now, if I really had a dime for every time I... Never mind. Let's go."

Rabbit followed Ucktock into the ship and ran through the checklist. Then, he stated, "See ya in space, Uck."

"Bye, Rabbit," came from a more than elated orc. He lifted off and shot anything between Rabbit and Rabbit's fighter from the cannon on the front of his ship, clearing a path for his friend's safety. He watched as the *Outcast* destroyed parts of the prison and took out other troops.

Rabbit ran his own checklist and left the prison world behind. He began evasive maneuvers ahead of the others as he entered the blackness of space. His friends accompanied him in their joint quest for freedom.

Sixteen
Big Green Planets

Twenty-one months after the cataclysm, Cypra was well on its way to a rebirth. Life began to take hold soon after the atmosphere began to clear, and the sunlight of her star pumped energy to the surface, promoting photosynthesis in plants. Seeds, already deposited in the soil during the great fires, sprouted into seedlings almost immediately, bearing fruit and offering food to any surviving animal life soon after that.

No longer were there trees towering above the grasses, blocking out the necessary light from plants below. Now every form of vegetation had a shot to become plentiful, and with them, any animal to become the dominant species, at least in theory.

However, Cypra had lifeforms on her who weren't indigenous. If anything, these aliens were stunting the natural order of Darwinism, greedily towering above everything below, and blocking out the light.

A force of orcs came to this new world to stop such an occurrence. They landed by the thousands in ships, much like they had on Plenna, to thwart the humans' attempts to change nature's predetermined course. Not that orcs cared about grasses and shrubs getting a fair shake at life. No, they cared about protecting orcs, their brethren, tortured by the barbaric humans and then destroyed in an act of genocide.

Nuttybomb stormed down the walkway of his ship before his bloodthirsty army. He simply directed to his officers, "Spread out and get all da humans, alive if you can anda bring dems to me."

Sirens screamed, the cue to initiate that the end of human existence was here. Orcs screamed at the top of their lungs, their primordial traits rising above their tempered anger, arms in the air, and fists clenched.

Several fights broke out among them as often did with such a savage race. It was okay, however. Nuttybomb understood his men, their need for combat at every level. He had subdued them to a point where he could generally control them and that was enough. Now, he would unleash them on the bastard humans!

***

"That's three for me," Leroy chanted.

Rabbit boasted, "And that last one was a hell of a shot. Good to have you back in a fighter."

Leroy agreed, "Sure makes it easier to hunt than to be hunted."

Jon broke in, "A little less chatter, guys. We are taking a pounding again."

Leroy replied, "On my way, Jon." He leaned hard on the throttle and swung around toward the *Outcast*.

Ucktock screamed in anger, "Dese ships too fast anda move around too much. I can't get 'em."

Rabbit, after the experience against orc fighters several months before, stated, "Uck, these are human fighters in human ships. Pilots are trained for years and the ships are maybe the best in the star cluster."

Ucktock asked, "So, you tink dat humans are better?"

Rabbit didn't want a confrontation with his orc friend, but he stated the truth, "Yeah. These guys are just good, maybe better than you've seen."

After a brief silence, Ucktock acknowledged, "Ok."

Somewhere in all their brains, even as busy as they were in this dance for survival, the Troublemakers took note of Ucktock's acceptance of Rabbit's information. For an orc to hear and accept his inferiority to humans in any way, it conveyed a level of trust between Rabbit and Ucktock that seemed highly unlikely. Maybe it was that Ucktock was already accepted by the Troublemakers and sprung from prison. Maybe it was that they chose him to live instead of other humans that gave Ucktock the ability to understand without losing control in anger. Whatever the reason, it expanded trust on both sides.

Leroy's fighter soared over the *Outcast's* port side and caught a Humania fighter with a burst of fire. "That's four!"

Rabbit shouted, "They're bugging out. Nice job, Leroy."

Once Jon was sure the opposing ships were in retreat, he instructed, "Bring 'em home, boys."

The *Outcast's* two fighters connected to her, as per usual. Ucktock brought his much larger fighter/bomber over the top of the *Outcast* and docked at one of her airlocks. The men came below.

However, Rabbit was trouble shooting some problems with his ship. He changed out some relays and reran his checklist. He rerouted power and tried to get his scanners to reset, but he was having trouble. "Jon, I'm having some problems here resetting my scanners."

"Did you reroute power?

"Yeah. I think I need to get into the secondary computer. This is my last attempt, like cutting Nuttybomb's balls off. If I can pull that trick outta my ass, this should be easy."

Jon quietly said, "Rabbit...prying ears."

Rabbit closed his eyes when the stupidity of his words sank in. He answered, "Sorry, Jon."

As he suspected, the secondary computer system did need to be updated. He completed the necessary updates and reconfigured everything back to original settings. He made his way to his mates in the computer area and sat down. "Hey, guys."

"Hi, Rabbit Harrison," came from the oversized lips of a very enthusiastic Ucktock.

Rabbit smiled. "Ucktock, my friend...I see that you programmed your planet information into our database. Nice job."

"Tanks. It was pretty easy." Ucktock furrowed his brow in visible concern as he continued. "Rabbit, did I hear you say befo' dat you cut a Nuttybomb balls off?"

The guys chuckled. Pretty closed her eyes. Rabbit replied, "Yes. I don't know that they were completely cut off."

Ucktock frowned. "Dat bad, very bad."

Rabbit explained, "He was gonna kill me. He is strong as hell and he was very angry."

261

"But big, green planets are da mostest importanest tings to male orcs."

Leroy couldn't help but laugh along with the others before he spoke. "Wait... Big, green planets? That's what you call your testicles?"

Ucktock seemed puzzled. "Testicles?"

Pretty glanced at Rabbit and smiled, then dropped her head in silence.

Leroy explained, "Yeah, the things that sit behind your penis."

Ucktock's eyes lit up as he had a revelation of sorts. "Oh, you mean da happy stick."

As if their victory and safe return wasn't enough, Ucktock's uncanny orc-like words and mannerisms added to the jubilation. The room erupted in hilarity. Rabbit caught a girlish smirk from Pretty.

Ucktock was baffled again. "What so funny?"

Rabbit asked his green friend, "Why is it called a happy stick?"

"Dunno. But, sumptimes, it really happy. Like, look." Ucktock dropped his trousers in front of the amazed humans."

Harry blinked twice and widened his eyes. Pretty, too. She shrugged at Rabbit.

Jon blurted out, "Holy shit," before looking away.

Leroy's jaw dropped with, "What the fuck?"

Rabbit stared in disbelief. "Okay. Well, I can see how it would be happy. I think your females would be really happy with the happy stick."

Ucktock tried to clarify what was the most important. "Well, it not really happy now. But, sumptimes, it get really happy fo' da females. Oh, anda when it not happy or lika when it is a kids, it called a pee. Yep, just a pee. It don't matta tho. Da big, green planets mo' important to females."

Leroy chimed in. "Okay, I gotta hear this. Why are big, green planets more important to females than the happy stick?"

"Cause da happy stick just do da work to delivva da baby stuff. You know, da stuff from da big, green planets. Dems is mo' important 'cause dems maka babies. Females luvs dat…makin's babies."

Rabbit was flabbergasted. "So, the size of your happy stick doesn't matter at all to the females?"

Ucktock shook his head and stated firmly, "Nope. Why would it?"

Rabbit wearily stood up. He whimpered, "You're gonna put me out of business." He turned and exited the room.

Pretty followed, "It time fo' Rabbit checkup." Then, she left.

"Wus it sumptin' I said?"

Leroy addressed Ucktock's concern, "Don't mind Rabbit. He thinks too much about what females like. Anyway, speaking of green planets, we should probably make a course change to evade detection near the twin planets, Vermyth and Dula."

"Huh?"

"Never mind. I need to discuss something with Jon."

Leroy left the baffled orc and met Jon on the bridge to advise a change in direction. Jon agreed and made adjustments to the auto pilot. The *Outcast* would take a different route back to Cypra than the one that brought them this close to home in an effort to thwart any attempts of pursuit by whomever wanted them dead. They solved the problem of being prohibited from jumping anywhere they needed to, but why enter systems that were teaming with warships?

Pretty caught up with Rabbit. "Hey, Rabbit."

He turned and smiled, "What's up?"

"Nuttin'. Just time fo' you a physical. Come on." She swayed her body with her hands and clasped them together.

Rabbit was astonished at the unanticipated likeness of Pretty to human women. Her stance was surprisingly feminine and somewhat flirtatious. Her rocking motion, akin to a slow dance between partners, drew his attention to her hips, her eyes, her hair.

Yet, she was unlike any human woman he'd ever been with, for she was minimally animalistic in a playful way. Her muscular body was toned and firm, not very different from human women, but had the slightest contrasts he couldn't explain. Aside from her light green skin and darker green hair, her overly curvy silhouette appealed to the orc in him. She seemed to be the best of both worlds.

She continued, "Why you starin's at me?"

Rabbit sighed, "Oh. I was just looking at you. I don't know if orcs say that you are beautiful or how I'm supposed to say it, if at all, but you *are* beautiful."

Pretty lowered her head as she looked up at Rabbit. "Tanks. Dat so nice."

Rabbit thought to himself, "Oh my gods, I'm in real trouble here." He was gonna have a hell of a time doing his job with Pretty around. He had to be on his best behavior and not let on to the other guys about his affair with her, not that he even knew why. Maybe because he would be seen as a scoundrel, fucking anything that moved? Maybe because he did have a job to do and couldn't let feelings for an orc get in the way? As of right now, like it or not, orcs were still Humania's enemy. He complied with her earlier request. "Okay. Time for my physical."

***

Moonoak, Nuttybomb's trusted shaman had been summoned to join the other officers. He sat down amongst the grumbling between Gunza, Nuttybomb's top officer, and Guthrak, another general. He engaged, "Nuttybomb, I seen a vision of humans comin's in great numbers."

Nuttybomb smirked. "Me, too. But dems will face most a our army. We be ok, I tink."

Gunza snarled, "We kill all da humans dat face us. All da udders on Plenna be our a prisoners." He laughed.

Nutty addressed his finest officer, "Gunza, we know where dems all are?"

"Most a dems. We see places fro' space. Our a armies on der way der now."

Guthrak interrupted, "My army already at one place now. Found humans and orcs in prisons."

The orcs all looked stunned. Nuttybomb questioned, "Humans do take der own as prisoners?" He paused, then continued, "Dat surprising. Bein' a smart race, I would tink dems wouldn't see da benefit."

Moonoak interjected, "Maybe dems not so smart and a lil more mean lika us."

"Or both. Dems seemin' mo' dangerous dan I thought."

Guthrak snapped, "Boss, dems not a problem fo us. We smart and not squishy lika dems."

Nuttybomb corrected his subordinate, "Dat Rabbit Harrison not squishy at all. Hims one a da hardest fights I evva have." When he realized his visible concern left looks of vulnerability, he lightly continued, "He choppa my pee into strings. Doc put it back togetha, but now it looka lika puppy dawg." He forced a hardy laugh to ease the tension.

His men reluctantly followed in fun. Gunza seized the moment to attempt an unoffensive joke. "Do it bark now?"

"No, but it find it way out to pee on evvy tree it come past now."

Levity of the total situation was lost for the moment. Some lighthearted jeers and laughs were exchanged between them. Only Moonoak remained perfectly respectful and careful not to engage in the group's banter. His job was to be the straight man, to command respect as a healer and a visionary. He wasn't a warrior like the others. His demeanor and reputation seemed to keep trouble at bay. Besides, his intellect rarely allowed him to see the same things as funny like his simpleminded cohorts.

As the orcs settled down, Nuttybomb asked Guthrak, "What else you find out 'bout dese humans?"

"Um, dems shoot good, but dems squishy. So dems don't hurt as much as our a guns. Dems don't fight sloppy, too. Dems stay togetha and kinda fight togetha. Hard a explain."

"Ok. Any weaknesses?"

"Dems all seem weak to me," the confident orc boasted.

Booma, now healed from his wounds received at Rabbit's hands, entered the tent to join in the discussion. "Hi, all. Nutty, I gots some stuff."

Nuttybomb rubbed his large hands together in anticipation. "Is it good?"

"Not all a it. Lots a big human ships a comin'."

"We know dat part."

Booma nodded in affirmation and continued, "Ok. Anda so far, we mostly fight um...prison guards, I tink. But now, human armies movin' in east to attack us."

Nutty leaned forward, his massive frame causing the crate he sat on to creak as the enormous weight pushed it to near breaking point. He asked, "How many troops?"

"Dunno, but a lot."

Guthrak spat, "Dems squishy. Dems need lika twice wut we got to even try anda beat us."

Booma advised, "Ya, maybe twice wut we gots. Maybe lots mo' dan dat. Dunno. Anda mo' comin's, maybe."

Nuttybomb ordered, "Guthrak, pull you army to join our main force to da north. We try to circle dems. I keep da main army goin' east to meet da human bastids anda you head south. Got it?"

"Yessir."

"So, we beat da humans here anda new ones comin' won't outnumba us. Anda when dis all done anda dis planet gots no humans, we make real colony on Plenna. Once I kill Rabbit Harrison, dems will be finished. Now, go anda kill da humans!"

***

"I have Evelyn Dulcey," the sinister voice taunted.

Jon replied, "You are in direct violation of the very laws that govern us, Zen. Your career is over."

"Your laws, Jon, your laws. They don't apply to me."

"And why is that, Zen?"

Zen was becoming more power hungry and off-center by the day now. His arrogance, coupled with the promise of promotion, was driving his sadistic behavior even further. Furthermore, he withheld crucial information about Cypra, Plenna, orcs, Spidanoids, Colonel Taggart, and what was to come. He spat, "You will see soon enough, my friend." He continued, "I see you jumped to Remoir. Count the ships, Jon."

Leroy announced, "Jon, huge number of capital ships near the actuator to Cypra."

Jon asked, "Are they ours or orcs?" He couldn't rule out that Zen had somehow formed an alliance with the orcs, however improbable. His mind reeled.

"They're Humania. What do you make of all this?"

"Lemme reply to the asshole first." He engaged Zen with, "I see 'em, Zen. What's the deal? I didn't know we had a force out here."

Zen coughed, "We don't. Or should I say, you don't."

Leroy looked at Jon. "A rebellion?"

Jon surmised, "That's my thought."

Zen stated, "I'm done playing, Jon. I can see you. I'll meet you shortly." He cackled before disconnecting.

Jon asked, "Can you seen him?"

"No. He either changed his cloak pattern or he's got to be on the surface. How else could he see us?"

"He can't change his cloak pattern. Maybe he's trying to scare us or get us to the surface. I don't know."

Leroy growled, "I hate this guy." Anger welled up inside him.

Jon said, "Easy, Killer. I need you to keep your shit together. Rabbit's gonna lose his."

Rabbit came up behind Jon. "Why would I lose my shit?

Jon and Leroy looked at each other for an answer that might put Rabbit's mind at ease. However, there was none to be found, other than the truth.

Jon spoke softly and quietly. "That was Zen. He has Evelyn."

Rabbit cursed, "Fuck! Are you sure?"

"No, I'm not sure. But we haven't heard from her in some time."

"Where is he?"

Jon shrugged his shoulders and winced as he obliged, "I don't know." After Rabbit sighed in disgust, Jon added, "But he says he can see us."

"And we can't see him?"

"No."

Rabbit jumped into Jon's captain's chair and fiddled until he asked, "Leroy, can you pull this up?"

Leroy answered as he did whatever he did to receive Rabbit's data, "Got it."

"If you can trace that, evaluating the smallest numbers to the biggest, we can get Zen's last heading. That would be his path."

Jon asked, "The largest numbers essentially being his newest exhaust with the smallest being the oldest?"

Rabbit replied, "Yeah. Since we got his engine signature when we decloaked him, we can use that to come up with the engines' waste product. The smallest numbers would have the longest time to dissipate or spread out. If he is here, we should find him."

Leroy announced, "I got it; I got it. He's at one o' clock. Distance, ten minutes." The chip on his shoulder hadn't left, but it was a bit more manageable.

Jon admitted, "Good. We don't have to get near those capital ships. We need to be careful, though, assuming Evelyn's on the *Paragon*. Let's get Evelyn."

Seventeen
OMG! Cypra Again!

Colonel Taggart stood on a platform next to the command chair with subordinates scrambling below by several feet. His light gray uniform contrasted nicely with the dark gray walls and black, shiny floor. The huge multi-layered windows wrapped around him from port to starboard, the view giving him great delight.

He ordered the commencement of the final elimination of orcs on Cypra. Standing on the bridge of his flagship, the *Vindicator*, he oversaw the large fleet he had conveniently amassed, so he could quickly counter the orcs' movements. Along with three other colonels and four admirals, his fail-safe plans were set into motion.

The first group of two carriers, six battleships, four cruisers, and six destroyers jumped first. Seventy-five additional fighters were sent from Remoir as well, giving the group well over two hundred to throw at the orcs.

During the twenty-two minutes it took for the first round of ships to jump, the orcs began moving ships of their own to confront the humans. They were fairly equal in number to the humans, although severely outmatched in technology and training, giving the humans a marked advantage.

Over the next hour, however, another twenty-two capital ships and nearly a thousand fighters would add to Taggart's imposing force. They gathered and formed into their respective battle groups, readying for the onslaught that was to come.

***

Once again, the *Paragon's* cloak was compromised by a small nuke from Leroy's fighter. How the *Paragon* changed its cloaking signature was of concern, but on the back burner for now. The main thing was, she was visible again.

However, fighters couldn't launch actual nuclear devices to destroy enemy ships. If that was the case, a fighter could easily destroy even the largest warships. In essence, it was just an EMP device. This was going to be a fight for their lives.

Jon announced, "I see him." He shot past the *Paragon* with guns ablaze. There was little damage to Zen's stronger vessel.

Rabbit circled the *Paragon*, firing again and again, hoping to cut into her weapons systems. "No effect," he exclaimed.

The *Paragon* went on the offensive, now turning to follow the *Outcast*, her weapons coming to bear.

Leroy said, "She's launching fighters. I count three."

Rabbit scoffed, "Are we ever not outnumbered?"

Jon stated, "Paragon is fully functional and pursuing us."

Rabbit's ship swung around to avoid Leroy as he passed the *Paragon*, firing again. He said, "We have to take out these fighters, Jon."

Jon, in frustration, barked, "I know, I know. Just make it quick!"

Leroy hollered, "I'm hit!" He was pissed.

"That didn't take long," was sarcastically shot from Rabbit's mouth.

"Shut up, bitch. I'm still in the game."

Rabbit, with somewhat a smile considering the way things were playing out, mumbled, "It's about time."

Ucktock finally separated his ship from the *Outcast* and made a run at the *Paragon*. "Don't worry. I on dis bastid." His cannon missed more often than not, but when it hit the *Paragon*, it caused the larger ship to shudder.

Rabbit instructed, "Uck, hit the main weapon in the front. Come in at an angle, so it doesn't hit you though."

Ucktock screamed, "Ok." His ship cut back around for another run.

Pretty was thrown to the deck from the same main weapon Ucktock sought to destroy. The lights flickered, and sparks shot out from a panel near her. She jumped up and reorganized medical supplies in case they were needed.

Harry bellowed, "Whatcha doin up there, Jon?"

A frantic response of, "I'm trying. I'm trying," was replied. He pulled hard on the throttle, looping the *Outcast*, and pushing her to her physical limits. This was both defensive, to cut inside the *Paragon's* turn radius, and offensive as he fired at the enemy's main weapon. Pretty was on the floor again. The Bridge's consoles lit up like a Christmas tree.

Ucktock also scored a shot, his inaccurate cannon somehow finding the same target. A small explosion ripped the bottom front from the *Paragon*, and with it, her ability to fire her main weapon. But Ucktock's ship was also under fire. He spat, "Fargin Creep," and something like, "Ugghhhh," as fire erupted from the port side of his ship.

Ship to ship combat was usually decided by the skill of pilots, the capabilities and strength of their ships, and to a lesser degree, a number of external circumstances. However, the percentage of luck, relative to outcome in dogfights with multiple ships, went up. Skill and ship attributes still played a large part in damage dealt and evaded, but a stray shot from an enemy in a blind spot could equate to death.

Rabbit wasn't sure how much his comrades knew this, but he used all his abilities to protect them as well as himself from errant, lucky shots. He pulled his trigger just a hair too late to help Ucktock, but he did eliminate the pilot fixated on the orc. The fighter exploded into pieces, the pilot never knowing he was hit. "That's one for me."

Leroy asked, "What about the one on your tail?"

"Oh, he's next." Rabbit timed his turn as he approached the *Outcast*, which was just ahead of the *Paragon*. He ordered, "Jon, turn hard right when I say."

"You got it."

Waiting, anticipating, judging, "Now!"

The pilot who was trailing Rabbit was momentarily shocked. His delayed reflexes put him between Rabbit and the *Outcast*. Zen's pilot was no quicker to react, putting the two on a path to impact.

The fighter blew apart against the *Paragon*, sending pieces into her mother ship, injuring seven, and causing fires to start on the front starboard side. the *Paragon* buckled, welds popped, stress ensued, as the most capable ship in the battle was damaged.

Zen fired, "Get us to the surface! Gods dammit! We'll kill 'em down there."

Nuttybomb was aboard his flagship, giving orders and evaluating what was unfolding before him. Several of his capital ships had begun to engage the first human group that entered the system. He saw damage to both sides occurring, although it appeared that his forces may have been getting the worst of it so far, but he wouldn't disengage, yet.

His eyes strained to see what was happening just beyond the battle. Dots appeared, confusing him, causing questions to be answered that he simply couldn't yet. "Wut are dose?" He erected himself and pointed.

An orc replied, "Dems looka lika ships."

As he neared the battle, his brain recognized the same grouping of ships that his forces currently faced. Only this time, the addition of enemy ships caused him to be outnumbered three to one. Nuttybomb ordered, "Do all da damage you a can, now!"

The bulky orc ships began firing at long range, their massive guns ejecting enormous projectiles toward the human ships. Most missed badly, predominately because of firing at these distances, but also compounded by the abnormally gracious spacing between targets. However, when the targets were impacted, spectacular damage resulted. Before long, the human fighters were swarming the orc warships.

Like ants on a giant beetle, each fighter did minimal damage. But collectively, they inundated the larger orc ships and began to pick away, one bite at a time.

While Nuttybomb used his complete arsenal to combat his foe, Colonel Taggart only used the first arm of his fleet. Nuttybomb called from his flagship, *Up Yer Ass*, to her sister ships, *Down Yer Throat* and *In Yer Ear*, to begin ramming the enemy as soon as possible. They could still fire their main guns at other targets as they neared, in an attempt to bring down additional vessels.

Nuttybomb's ships were just as large as their human counterparts. However, they were bulkier and thicker, their bows meant to sustain the brunt of damage while also being used for ramming. This complimented orc tactics too as their main weapons faced forward and were at the mercy of steering, usually facing enemies head on.

A lucky shot here and there crippled a couple human ships at long distance. But as the fleets drew nearer, the human ships had the advantage, dealing crushing blows to several orc cruisers.

Down Yer Throat was the first orc ship to shove her bow into the side of a human battleship. The collision was magnificent, opening a gaping hole in the human ship's port side. Orcs with huge handguns and swords poured from their own ship and into the belly of the *Dangerous*.

The *Bulwark* was impaled by *In Yer Ear* in much the same way, with orcs disembarking from their own ship, and invading the corridors of the enemy. A human cruiser and destroyer also sustained heavy damage from *The Orc Impaler* before she made contact.

The next casualty was an orc battleship. The *Deep Growl* was cut in half by fire from the *Insidious* and the *Treacherous*. The latter wouldn't enjoy victory for long though as it would soon be on the end of Nuttybomb's *Up Yer Ass*.

Nuttybomb ordered, "Troops, attack!" Orcs pullulated the *Treacherous*, obliterating anything that moved before them. They overran security and took control of vital areas. They even used the *Treacherous'* own guns to fire at other human ships. *Down Yer Throat* and *In Yer Ear* had similar success.

Taggart's full complement of capital ships, escorts, and fighters were readying to engage. He couldn't sit back any longer and allow the orcs to inflict any more losses. His confidence, momentarily shaken, began to rise as the remainder of his fleet engrossed the orc warships.

Soon the orc fleet would be eliminated and the green sub-humans on the surface would follow.

***

"What the hell is he doing?" Jon puzzled over Ucktock's ducking and rolling to avoid gunfire.

Leroy grinned, "How the hell should I know? He's an orc. Enough said."

Ucktock followed Rabbit, although much more slowly and in animated fashion. Human troops shot at them from three sides as they traversed a hundred feet of heavy woods, stopping them in their tracks as they came to a clearing. The two hunkered down around sixty feet from the *Paragon* and returned sporadic fire.

Rabbit asked on his radio, "Did the Electus disembark, yet?" He ducked down considerably lower as bullets raked metal containers above his head.

Leroy answered, "I only saw two leaving the ship as we landed." He, too, ducked as he made his way around to the right with Harry close behind.

Jon, remaining on the *Outcast* with Pretty, instructed, "Around ten troops to your right, ten to your right, guys. Look sharp." He shot the *Outcast's* smaller machine guns toward approaching troops.

Harry quarreled, "Sharp? My gods, I just took one in the helmet! That was close." He and Leroy struggled to make their way around to the far right of the fight.

Leroy pleaded, "Cover me." He dashed a few feet and dove for cover while Harry unloaded his weapon to dilute incoming enemy bullets.

Rabbit, stuck in the middle of the turkey shoot, begged, "If you guys do that again, let me know so I can move, too."

Leroy sighed, "Gonna move again in a few seconds." He looked back at Harry, who was just a few feet behind and at the edge of the woods.

Harry remarked, "Ready."

Leroy snapped, "Go!"

Harry and Ucktock shot at enemy positions from cover as Leroy and Rabbit darted a few feet and threw themselves to relative safety.

Rabbit commented, "I didn't get very far."

Leroy scoffed, "Me either." With that, he opened fire and knocked out two security officers who were somewhat exposed by his new position. He continued, "Ready to move again?"

Rabbit replied, "Ready."

Harry was also up to the task of shooting at his foe. "Ready."

Leroy tossed a grenade and ordered, "Now."

An explosion tossed a couple more enemy bodies into the air and stunned the others to the right. Leroy dove into an enemy position and cleared the area, but now found himself in trouble. The *Paragon* assaulted him with a machine gun mounted on her bottom port side. He screamed, "Gods dammit," a devastating swath of slugs allowing him no quarter.

Rabbit had made it all the way to the *Paragon*. He hurried up the ramp and cautiously entered, poking his head around the opening bulkhead. He turned the corner and proceeded.

***

Jon struggled to remove all danger from his team, allowing a handful of troops to get past his ship's bullets. He jumped from the safety of his rapid-fire weapons console and started shooting into the fast-moving crowd. But they were on him in an instant. Although he had dropped two, the other three made it to the *Outcast* and up the ramp.

A bullet ripped through Jon's right thigh, dropping him to his knees. Another found one of his ears, but luckily, it was only a glancing blow. His own gun was used to bash the face of an oncoming foe, rendering the unlucky chap unconscious. Another was tossed haphazardly over his shoulder and into the wall behind him. He, too, was immobilized.

But Jon wasn't quick enough to stop a hard punch to his face, especially being somewhat immobilized himself from being shot in the leg. Another fist hit the other side of his head, dazing him; his gun flew somewhere down the corridor behind him. He threw his hands up to block any more punches from landing to his head while he got to his feet.

Jon wasn't on his feet for long, however. The opposing man managed to work him to the ground, arms and legs vying to lock and/or choke him out. The strength and skill of the man surprised Jon as he gasped, "I see you've had some training. And you are strong, too." He freed an arm and gained enough leverage to obtain side mount.

The man managed, "Cypra will do that to a man, Jon." He grinned, not ready to be defeated. His gun had been shot from his hand by Jon's initial volley, rendering it useless. Now they would use strength and skill of hand to determine the outcome.

For several minutes, they grappled, neither having a distinctive advantage. Jon clearly saw the man's face for the first time and recognized it immediately from intel he had pulled. "Thomas Matthews."

"Seems you have top clearance, too, Jon... Unless you know me from my past," Thomas spewed.

Jon dropped an elbow into Matthew's forehead. Slight swelling above Matt's brow began. "No, I don't know your past. And really, I don't care."

Matt timed Jon's next elbow strike and wiggled down, beneath his hips. He finagled his way out of Jon's grip and freed himself. "I know your past. You're a renowned martial artist. Too bad it won't save you." Matt worked his way around Jon's back.

"Well, it's not gonna save you," Jon teased. He was always moving and applying pressure. His opponents didn't even know they were being compromised by being weakened or set up for the next move. Jon kept his balance and forced Matt to use his strength for several minutes, exerting more energy than was necessary. Jon easily maintained his position without wearing himself out.

Matt needed to readjust his hold, so Jon didn't escape. He was just a moment away from initiating Jon's perceived demise, when he found himself on his back. He was dropped into Jon's full guard position. "Nice move."

Jon landed some forearms and elbows, this time drawing blood on several strikes. The floor had actually dented from Matt's head being forced into space the two couldn't possibly occupy. His skull was cracked, but he was still in the fight. Jon commented, "I heard that. Not good to hear any bone break, let alone in your head."

Matt somehow landed a decent forearm of his own, something he was notorious for defensively. If Jon had only known, a gash wouldn't have been opened over his left eye, blood filling his face. Then came another and another. "I think I'm okay," he retorted.

Jon moved a bit to avoid the barrage from below. Matt swung under Jon for the second time, once again, freeing himself. The two got to their feet. Jon complimented, "Not bad."

"Do you think you're the only great fighter?" Matt asked.

"No. There's Rabbit Harrison. And if you get through me, you'll have to deal with him." Jon backed his way down the ship's ramp and stopped a short distance from the metal hulk, his boots finding steady ground to work on. If Matt had a gun, Jon would have stayed on the ship, keeping a tight grip on his foe. He didn't even know why Matt didn't have a gun to use. "No matter," he mumbled to himself. He briefly rubbed his wounded leg.

Matt kept pace like a big cat stalking its prey. "Won't matter to you after you're dead, Jon."

"Maybe," was Jon's response. He took up a defensive pose and waited.

Matt quickly moved forward and got his arms around Jon's upper body. Jon sidestepped and flipped Matt, controlling his head. The two came to the ground with Matt on top, but in a submissive position. Jon's legs were hooked around his abdomen.

Matt thought his saving grace was having a hand up at the side of his head to thwart Jon's attempt to choke him out. In this position, Jon wouldn't have been able to inhibit blood to reach his brain.

But Jon kept pressure on, the way he had done so many times in *his* past. Matt's arm eventually succumbed to weakness and was worked below his face- low enough, in fact, that his own arm was used to collapse the carotid artery in his neck. Matt struggled to escape, but was totally bound from behind. He passed out and went limp.

Jon heard more troop movement in the woods from the direction that Matt and the other enemies came. He released Matt and got to his feet, turned, and dashed up the ramp. He screamed, "Pretty, come here."

Pretty met him at the ship's entrance. "You hurt," she exclaimed.

"I'm okay...for now, at least. Here. Use this gun to shoot that guy down there or any others who try to get aboard. If any run past the ship, into the woods toward our guys, shoot 'em." Jon didn't kill Matt, that wasn't his way. He saw a skilled fighter in Matt, no matter which side he was on. He hated taking any human lives, but he needed to protect his ship and his crew. The lives he was taking were in self-defense, he reasoned, and they happened to be on the wrong side of things. He made his way to the ship's gun he used just minutes before.

Pretty took up position at the top of the ramp and stood guard. "Ok," she answered. Then, she uttered to herself, "I hope Rabbit ok."

***

Rabbit didn't know what was transpiring back at the *Outcast*. The ship was only a couple hundred feet away, but far enough that he couldn't possibly see. He needed to do his part, which was now becoming more difficult by the second. He grumbled, "Watch my rear, take out that gun for Leroy, save Evelyn, eliminate troops, guards, and the like, blah, blah, blah." He was silenced by gunshots just ahead. He broke to his right and ducked into a workstation alcove in a connecting corridor. He stuck his hand back around the corner and returned fire.

He was surprised by two crew members who were running right past him from the opposite direction. They had no idea he was aboard and ran right into his position. All three reacted in unison, shooting at each other hastily.

Rabbit's reflexes and aim were just a little better; enough so, that he shot both men at point blank range into their chests. He was hit in his left leg and right side, though; it was sufficient to slow, but not stop him. He grimaced and spurned, "I shoulda joined the circus." Upon realizing the bullet had passed through his leg, he quickly wrapped it to slow down the bleeding. To his relief, the wound in his side was a scratch.

He decided to clear the corridor and adjacent areas, so he wouldn't be surprised again. A grenade ahead and several tossed into some rooms on the way, secured his path from harm.

A guard fired from the *Paragon's* machine gun area. He was there only to protect the gunner whom was firing at Leroy and the other Troublemakers. Rabbit was grazed again, this time, one of his shoulders losing some skin and underlying tissue. Like Leroy, Rabbit was getting pissed. He wanted to yell, "You son of a bitch," but kept his mouth closed, instead tossing a grenade.

Machine gun fire ceased. Rabbit darted down the corridor and found the two men he had killed. He took a second to check his shoulder and only grumbled, "Man, I like this jacket." His finger wiggled through a bullet hole.

A coordinated assault by Leroy, Harry, and Ucktock, granted them access to the *Paragon*. Their trip to the ship wasn't without incident, but they were able to shoot their way aboard.

Ucktock, getting the worst of enemy fire as he climbed the ramp, hollered, "Rabbit!"

Rabbit heard his green friend's feet pounding the metal incline and instructed, "Get down and watch to your left. That area isn't cleared, yet."

Leroy shouted, "Got it."

Rabbit gleefully returned, "Hey, you made it."

"Thanks to you taking out that gun and Ucktock getting shot up to get us here."

"Is he okay?"

Leroy replied, "I don't know." He asked the bloody orc, "Are you okay?"

Ucktock nodded, "I'm ok, Rabbit."

Leroy semi-joked, "He's okay, Rabbit."

Ucktock bellowed in a grand laugh. "Da big, green planets be ok."

Rabbit was relieved. He smiled at Ucktock's and Leroy's comedic gestures, but also, because they were alive and seemed to be doing fairly well. He asked, "Harry with you?"

Leroy grinned as he replied in a goofy voice, "Always." He took Harry and cleared the area to the left, including the bridge. A few Paragon guys lost their lives in the process.

Rabbit threw a grenade around the corner and into the main corridor. Ucktock ran from the ship's entrance to follow the grenade. It detonated, leaving a mangled mess that marked the corridor in splattered, red liquid. Ucktock stopped at the mess and jeered, "Dis area a clear."

Rabbit came from behind and laid his hand on the orc's shoulder. He proceeded to hold back his green friend as he cautiously shot into a neighboring area.

Ucktock urged, "Use grenade."

Rabbit whispered, "Shh. I don't have any more. Evelyn must be in there." He pointed to a door at the end of the passage way.

**

Jon fired at anything that moved. But the gun's mobility was limited, hanging from the *Outcast's* body like a one-armed pugilist. A couple of troops evaded his lethal designs and came upon Pretty.

Pretty gripped the gun and pulled the trigger, the grunts of the fallen was music to her ears. Then, she aimed at Matt, who got to his feet, turned, and headed toward the woods. Her gun opened into him, dropping his wounded body to the ground. She raced down the ramp as he crawled ever so slowly toward the heavily treed area, just feet away. She warned, "Stop!"

He moved along the ground, ever closer to cover behind a tree. She cautioned him again, "Don't. Rabbit dat way."

Matt grinned in spite, blood spitting from his mouth, "Well, then that's exactly where I'm going."

"No, you not," was followed by a string of shots that finished the stubborn human. Pretty strained to see through the trees, hoping to find Rabbit returning safely, but the foliage was just too heavy and the danger of remaining outside the ship drew her in for protection.

Jon thought he heard footsteps on the ramp. "Pretty, you okay?" he asked.

"Yep. I killed da men anda da one you said to if he a moved."

"Okay. Stay there and look for Rabbit and the others. I don't see any more troops coming this way."

Pretty relaxed and peered into the woods, intently.

***

"Zen, it's over," Rabbit said.

Zen shouted in defiance, "No, it's not over." The door opened, and he came into the corridor with Evelyn in front as a shield.

Rabbit, concerned by the wild look in Zen's eyes and his erratic movements cautioned him, "Easy. Don't do anything stupid, Zen."

"Stupid? Stupid? How stupid are you to stand there with your weapons drawn while I have her?"

"I won't let you leave with her. Let her go." Rabbit saw how awful Evelyn looked. She didn't have orc blood, or Spidanoid DNA, or whatever he had that gave him a much better chance at surviving such brutality.

"Step aside or I'll kill her," Zen warned.

The other Troublemakers took their cues from Rabbit. Because Evelyn was *his* woman, whether past or present, he would decide how to proceed.

Rabbit looked around. "Guys, let him through." He looked at Leroy and led him to the area near the ramp with his eyes.

Leroy and Harry took a few steps back and stopped upon hearing, "Drop your weapons." Zen pushed his gun against Evelyn's face, just hard enough for her to grimace.

Rabbit and Ucktock were closest to Zen. They dropped their weapons first. Leroy and Harry were next, but they darted around the corner for safety. Rabbit and Ucktock dodged into the corridor nearest to them.

Zen yelled, "What the hell are you doing? I'll kill her."

The Troublemakers knew he couldn't kill her if he wanted to escape. And his only way out was getting passed them- Rabbit and Ucktock to the left, and Leroy and Harry to the far right.

Zen screamed, "Now, or I'll kill her." There was no sound or motion in response to his order. He screamed again, "Her death will be on your hands, Rabbit." Frantically, he rushed toward the ship's exit.

Leroy jumped from cover and into his path, gun in hand.

Zen said, "Get back, get back." His gun pushed hard against Evelyn's face. He jacked his head around to find Rabbit right behind him, but before he could defend himself, his neck was broken.

Leroy had grabbed Zen's weapon and pulled it away from Evelyn in case it misfired or if things with Rabbit didn't go well and Zen pulled the trigger.

Ucktock held Evelyn's weight until Rabbit could pick her up.

The few remaining enemy troops didn't pose much of a problem to the Troublemakers, who made it back to the *Outcast* without any more wounds. Evelyn and Ucktock were treated by Pretty, the latter requiring a majority of the makeshift nurse's time. Rabbit also received some attention, his wounds being the least severe of the group. Jon, too, got some needed help with his leg.

Beat up, but not beaten, the Troublemakers headed back into space and off in the direction of Cypra. How much they could accomplish against an entire fleet, was questionable at best, but they still needed to accomplish their mission of determining what was causing low production on Plenna. Only now, there were orcs, a possibly hostile Humania fleet, a rebellion, ties to Crystal Technologies, cover-ups and misinformation, and maybe Spidanoids as well.

Eighteen
What was to Come

Colonel Taggart was full of himself. His entire Second Fleet was now in the midst of battle against lowly orcs...and doing quite well. He ordered a cup of java and took a seat in the officer's lounge to view things in comfort. Also, he had some orders to give to other fleets and troops throughout Humania. He pushed a communication button and began with, "This is Lord Taggart. All officers, personnel, troops, fleets, and the like, under the command of myself and the Top Seven, it is time to execute the New Order." He continued, "Begin."

Only three of his battleships, a few cruisers, destroyers and maybe a hundred fighters were lost in the Cypra System. Conversely, around half of the orc ships were eliminated so far.

The visual spectacle was amazing, even tantalizing, to those who were caught in its deadly clutches. The amount of gunfire, which alone lit up the dark, black backdrop, paled in comparison to the mighty explosions that ripped enormous ships apart on a titanic scale. Everything seemed to flicker, a million beacons, shining intermittently, shooting through space at breakneck speeds.

Numbers aside, Taggart not only recognized the superiority of his ships and their crews, his eyes saw the difference between his sleek, slender, powerful ships against the orcs' stocky, boxy dung heaps. This was confirmation of what he already knew – complete and utter destruction of his enemy.

Taggart was thrilled by the sight. He was even giddy knowing what was to come.

***

Booma's troops rushed forward to meet their squishy opposition. His orcs screamed and beat their chests, running and shooting into the bush ahead, but before reaching the main line of the enemy, they were weakened by gunfire. Still, they lunged into combat against an invisible foe until the last second. Then, and only then, did they see the fear in the humans' eyes.

Arc raised his hands, his eyes taking on a glowing white. He lowered his hood with one hand and looked to the skies. Energy ran through his body and gathered in his hands. His fingers lit up, matching his eyes as he convulsed. His head twisted, like a dog straining to understand. He leaned forward and pushed his arms out ahead of him. Bolts of bright blue and white lightning shot forward, into the enemy lines. Humans screamed in pain and horror as this new weapon of destruction overwhelmed them.

Other than Arc, the green monsters slashed and bashed everything around them to oblivion. But as the enemy's front line was cut down, the orcs were confronted with a second, less squishy force.

Humans in armor smashed into the orc line. Their power was equal to the orcs in virtually every way, their intelligence, superior. Twice as many orcs than humans began falling.

Arc unsheathed a thin short sword from his side and engaged several humans at a time. Between thrusts and parrying, he unleashed a furious magnitude of electrical energy. He was a skilled warrior, not only relying on his unique ability to manipulate the elements, but to operate his weapon with precision as well. He grew tired. Summoning the otherworldly mayhem drew upon his own energy, too.

Booma fought alongside Arc, protecting him at times when the smaller orc entered into a trance or became visibly slower. While somewhat calmer, he lowered his weapon and took a moment to radio his brother. "Nutty, da humans are killin's lots a our troops. Dems not squishy."

Up Yer Ass had just finished its business of taking over the *Treacherous*. Dozens of orcs remained aboard the enemy ship, so they could use the enemy guns to add to their own firepower. The massive orc ship reversed and freed itself from the human ship.

Nuttybomb replied to his brother, "Booma, none a dems are squishy?"

"Dunno. Looka lika we got thru da first line a humans, but next ones be real strong."

Between giving orders to his fleet, Nuttybomb asked, "We gonna win?"

Booma stated, "Dunno. Takin' heavy losses. Guthrak troops startin' fight to north."

"Listen," Nuttybomb ordered. "Orcs on our ships beat humans hand to hand easy up here. Der are squishy ones. Not all da humans are strong. Keep fightin' anda lemme know if better when Guthrak meet up wit' you."

"Ok."

Nuttybomb rubbed his eyes and forehead with his palm. Perhaps Rabbit Harrison's amazing strength wasn't a one off. Apparently, humans came in varieties, and not in forms he wanted to deal with. Rabbit Harrison was a handful, more than a handful. Was he typical of what orcs should expect? How could intelligence reports have missed these powerful humans? How many orcs would Nutty allow to die before he might have to retreat? And how would he protect orcs against a masterful foe? He was startled by the next report.

"Sir, more ships jumping to here"

***

Leroy snapped, "I see him, I see him." He shot through a wall of Humania fighters. "Gods dammit!" He brought his ship to the left, then the right.

Jon yelled, "Doesn't look like they want us here." Sparks flickered, zapping his right hand.

Rabbit followed Leroy through the maelstrom of bullets. "Holy shit, that was close!"

The *Outcast* and Ucktock's ship kept up the best they could with their fighters leading the way. Jon spat, "They're coming around."

Leroy hollered, "Dammit, Jon. We aren't even to the fleet, yet. Was this a good idea?" He ducked his fighter to the right and pulled his trigger. "One for me."

The Troublemakers' ears perked up and listened carefully to a Humania wide transmission. What they heard, confirmed many of their earlier suspicions. A handful of Humania planets were being invaded by other humans. Communications, military bases, and government centers were reported as being attacked.

Jon, although aware of fighters swinging around behind the *Outcast*, hung his head. His words changed to a very depressed tone. He said, "Looks like we are at war, boys."

Leroy questioned, "With who?"

"I don't know, but these guys must be them." Jon lurched forward, his harness keeping him from leaving his seat.

"But why would they attack orcs? Wouldn't they need all of their forces to take the rest of Humania?"

Rabbit chimed in with, "Probably still testing on Cypra and building a super army. I can't help but wonder why they went to war now, though?" He opened into the back of some unsuspecting fool. He added, "One for me."

Harry spoke from the *Outcast's* engine room. "If all of this is true so far, Rabbit was probably right about releasing Spidanoids and insecticides too. Maybe they went to war now, because we caught 'em with their pants down."

Leroy grinned, "I hate you, Rabbit. Just the thought of you being right and all of their pants down..."

Jon interjected, "Ummm...hey guys...There's a whole other fleet over there."

Colonel Parker said, "Hello, Jon."

Jon, a little surprised to hear Parker's voice, still greeted, "Colonel?" The *Outcast* rolled between an enemy frigate and destroyer.

Parker conceded, "You were right, Jon. Unfortunately, you were right."

"Sir, where are you?"

Parker held the fleet until further notice. He said, "Jon, talk to me. What's going on with the orcs?"

"They seem to be fighting a common enemy, sir," Jon said, his hand pulling on the stick to skirt the comm tower above a battleship.

"There are a lot of ships out here, son. Will they attack us?" Parker asked.

Jon replied, "Not if we ally with them. I don't believe so."

Unconvinced, Parker questioned, "Are you willing to put your career on the line?

"Sir, my career hardly amounts to much with all things considered," Jon assured.

"So, who the hell do we shoot at?" the targeting officer on the bridge with Parker queried.

Parker ordered, "All Humania warships, this is Colonel Parker. Engage the human fleet that is currently fighting orcs. Do not attack orc ships. I repeat, do not attack orc ships."

***

Nuttybomb's orcs were about to retreat. News from the surface had been inconsistent, but troubling. Things in space looked perilous and probably more than enough reason for the orc ships to disengage, but he didn't order a retreat, yet. He hoped Booma might have told him something promising.

Booma reported, "We thru da second line, Nutty. Guthrak tella me da same ting. Der wus squishy humans wit' guns, den der beed strong humans wit' swords, dens squishy again. We doin's ok."

Most surprising of all, was hearing and then, seeing human ships attack other human ships. With things going well on the planet, and the odds in space looking a bit more favorable, possible retreat or defeat became less likely.

Nuttybomb needed to know who his enemies were and who were his friends, though. He said aloud, perhaps uselessly into space, "I am Nuttybomb, Warchief of Hotta, Angra, Lilst, and Plenna. Who are you, Colonel Parker?"

The human replied, "This is Colonel Parker. Hello, Nuttybomb." He didn't care for the orc's title, including Plenna, but he was diplomatic enough and aware of the current problems.

"Why you shoot at udder human ships dat I fight, too?"

Parker chose his words carefully and tried to be as direct as possible, without divulging too much information. He also used small words, so the orc would understand. "I think you and me can be friends. The other humans are bad. They want to kill you and me."

Nuttybomb quizzed, "Why you?"

Parker didn't indulge his green comrade. He simply stated, "Nuttybomb, I have a war to win. How about this? I don't shoot at your ships and you don't shoot at mine. We can talk after we win."

Fully understanding how every thought, movement, and emotion needed to be controlled to bring his orcs to victory as well as not feeling threatened by Colonel Parker, he agreed, "Ok. We no fire at each other. We talk when dis over."

Taggart clenched his fists as he spat, "Parker, I should have had you killed, too. I was hoping you would see how things *should* be and you would fall into line, but I always knew you were weak."

Things were becoming clear to some – and confusing to all. There were two major Humania fleets, one currently allied with orcs, and the other trying to impose its will on them, in a conflict above Cypra. Over two thousand ships, mostly fighters, tried to determine who was friendly and who wasn't. Communication was all but impossible. Hundreds of voices gave commands, targets, and reports, all on a small number of different channels.

It was later determined that at least two hundred fighters and a few capital ships were lost to friendly fire around Cypra. Moreover, many humans died with the belief that they were fighting for Humania. However, Humania was a term to be used lightly, or maybe more precisely, until they understood which Humania they were fighting for. Was the rightful human government led by Orson Korgue or the self-proclaimed Lord Taggart? Did Orson Korgue and/or a corrupt government lay out the plans for Cypra? Was General Amadas simply following orders? Was Humania the problem or was it the rebellion? The government had given Crystal Technologies the ability to do anything it wanted. Was this done unbeknownst to the politicians who granted such things, or were they kept in the dark by elements in the rebellion?

The *Outcast* strafed the *Vindicator* all the while dodging thousands of bullets from pursuing fighters and other typed of ships. Harry screamed, "Dammit, Jon. What the hell is going on up there?"

Rabbit and Leroy had both been hit, but neither had sustained major damage. They worked together, Rabbit engaging enemy targets, and Leroy protecting them as wing man. "Two for me," Rabbit squawked.

Leroy announced, "Fucking gods damn mother fucker! I'm hit again!" Smoke billowed from the front of his fighter and past his cockpit.

Rabbit asked, "You okay?" He took out another fighter. "That's three."

"I think so. This is unbelievable."

Leroy heard a familiar voice say, "Watch the language, Leroy."

He asked with joy, "Lenny? What the hell are you doing here?"

Lenny explained, "I'm back on the *Renown*. Hey, was that Rabbit?"

Rabbit greeted, "Just like old times, except Leroy is getting his ass kicked in a little fighter this time. Four."

Nuttybomb's angry voice filled their ears. "Rabbit Harrison?" There was silence. He asked again, "Rabbit Harrison, you der?"

Rabbit sighed and took a few seconds before responding, "Nuttybomb, Leader of This and That, I haven't seen you in what, a couple months?" He cleared his mind in case the orc leader tried to use his special powers. The truth was, he couldn't conceal, nor rid himself of the fear Nuttybomb brought upon him.

Jon ordered, "Knock it off, Rabbit." Jon threw the *Outcast* into a terrific spin, hurling anything to the ceiling that wasn't secured. Bullets ripped into the ship's starboard side and bottom.

Nuttybomb spat, "Wer are you, so we can finish our fight."

Rabbit laughed, "Hey, we're on the same team now." Another ship exploded before him.

Nuttybomb wasn't convinced. "Wer be my sista?"

Jon intervened, "Nuttybomb, she's safe on my ship, relatively speaking."

"Meaning?"

"Meaning, we didn't harm her. She's actually been part of our crew. As long as my ship isn't destroyed, she will join you when this is over."

Nuttybomb commanded, "I speak wit' her, now."

"Nuttybomb, dis Ucktock."

"Ucktock?" Nuttybomb quizzed.

"Yep."

The orc leader asked, "Wer you beed?"

Ucktock explained, "In prison till my friend, Rabbit Harrison, freed me."

Nuttybomb scratched his head in disbelief, believing some sort of ulterior motive behind the hated human. "Rabbit Harrison freed you?

"Yep. Anda him not so squishy. He tried lika free times, but he so stupid." Ucktock bellowed a big belly laugh, forgetting to disconnect from the open channel.

"You see Pretty?"

Ucktock acknowledged, "Yep. Her beed goods."

Nuttybomb addressed the leader of this new alliance, although only held by a string, "Colonel Parker, you fight fo' Rabbit Harrison?"

Parker laughed, "No, he's only a captain."

With brows furrowed, Nuttybomb exhaled, "Captain? You give me Captain Rabbit Harrison wen dis fight be ova."

Jon cut in with, "Colonel Parker, I'll handle this if that's okay?"

Parker allowed, "Go ahead, Jon."

Jon began, "Nuttybomb, I'll allow you to see Rabbit Harrison when this is over. We can meet on your ship or down on the planet. We have no reason to fight you and I think there are things we should discuss. We will bring Pretty, of course."

Nuttybomb pushed, "Ucktock, too."

Ucktock smiled, "Yep."

Among the diplomatic chatter and arrangements, The Troublemakers, Parker's fleet, and Nuttybomb's forces had gained the upper hand. Ships still flew in erratic patterns, sometimes missing each other by mere inches, other times colliding in balls of fire. Titanic projectiles launched every minute or so from the front of each orc ship, lighting the silhouettes of their massive hulks against the night sky. Gargantuan explosions ripped battleships and carriers apart, sending massive parts of their hulls and superstructures into neighboring ships. The fact that any conversations were even capable under such chaos, was a testament to the skill of the pilots who survived to this point. Sprinkled in was some good old-fashioned luck.

Leroy heard a greeting from another familiar voice, this time from his older brother. "Lou?" He banked left to avoid fire.

"Yeah, I couldn't talk earlier with all the other stuff going on."

Leroy was glad to hear from another member of his family. He felt lighter, somehow invigorated. He took a calculated shot at a fairly long distance. "That's three. I can't tell you how good it is to hear your voice."

Lou joked, "Let's wrap this up while we still have voices. It looks like Taggart's fleet is splitting, some heading to the planet and the others shooting for the actuator."

Leroy tensed a bit. He stated, "We gotta get the prison ships and the chemical ships heading to the planet." He fired at a fighter heading toward him, then continued, "If they land, they will kill all the orcs."

Jon said, "I'm on it."

Ucktock followed, "Me, too."

Nuttybomb, not wanting his orcs to be annihilated on the surface, ordered his destroyers, *Night Killa* and *Da Massacre* to halt the prison and chemical ships. His capital ships remained to weaken Taggart's fleet further.

Adolph Gruber, aboard the *Vindicator* with Colonel Taggart was to oversee the release of Spidanoids on Cypra's surface, and then their destruction by chemicals - chemicals engineered and tested on places like Libel, Plenna, and Cypra.

There was a blurred line between duties, responsibilities, and command between Humania's space and ground forces. Things were sketchier under Lord Taggart. Admirals found generals or colonels giving orders pertaining to targets, when they should have been limited to the scope of battles below. Special advisers complicated the matter even more. Gruber was the lead scientist at Crystal Technologies, not an officer, yet he commanded the movement of ships so as to place them on the surface.

A damaged prison barge, under Gruber's command, crash landed on the planet, releasing hundreds of the deadly creatures. The human crew was quickly devoured. Another made it safely, unloading nearly three thousand spidanoids onto Nuttybomb's orcs.

Jon, Ucktock, and Nuttybomb's destroyers couldn't stop all the ships from getting to the surface...and it was too late to try. Several more landed with different degrees of damage. In all, over ten thousand Spidanoids were let loose.

Jon called, "Nuttybomb."

"Dis Nuttybomb."

"We couldn't stop some ships from getting to the planet. I believe your orcs will be attacked by Spidanoids, giant bugs."

Nuttybomb wasn't pleased with this new information. He was inclined to believe that this Jon, working with Rabbit Harrison, may have designed plans to drop Spidanoids on orcs while covering up with their words. He growled, "You failed."

Jon stated, "Spidanoids are bad, but the chemical ships can still be stopped."

"Wut do chemical ships do?"

"They kill Spidanoids."

Nuttybomb questioned in suspicion, "Den why stop dems?"

Jon explained, "Because even though the chemicals are designed to kill Spidanoids, they are probably harmful enough to kill tons of your troops. They'll almost certainly kill any orcs who were living on the planet."

"You know dis fo' sure?"

"No, I don't," Jon admitted. He continued, "I'm trying to save orcs. Any humans on the planet are probably our enemies. I'll leave this decision up to you."

Nineteen
The Void

Gunza was cleaning up any remaining humans in the area when he was startled. He reported back to his superior, "Nuttybomb, dis Gunza."

Nuttybomb replied, "Wut is it?"

"Der be giant bugs here. Nasty, too." Sounds of screaming orcs, growls from gods know what, and gunshots tried to drown out Gunza's words.

Gunza swung a battle axe, taking two legs from a spidanoid in front of him. He ducked to his left to avoid being bitten as the creature lunged forward. He swung upward, slicing through the beast's exoskeleton and into its exposed organs. It fell in death's grip. Gunza stumbled backward as his eyes saw several of his troops being eaten by Spidanoids.

Nuttybomb asked, "Bugs come fro' da ships dat landed?"

"No, fro' under da ground. We find buildin's cut into da mountains. Dems all come outta der."

Booma had already reported thousands upon thousands of Spidanoids that he and his troops were fighting. They had come from ships. Nuttybomb didn't know how many more Spidanoids were from inside the mountains, but he needed to decide on whether to attack the chemical ships or to allow them free passage. If the ships would only eliminate the Spidanoids, his troops would be much better off. However, if they killed his troops, too, as Jon suggested they might, he would be condemning his own men to death.

Nuttybomb hailed Jon, "Would chemical ships kill all Spidanoids?"

"Maybe. Maybe not. These are big ships, but that makes them slow, too. Could you get your troops to board the chemical ships? Maybe we could take them over and use the chemicals after your troops leave the planet. I'll help."

Nuttybomb barked, "Orcs no leave da planet you call Cypra. Humans kill orcs no more."

Jon reasoned, "Nuttybomb, we are helping you. We could have let you and all orcs die here in space and down on the planet. Cypra belongs to Humania."

"I tink a planet is worth millions a orcs dyin'. Besides, we beat da humans on Cypra and control it."

"This is what I think," Jon began. "If these chemical ships get to the planet, you could lose everyone down there. I'm not sure, but you could. I'm hearing estimates of up to fifty thousand Spidanoids down there. They will cause considerable losses to your troops, if not kill them all. The chemicals will probably wipe out most surviving Spidanoids and possibly any surviving orcs. Is that worth saying the planet is yours? If there aren't any orcs to defend it, how can you claim it and defend it?"

Nuttybomb thought for a few seconds. He resisted the thought of leaving Cypra, but finally agreed, "I begin to withdraw troops *fo' now*. Dis topic still open fo' us to talk about."

Jon breathed a sigh of relief. "Okay, Nuttybomb. There are two chemical ships. Let's board them and take them over. Pull your troops so we can use the chemicals on the Spidanoids."

Nuttybomb gave the order for his destroyers to stop the chemical ships and to vacate Cypra. He couldn't take a chance on killing his own men. He just hoped he made the right decision.

***

Rabbit had an idea. He hoped a plan would materialize if he could get others to commit. "Colonel Parker?"

"This is Colonel Parker."

"Can you slow the fleet trying to escape to the actuator? It's imperative to try." Rabbit steered his fighter between some enemy support ships. The vessels didn't dare fire at fighters passing between them. That would open them up to firing on each other errantly.

Parker questioned, "Who is this?"

"Captain Rabbit Harrison, Sir."

Parker obliged, "Be careful, Captain. You don't have a very clean history in situations like this."

Lenny barked, "We got your back, Harrison." The *Renown* put itself between two of Taggart's cruisers. The battleship was heavily damaged, but decimated the lighter warships that were left behind to ensure Taggart's escape.

Colonel Parker and Lou set a path to block Taggart, throwing what they could at his remaining capital ships. At top speed, their battleships would arrive at a point in space just before Taggart's.

Leroy said, "I'm with you, Rabbit." He continued to call out targets to Rabbit as he eliminated threats to them both.

Rabbit replied, "Let's get to the actuator."

Lou positioned the *Repulse*'s starboard side in front of three enemy battleships as they approached in line. He ordered, "Fire."

A thunderous barrage tore across the bow of the *Contemptuous*, raking her bridge, and sending her adrift. Her front turret still fired, tearing holes into *Repulse*'s side. This turret was silenced by *Repulse*'s next salvos, however.

The *Repulse* was slowed by the combined firepower of the other two enemy battleships, one being Taggart's. She was an older vessel, and as such, lacked some of the modern armor plating other battleships had for protection.

Colonel Parker and Lenny were there to keep the *Repulse* from suffering catastrophic damage as they received their share of damage as well. They positioned themselves to deal some damage while drawing enemy fire.

The *Vindicator* unleashed all her main batteries on Parker's *Crusader* at point blank range. At this distance, any battleship would have been crippled by even the oldest battleships in the fleet. But the *Vindicator* was Humania's newest and most powerful, as well as, most advanced. Taggart had himself a monster of a warship! He headed for the actuator's safety, leaving Parker in a twisted wreck of flaming Swiss cheese.

Taggart left a few frigates and corvettes, as well as a hundred fighters to escort the chemical ships to Cypra. This was the final thing he could do to destroy as many orcs as possible. Spidanoids weren't considered collateral damage, but he figured he could mop up the rest of them if necessary. The ships he brought with him laid mines to keep Parker's and Nuttybomb's forces from catching him.

Parker and Nuttybomb could no longer avert Taggart's escape. They were to his rear, watching helplessly as he and ten of his largest ships widened the gap. Fighters still flew in zigzags, strafing each other in an epic dogfight.

Reports of more worlds, either being attacked, or swearing allegiance to Taggart, were being received. Colonel Parker decided to lick his wounds and rally his fleet somewhere near the home worlds. He thanked Nuttybomb and left negotiations to Jon. A couple battleships and a carrier as well as some cruisers and destroyers were brought along.

Lou and Lenny said their goodbyes and prepared to bring their damaged ships to the nearest shipyard for repairs. Leroy was pleased, the weight on his shoulders feeling somewhat lighter.

Rabbit and Leroy were first to reach the actuator. They docked and entered its empty innards. Rabbit asked, "How long 'til Taggart's ships arrive?"

Leroy answered, "Maybe five minutes. Is that enough time?"

"I don't know. I wish I had more." Rabbit used the computer's calculator to run calculations. He scribbled some figures on the counter in front of him and continued, "I can't get this wrong."

"Can I help?" Leroy queried.

Rabbit replied, "Yeah. Two things...One, get me how many and the mass of each ship coming in order of arrival and two, keep me updated on how much time I have."

"Seriously? All in four minutes?" Leroy scoffed.

"Hurry."

Leroy began, "Ten ships." He added each ship's mass and updated how much time Rabbit had to complete a set of numbers, unique to each ship. "Three minutes left."

***

Night Killa was able to knock out the lead chemical ship's propulsion system. She came alongside and docked with the drifting vessel, her orcs overrunning the human crew.

There were no super humans aboard, really no defense to speak of. The ship was taken in several minutes.

Da Massacre wasn't able to stop the trailing chemical ship. It entered the planet's upper atmosphere and began its descent. Even with her navigation knocked out, gravity began pulling the vessel to the surface.

Jon hailed the orc leader once again, "Nuttybomb, one chemical ship is entering the planet's atmosphere. It has to be destroyed. If the chemicals are released this high, I think orcs will be okay."

Nuttybomb ordered his destroyers to shoot at the ship before it made it to the surface, but neither could catch up to it as it sped toward its eventual destination.

Jon asked in desperation, "Ucktock, can you fly your ship into the chemical ship?"

"Uh, ok?" was replied.

"You need to get out right before impact though."

Ucktock was confused. It didn't stop him from pursuing the enemy ship at top speed though. As he closed the gap, he questioned, "Not sure if my suit will keep me live, tho."

Jon explained, "You are our only shot. All the orcs down there might die if you don't do this. I'll be right behind you to get you aboard as soon as I can."

Being an orc, Ucktock didn't hesitate. Death would happen eventually, anyway. At least he would die in battle, so he agreed, "Ok, Jon. Good fightin' wit' you."

"You, too, Ucktock. Hey, good luck."

Ucktock laughed, "I no need luck, I need suit." He steered his ship, the only home in freedom he had known over the last several years, into the falling chemical ship.

Jon watched his body shoot from the rear, upward toward space, as the orc ship impacted the aft-port side of the chemical ship. A terrific explosion temporarily blinded Jon, but he was near Ucktock's lifeless body in an instant.

Pretty emerged from the lift to pull Ucktock to safety. Goggles and an oxygen mask gave her minimal protection as there were no orc helmets and space suits aboard the *Outcast*. At this altitude, on the border of space, her blood began to heat, and her body fought against the inevitable expansion from water accumulating beneath her skin. This was mild during the few seconds she was exposed to the elements, or lack thereof. "Hatch closed," she said, the lift bringing her and Ucktock to the main level.

Jon Asked, "Is he okay?"

"Dunno," Pretty answered. "Him not conscious." She pulled the oxygen apparatus from her face with one hand and lugged Ucktock with the other.

"Do you need help?"

Pretty replied, "Nope." Now, both hands free, she threw Ucktock over her shoulder and clumsily trudged to the medical area.

With Ucktock aboard, Jon turned his attention to the chemical ship. The data on his screen showed dispersion of pernicious materials into the upper atmosphere of Cypra. The explosion spread it out so thinly, that very little would make it to the surface in harmful levels. He breathed a sigh of relief.

Jon pulled the *Outcast* away from Cypra. It was time to meet up with Leroy and Rabbit. He hailed the engine room, "Harry." There was no response, so he engaged the ship-wide intercom, "Harry." Still, there was no response.

"Pretty, is Harry with you?" Jon inspected.

"No. Just a me, Ucktock, and Evelyn."

"Dammit. Is Ucktock stable?" Jon wiped his forehead with his sleeve, sweat breaking on his forehead. "The air system must have been compromised," he mumbled.

Pretty said, "Ucktock doin' ok. Him wakin' up."

Jon was partially relieved and stated, "Good." Then, he urged, "I need you to check on Harry."

"Ok," she responded. She left the medical area and made it to engineering where she found Harry collapsed on the floor. She tried to revive him, but was unable.

After a couple minutes, unsure of whether Pretty had even left the medical area, Jon asked, "Pretty, you find Harry, yet?"

Pretty tried to answer in a way that made sense, but sense seemed in short supply currently. "Harry, ya. Him sleepin' or sumptin's. Or him lyin' down wit' eyes open. Dunno."

"Fuck, I hope we don't get attacked. I'm on my way."

***

"Now," Leroy ordered.

Rabbit's hands worked the controls. Even if his plan didn't completely work, maybe he would be successful in sending parts of the enemy ships out of phase, like what had happened to Harry on the *Outcast*. He was able to get Harry and the ship back to normal, but sending a ship deliberately, without knowing how these things worked exactly, was suspect at best. He said, "First ship is sent. Did it come out in Plenna?"

"Um," Leroy muttered.

"Well, did it or not?" Rabbit hastened.

"No. I don't see it."

Rabbit smiled, "Maybe this is working after all." He worked the controls again and stated, "Second ship sent."

Leroy whistled before calmly saying, "Nothing. They aren't jumping to Plenna."

"Good," Rabbit scoffed. Then, he asked with skepticism, "Do you think there is a chance they are cloaking."

After a short pause to think, Leroy said, "Nah. If they could cloak, they would have earlier. Right?"

Rabbit shook his head back and forth agreeing. "Right. I hope. Okay, next ship has been sent."

Leroy asked, "Where do you think we are sending them?"

***

The *Vindicator* lunged ahead several times and halted abruptly each time. The gravity inducers failed twice before kicking back on with backup power. The engines failed for good, leaving the ship adrift in a starless sky. An eerie calm settled like the mist and smoke that hung in the bridge.

Taggart shouted, "What happened? Report." He wiped his bloody nose on his sleeve.

A subordinate on the bridge found his way through the thin cloud that shrouded the damage. He, too, was injured; his hand cupped a gash over his left eye. He stated, "I don't know, sir. The star patterns aren't what we should see in Plenna."

Annoyed, Taggart snapped, "Well, where the hell do the star patterns say we are?"

The confused man choked, "I don't know, sir. We aren't seeing any stars."

Taggart asked the admiral of the ship, "Admiral Lindsey, what the hell is wrong with your crew?"

Lindsey turned on his heels with, "Nothing, sir. We will figure this out."

Voices could be heard through the fog saying things like, "No, parts of the ship are just gone," and "Total checklist failure."

Lindsey ordered the checklist to be done again and discussed point by point. He directed his engineers to get the ship moving and to divert any other power to essential life support systems. He stumbled from his chair to the environmental station, but to his surprise, it wasn't there. "The whole damn thing is gone," he said aloud to himself. He looked out into the blackness of space, the whole port side of his ship missing.

He shouted to Taggart, "Sir, we are experiencing a complete structural failure."

"What the hell does that even mean?" Taggart followed Lindsey's voice to the gaping hole that ran the length of the massive ship. He was astounded. "My gods."

The admiral explained, "I would call this complete structural failure." His eyes ran from bow to stern.

The communications officer interrupted, "Sir, other ships are reporting similar damage."

Taggart clenched his fists and growled, "What system are they in?"

"No idea, sir. They can't determine location either."

Taggart waved his hand in front of his face. "Admiral, this is not the time to shit your pants." The odor built in strength.

Lindsey rebutted, "That wasn't me, sir." He began to gag, his mouth watering involuntarily.

As the aroma of putrid rot grew, so did the muted sound of rumbling. It was maybe a large ship engine or a deep bass sound from an orchestra. Taggart thought it sounded more like a million heartbeats.

Screams filled the back side of the bridge. Through the mist, shadows fooled the unaware, and insanity struck the minds in those alert. Terror ran amok!

Radio chatter cut in and out. The lights flickered. Sparks gave a yellow hue to the greenish fog that enveloped everything. The smell of death was everywhere!

A large, dark gray creature came from the fog and upon Admiral Lindsey. It grabbed his shoulder and took him easily, like a child's nightmare, the monster grabbed the man and went off with him. Lindsey kicked and screamed in absolute terror. He swung at the mighty beast, but caused nothing that remotely deterred death from coming.

Taggart fell to his knees, weakened by fear. He shook, fighting back the sensation to vomit at the horrid creatures' hideous odor. He crawled near a console and ducked beneath it, praying for salvation.

He watched, trembling uncontrollably, as Adolf Gruber was dragged by a leg into the darkness. Gruber begged like a homeless boy on the corner of the old city, praying salvation would come for him, too.

Instead, he was lost in the void, at the mercy of these beings.

Silence befell Taggart. It seemed his chances at winning a war had changed somewhat. His war, his glory, the orcs...all of it meant nothing right now. It was what he couldn't see or hear that plagued him currently.

He would hear a possible footstep, maybe see the slightest movement out of the corner of his eye. He fought back the notion that he thought he heard children playing as well. How outrageous a notion on the bridge of a battleship!

Hot breath on the back of his neck caused him to turn suddenly, only to find nothing. His eyes peered into the mist, hoping not to find what might be coming for him. He hunkered down on his hands and knees with his head between his palms.

No more silence. The blood curdling screams, putrid smell, and dreamlike aliens preyed on his psyche. Something caught his attention, a shadow out of the corner of his eye, like the movement we've all seen in our periphery that startles us, so, too, did it frighten Taggart. He slowly turned his head to find a beast towering above him. He yelled, "No!" and fought to get away. His arm was lost in the process, being tugged on while his body clung to a power cable beneath the perceived safety of the console.

The pain and unbelievable assaults on his senses rendered him unconscious. Many crewmen of his and other ships would phase in and out of consciousness that fateful day. Who could have really determined what was reality in such confusing states?

Nobody ever came back from the Void to tell of their experiences. Nobody ever determined what was awake, asleep, alive or dead in...

The Void.

Twenty
What's in a Name?

The battle above Cypra was over, leaving in its wake debris of every kind. Strewn from the planet to the actuator were destroyed ships, partial hulls, and bodies. Any of the late Taggart's remaining fleet had been captured or managed to escape via another actuator that propelled them to a different system than Plenna. Many who crash landed or hoped to find safety on the planet were forced to face the Spidanoids. For the victors, the spoils included salvage and rescue, a far cry from the tales of wealth attained by winning battles. It was agreed that orcs and humans would only salvage their own parts, respectively.

Harry was fully awake and aware. He looked around, a bit confused to find himself lying in the medical area. "What happened?" he asked.

Jon, with arms folded, replied, "I think it was just a good old-fashioned seizure."

Harry sighed, "Great."

"All things considered, it could have been worse."

"This can't be allowed to happen. I can't have these while on duty."

Jon rationalized, "It's never been a problem before. And listen...We all have stuff that comes up. Leroy takes on a whole squad of Marines. Rabbit accidentally blows up a planet. It happens." He laughed out loud.

Ucktock spat, "I just shot myself to space." He grabbed his gut and cracked up.

Harry questioned, "What? Wait, never mind. It doesn't matter. I have to think about what I'm gonna do." He dropped his face into his hands, rubbing his thumbs on his temples.

Jon said calmly, "There's nothing to do. It will be fine."

"Fine? Just a thought, do Spidanoids have seizures? Do orcs? You would think I would have enough of one or both in me to not have seizures."

Jon cautioned with eye movements in the direction of the Troublemakers' new orc friends, "I don't know, but this is a discussion for another time."

Harry understood. He sat up and asked, "Where's my cigar?"

Leroy and Rabbit, who were waiting around the corner, found it was time to enter. Leroy held out a fresh cigar and handed it to his best friend. He chuckled, "You're gonna have to break this one in."

"Thanks. I'll suck on it a while."

Rabbit started, "If I had a dime..." He looked around with a smile, caught himself, and cleared his throat with a serious look on his face. He asked, "How are you, Evelyn?"

Evelyn had tubes and wires running from her arms, nose, and chest. Everything from antibiotics to drainage for her lungs was hooked up to or sticking out of her painful body. Her face was bruised and swollen with some visible cuts to her lips, nose, and forehead. She slowly replied in a gravelly voice, "I feel like shit."

Pretty watched the interaction between her and Rabbit. She hoped to gain some understanding about their relationship, and in so doing, understand her relationship with Rabbit.

Rabbit joked, "Well, you look great." He saw the scowl on Evelyn's face and continued, "Never better, in fact."

Evelyn spat, "Go fuck yourself, Rabbit."

He smiled and leaned over to kiss her cheek. Evelyn's eyes looked up into his, longing for his comfort, for as much as she disliked him, she loved him even more.

Rabbit rested his hand on hers and smiled. He said, "Get better soon. We will have awards dinners and celebrations to attend for this one. This was a big deal. Orcs, Spidanoids, torture, rebellion, invasion, Crystal Technologies; you helped us solve most of this."

Jon cut in with, "Don't forget cloaking technology."

Rabbit added, "Cloaking technology," with a broad, goofy smile.

Pretty heard, "Dinner," and saw a kiss, smiles, and holding hands. Her heart sank.

"I don't think I'll be attending any of those things," Evelyn muttered.

Rabbit asked, "Why not?" with concern showing in the lines on his face.

"Duh," she grunted. "I'm an operative. We don't reveal who we are."

"Oh. I thought maybe you hated me." Rabbit winked.

Evelyn sighed. "You're fine. Now, leave me alone."

"Sure thing, Eve."

"Don't call me that."

Rabbit acknowledged, "Okay. Sorry." He turned to leave with the others.

Evelyn stopped him though with, "Wait. Thanks for saving me."

Rabbit smiled, "You're welcome. Any time."

Harry murmured, "I helped some."

Ucktock shot, "I helped a lot."

Everyone left the medical area with smiles on their faces, everyone, except Pretty that is. They began huddling in the computer area, waiting for Jon to go over how to handle Nuttybomb.

Leroy asked, "Rabbit, how many kills for you?"

"Do all of the capital ship guys count?"

Leroy shot back, "No! We don't even know if they are dead. Besides, you didn't shoot them in your fighter. Doesn't count."

"Seventeen, I think. Yeah, seventeen. You?"

"Nine, but I was tasked with protecting your ass!" Leroy complained.

"And a fine job you did, too," Rabbit teased.

Ucktock revealed, "I gots two lil bastids and one giant ship."

Rabbit complimented, "Nice work, Uck."

"Tanks."

Pretty joined the group and sat down in time to hear Ucktock ask, "Heya, Rabbit. Why you got name of a small, fuzzy animal?"

Rabbit kidded, "Just lucky, I guess."

Ucktock tipped his head in confusion. "Dat a lucky name?"

"I'm not sure. I guess I've been lucky so far."

The orc scratched his head while he leaned forward, obviously anticipating some kind of explanation to clear up the confusion.

Rabbit explained as he shook his head, "It's not that it's a lucky name. Forget that I said anything about it being lucky." He continued, "When I was born, the nurse asked what my parents were naming me. I'm not sure if it was my mother or father who said my name was Robert. The nurse thought they named me Rabbit."

Leroy interrupted, "They should have named you asshole."

"Women started giving me that name much later," Rabbit admitted.

Harry added, "I don't think you're an asshole, Rabbit."

"Thanks, Harry."

Ucktock asked, "Anda dat why you called Hairy? Cause you gots hair all ova you body?"

Leroy shouted, "Yes, he's a hairy bastard."

Harry and Rabbit both chuckled. Harry said, "It doesn't mean hair all over my body. Harry is just a name."

Leroy choked, "He's lying. Don't listen to him. He came out of his mother with that much hair."

Randomly, Ucktock asked, "Hey, how come we all talk orc?"

Harry blurted out, "I thought we all talked Humanian."

"Ut uh, we talk orc."

Rabbit explained why he thought these two races, separated by billions of miles, were able to engage in mutual conservation. "Our history says that we all had contact with each other thousands of years ago. Maybe we learned each other's languages and combined them. Maybe we spoke, and taught orcs or you guys taught us."

Ucktock laughed, "I not too stupid a tink dat we taught you. You definitely taught us."

Leroy queried, "So, why do the other races speak a common language, too?"

Harry answered, "Maybe the gods had something to do with it?"

Leroy teased, "The gods? They can allow billions to die in war, famine, and disease, but they care enough to give us all one language?"

"Maybe. Don't you think we would all have different languages?"

"I think you have a different language," Leroy taunted.

Harry smiled. "I'm gonna forget you said that."

"That shouldn't be too hard," Leroy joked.

Jon met his men and the two orcs. He looked at Pretty as he spoke. "How's Evelyn? I mean, really, how is she?"

Pretty said, "Not good. I tink she be ok in time, tho. Gotta wait to see."

Rabbit stated, "She's stable, doing better."

"Yeah, that's good," Jon hastened, trying to keep the mood and outlook positive. He continued, "What about the blood work you ran for me, Pretty?"

323

"I get it. Be right back."

Rabbit asked, "So, we're meeting Nuttybomb?"

Jon elaborated, "Yeah. I spoke with Colonel Parker and he's in agreement that we should offer an alliance. The catch is that we offer Plenna and not try to retake it. I think allowing Cypra to go unchallenged is a bit much, though. I'll do the talking on all that. The main thing is that we hand over Rabbit."

Rabbit mewled, "I knew it."

Jon smiled, "Well, I guess we can keep you around a little longer."

Pretty returned. "Here, Jon."

After seeing each of his men's blood work results, he quietly passed them around.

Rabbit said, "That's what I figured."

Harry agreed, "Me, too. Odds of false positives were too high for two of us."

Leroy asked jestingly, "Am I eventually gonna turn red and yellow, too?"

Jon answered, "I think your family is okay with you being black. Let's keep you this color for a while."

Harry agreed with his superior officer. "Yeah, and it's great that your brothers came to help."

Leroy said, "Yeah. I guess beauty **is** only skin deep."

Harry removed the soggy cigar from his open lips to comment, "We never said you were beautiful."

"We never said he wasn't either," Rabbit added.

Pretty seemed to randomly ask, "Is Evelyn beautiful?"

Ucktock, without a moment to fully digest the question, and no sense of how loud he was responded soundly, "Nope."

The guys all looked at him, back at each other, and then back to him again.

Ucktock clarified, "She not even all green. She gots green around da eyes and udder parts, but she lika all spotted."

To Rabbit's surprise, Jon sighed, "Yes, she's beautiful."

Pretty asked Rabbit, "You tink she beautiful?"

Boy, did Rabbit feel like he was in a pickle. He shrugged his shoulders and said, "Um, I guess."

Harry broke in with, "She's a good lookin' woman if you ask me. No offense, Rabbit."

"None taken."

Leroy scoffed, "She might be the most beautiful woman I've ever seen."

"Okay, Okay," Rabbit warned. "I see what you're doing here." He crossed his arms and stated, "It was a long time ago. Things will never be the same. Let's get her to a medical ship."

Jon stated factually, "All joking aside. Things will never be the same anywhere for anyone."

Leroy said, "I can't believe we are at war."

"And not just any little war," Harry added. "A huge war against ourselves."

Leroy punched Harry in the upper arm. "That's the stupidest thing I've ever heard. A war against ourselves? What does that even mean?"

Harry appeared perplexed. "You know, against other humans. And by the way, you've been at war with yourself since the first time we ever got to Cypra. Stupidest thing you ever heard? You *saying* it's the stupidest thing, *is* the stupidest thing *I've* ever heard."

Jon interrupted, "Ladies, are we done?"

"Not yet," Leroy spat. "I've been in a good mood today. Fighting myself? You don't know what the hell you're talking about."

"Yeah," Jon said. "I think you're done."

Rabbit nodded and began, "Stupidest thing I ever heard, other than this conversation, was the night I was with those androids. You know? The one who lost an arm? She was arguing with the others to stop so she could put her arm back on. Really put a damper on the whole thing. Androids...Who knew they'd be so high maintenance in the bedroom?"

There was no more arguing.

Harry said, "I guess that sounds pretty stupid."

Begrudgingly, Leroy agreed in jest, "Yeah, okay. I guess that's pretty stupid, too."

Jon shot a look at Harry. He pointed a finger and said, "You said we were all geniuses. You should be ashamed of yourself."

"Every day, Jon. Every day."

The group laughed.

***

The retreat of Cypra was well underway with fighter craft strafing behind the evacuation to hold back Spidanoids. Orcs were still fighting in pockets, defending against the equally brutish spidanoids. The green mass of orcs worked their way onto hundreds of spaceships, eventually finding themselves in the star-dotted sky above.

Nuttybomb sat with his officers beside him in that sky above. It was time to hear reports and updates from leadership about casualties, Spidanoids, future plans...and time to talk about the humans. He looked around at these fine orcs, seeing them as loyal, tough, and smart for their kind. He began, "How many orcs die so far?"

Booma replied as accurately as he knew how, "Abouts thirty-seven thousand."

"Just on da planet?"

"Yup," Booma confirmed. "Ova ten thousand mo' in space."

Nuttybomb quizzed, "How many wounded?"

"Woundeds so bads dems can't fight no mo', or all?" Booma asked.

"Woundeds so bad dems can't fight. We can fix up da udders."

Booma stated, "Um, ova fifty thousand bad woundeds."

Gunther took his turn and asked, "Boss, we leavin's Cypra foevva?"

"No," Nuttybomb replied. "Dat not da plan."

"Wut is da plan?"

Nuttybomb explained, "I tink dis depend on Rabbit Harrison and da humans. We nevva run fro' a fight."

The officers hooted and hollered.

Nuttybomb waved his hand to quiet them. He continued, "But dems smart as a hell and lots not very squishy. Plus, dems got mo' better ships. We needs to a regroup."

Gunza chimed in with, "So, wut 'bout dis Rabbit Harrison?"

Guthrak added his own question. "Ya, we really gonna meet him?"

Boomer spat, "Dunno why. We should a kills him fo' evvyting he done."

"Enough!" Nuttybomb ordered. "Da humans helped us beat da bad humans. Dems didn't have to. Dunno 'bout Rabbit Harrison. He on da side a da humans we gonna talk wit'. If I no lika wut I hear, I kills him. Dat's all."

Subdued cheers erupted at a low decibel, so as not to anger Nuttybomb. Actually, he relished the thought of finishing Rabbit Harrison. The approval from his subordinates tasked him with an uneasy decision though. The humans had offered a temporary alliance, thin at best, but possibly something to build on diplomatically. Killing Rabbit might kill that possibility too. Nuttybomb looked at Moonoak, who quietly waited his turn.

Moonoak answered without being prompted, "No. No killin's Rabbit Harrison. I tink we see wut da humans offer and find out wut really a happen on Cypra and Plenna."

Booma asked, "Why we call dems Cypra and Plenna? Dat wut humans call 'em."

Nuttybomb explained, "Just mo' easy to call dems da same ting when we negotiate."

"So, we gonna rename dems?"

"Dunno," Nuttybomb answered scornfully. I not tink 'bout it, yet." He corrected any doubts about his intentions with, "I not givin' in to da humans. Our ships stay here in dis system till we talk wit' humans, Jon and Rabbit Harrison. Dis hard a understand, but we might leave Cypra. Dat part I dunno yet. I wait anda see wut humans say. We not givin up Plenna fo' sure. We fall back der wit' our troops. If I no like wut I hear, we take Cypra too anda maybe mo'. Humans be fightin' against humans. Dems weak. We use dat to our advantage. I tink da good humans need us."

Booma queried, "Negotiate?"

Moonoak quieted the room when he jumped to his feet and slammed his walking stick on the floor. He pulled his hood back from his head and said, "Nuttybomb da greatest leader and greatest warrior orcs evva knew. He bestest fighta and smartest, too. Him know dat der be time to negotiate. We maybe can gain so much workin' wit' dese humans. And if dems are no goods fo' us to work wit', he will know."

Nuttybomb asked, "Anyting else? Good. Let's meet Rabbit Harrison."

Twenty-One
Rabbit Harrison!!!

The *Outcast* set down on the planet in the Plenna system where the great fight between Nuttybomb and Rabbit Harrison took place. Only the Troublemakers were there to represent Humania. However, over a million orcs were on the surface, and many of those were close to the landing sight.

Rabbit gulped as he said, "I don't like this."

Jon asked, "Is Nuttybomb trying to read your mind?"

"No, nothing like that."

"Then, what?" Jon questioned.

Rabbit started, "Well, he does hate me."

Leroy asked, "Who doesn't?"

The joke was lost on Rabbit as he failed to find humor at the moment. "I'm freakin' sweating. Look, they all hate me. They blame me for all the orc lives lost on Cypra."

Leroy tried again, "Hey, it's been nice knowing you, Rabbit."

Rabbit turned and shot darts back into Leroy's eyes. He asked, "Ever heard of guilt by association?"

Leroy stopped smiling. "Yeah, I've heard of it. I was only kidding. You don't have to make believe kill me, too." He, too, was worried, although he seemed to hide it better. He also hid the bit of anger he felt toward the orcs. It was wrong to categorically hate them all because their invasion brought him and the other Troublemakers back to Cypra and everything that happened recently. Now, they were gonna risk their lives *again*, outnumbered hundreds of thousands to one. It was easier to be angry than scared. Anger gave him an edge, he thought.

Jon stated, "Look, we get in, say what we have to, and leave. Simple."

Harry was stunned. "Has anything we've ever done been simple?"

"No, but this will be," Jon assured his men with a quick, decisive nod of his head and stern voice.

Leroy quarreled, "You've gotta be kidding me."

Jon said, "You're procrastinating. Let's go."

On the way out of the ship, Rabbit mumbled, "Fuck me."

Pretty ordered, "It ok, Rabbit. Stay wit' me."

The group stood at the top of the ramp. Jon squinted with his hand protecting his eyes from the glare that the planet's closest star caused. Furthermore, the difference in light between the inside of the ship and the outside was staggering. The other Troublemakers did much the same, shielding their eyes.

Jon's eyes focused. There was an ocean of vicious orcs, waiting for the opportunity to rip the humans apart. Beyond and elevated by maybe thirty feet were Nuttybomb and his officers. A chill rushed through him, goosebumps breaking on his skin. He began to walk, steadily, but carefully. He would show no fear, regardless of how he felt.

Ucktock walked alongside him, a posture meant to show good will. This was the orc Jon and his men saved from captivity, albeit at the hands of

331

humans. The orc lumbered down the ramp, smiling all the way, happy to be among his own kind.

Rabbit and Pretty walked side by side, another attempt at choreographing the proper return of Pretty to her brother. Rabbit's knees were weak, his legs trembling beneath him with every step.

Leroy and Harry were last. Leroy popped on some sunglasses and began walking before his stunned comrade. Although his eyes were shaded, he would never admit that the spectacles were to hide them from the orcs and give him a sense of security. It just so happened they protected his pupils. Harry's damp cigar fell from his opened mouth, a feat rarely seen, if ever. He stepped in double time to catch up with Leroy.

They strode among their long-time enemy from millennia gone by. The green mass parted, like the sea, for a prophet to bring his people to salvation, but these humans weren't prophets. They felt more like lambs being brought to slaughter.

Jon heard the orcs growl. He felt the tension as he slowly walked passed each onlooker. It was at this moment he questioned his decision to be here.

Rabbit began drawing his own grunts and sounds of detest from the massive mob that completely surrounded him. He peaked back to see that he and the others were cut off from the *Outcast* as the orcs behind him had begun to follow the group.

Each Troublemaker, unique to their own way of thinking, yet tied to possible death together, had overlapping thoughts. Most felt uneasy. Rabbit had never been so terrified in his entire life. Only Harry thought he might pee his big boy pants. He kept that to himself.

And Leroy...well, he thought a little differently. Since the chat with Rabbit and Jon aboard the ship, his anger had welled up, close to the surface. If not kept at bay, held deep down inside, it might send him and the others to unquestionable death.

It didn't help that the orcs really seemed to dislike him. They became louder as he approached, swaying like caged animals, their fists and teeth clenched. They felt particularly threatened by him – He was darker than the other humans, darker than they were in fact. He was large as well, a common physicality that separated the strong from the weak. In Orcdom, he would be challenged to see how powerful he really was.

The hair on Leroy's neck and arms stood on end. He removed his sunglasses and halted his forward movement. He snarled and cracked his knuckles.

As if on cue, the orcs moved toward him, animalistic urges pushing them into an inevitable fight with this human. Many orcs assumed he was *Rabbit Harrison, the Orc Killer*.

The real Rabbit Harrison, a bit panicky and unsure, said loudly, "Warchief Nuttybomb, this is like old times. Good to see you."

The orcs quieted in a combined mass of befuddlement and stopped following.

Jon closed his eyes for a second with a "holy shit" look on his face. He turned and whispered, "Knock it off, Rabbit. You trying to get us all killed?"

Rabbit replied, "It's the first thing I thought of to stop Leroy from being provoked into a fight."

Harry sighed, "Can we not do this now? Huh? Please?"

Leroy put his sunglasses back on. "Better to die up there?"

Angrily, Jon shouted, "Nobody's dy-" ...He continued in a whisper, "I mean, nobody's dying. Let's go."

Nuttybomb was having trouble figuring out these humans. Were they totally unaware as to how precarious their situation was? This Rabbit Harrison sure was brazen. And who was the dark human who seemed to instigate his orcs? He decided to reply to Rabbit's sarcastic greeting with a bit of self-control. "Rabbit Harrison, it beed a long time I wait to see you."

Against Jon's silent wishes, Rabbit said, "That was one hell of a fight we had. You are a great warrior, Warchief Nuttybomb."

Jon whispered, "Okay, you talked. Now, shut up."

Nuttybomb wasn't sure if he had received a real compliment or if he was being patronized. He simply said, "You pretty good fighta, too, Rabbit Harrison."

Jon cut in with, "But we aren't here to talk about fighting against each other." He began climbing the steps to the massive orc and his officers. He continued, "We have a common enemy, Warchief Nuttybomb."

"So, it seems," Nuttybomb concurred.

Jon was the first Troublemaker to the top. He presented, "You know Ucktock?"

Nuttybomb answered as he looked over his long-lost friend, "I do."

Ucktock was grinning ear to ear. His head bobbed as he took his final step to reach the platform. "Hiya, Nuttybomb."

Nuttybomb nodded. "Good a see you, Ucktock."

"Boss, I beed in prison, but I killed da warden. Rabbit Harrison jail breaked me. We fought udder humans and," ...

"Enough! Nuttybomb commanded. "Glad you ok. We talk 'bout it later."

Ucktock straightened up. "Yessir, Boss."

Rabbit stepped up and held Pretty's hand. He walked before his nemesis and stated, "Warchief Nuttybomb, your sister, Pretty. She's a great orc, strong and smart. She helped us to figure out who the bad humans were, and she fought like a great warrior." He released her hand and bowed to Nuttybomb.

Nuttybomb stepped forward, his enormous frame standing before Rabbit and Pretty. "Pretty, dems hurt you?"

Pretty smiled, "No, Nuttybomb. Dems were nice to me."

Rabbit felt Nuttybomb's presence, not just physically as the huge orc stared down at him, but mentally as well. He managed to guard against the intrusion and spoke. "You are gifted, Warchief."

Nuttybomb replied, "As are a you, but you ascareds and I not."

335

"Humans seem to feel fear more than orcs. Sometimes we have to confront things, even though we are afraid." Rabbit felt the perspiration grow on his chest and back beneath his clothes. He wiped his brow with a sleeve.

Nuttybomb took a step back and stated, "Dis a honorable trait in humans, one I did not know. Too fight when ascareds be heroic." He paused, then continued, "But der be bad human traits, too."

Jon didn't like the possible direction this new sentence might be leading to, so he asked, "Nuttybomb, may we talk about being friends?"

Nuttybomb slowly and deliberately turned and approached Jon. He closed his eyes and focused. "You ascareds, too. Not lika Rabbit Harrison, but still ascareds."

Jon was feeling the same intrusive presence Rabbit had explained in the past, but he wasn't able to halt Nuttybomb's invasion of his mind. He commanded, "Nuttybomb, stop."

The connection was lost. "You gonna tell me wut to do?"

"Friends don't do that to each other," Jon explained as he caught his breath.

Nuttybomb casually waved his hand in defiance. "No matta. I already get wut I want fro' you."

Leroy growled, "Yeah, what's that?" He stepped between Jon and Nuttybomb.

Nuttybomb laughed, "It ok, brown man. Jon brain and heart be good."

"What?" Leroy barked.

"I needed a see if he really be a friend," Nuttybomb explained.

Leroy stepped forward into Nuttybomb's space. "Well, he is."

Nuttybomb's smile faded into a scowl. "But you not friend. Not how you stand to me."

"I will protect my commander, even if it means risking my own life." Leroy's anger had built to a pinnacle, ready to explode.

Jon cautioned, "Easy, Leroy." He pulled Leroy back and stepped forward to occupy the space of his angry friend. He said to Nuttybomb, "He's okay. You have orcs that defend you, too; don't you?"

Nuttybomb understood. "One mo' ting befo' we talk fo' real."

Jon asked, "What is it?"

"Why orcs tortued and killed by Rabbit Harrison?" the massive orc asked. His eyes changed into fiery balls, his body tensed.

Jon corrected, "Rabbit didn't torture anyone. The bad humans did. I'm not even sure who all the bad humans are. Anyway, they were testing the chemicals that those ships had on orcs and humans. It was all done in secret – most humans didn't know about it." He paused to gather his thoughts, and being careful not to divulge the facts about a super army or how he and his men were super strong, he continued, "Rabbit tried to blow up one of the torture places. But the way the pressure in the atmosphere was, combined with all the chemicals, the whole planet ignited. That's how so many orcs and humans were killed. It was an accident, a huge one, but just an accident."

Nuttybomb lumbered back over to Rabbit. "Dis true? You try and stop da tortues?"

Rabbit shook his head and said, "Yeah. It doesn't change what happened, but I'm sorry for the orcs I killed. That wasn't my intention. I'm sorry every day. I tried to save them. Nuttybomb, it's my fault."

Gunza yelled, "Him lyin's!" The other orcs readied for bloodshed.

But Nuttybomb was calm. He looked into Rabbit's eyes, without aid from his abilities, and saw the truth. He took a deep breath and sighed. He exhaled a huge breath and proclaimed, "Him tellin's da truth."

Jon asked, "So, now we talk?"

Nuttybomb laughed. "Now, we talk."

The humans were directed to sit alongside the orc officers. shlogger was served and food was offered, although the men turned down the latter. They weren't inclined to eat snail or bugs, or gods knows what might have been on the menu.

Finally, Jon began, "Nuttybomb, Humania would like to offer you an alliance. We will fight alongside you against common enemies. If we need help in a fight, you help us. If you need help in a fight, we help you. You may keep Plenna, but we will keep Cypra. Also, we will try to stop any further torturing or testing on orcs. Humania is against it. That's the deal." He sat back and waited.

Nuttybomb retorted, "I hear you. Now, you hear me. You tell me all bout bad humans; wer dems are, der armies, ships, and planets. Den, orcs will stay away fro' Cypra. But if we fight wit' you as friends, we claim bad human planets we take. Dat's da deal."

Jon disagreed, "No."

"No?"

Jon was more assertive in his tone. "No. These are Humania planets being controlled by bad humans. There are good humans on these planets. Bad leaders took over. You can't have any of those planets."

"No good," Nuttybomb rebuked.

"Look, it's like me saying that I'll help you, but your planet is mine then. I'll try to get you better technology for your ships if it helps, but no more planets. That's it."

The orc officers didn't like giving an inch. They weren't even sure why Nuttybomb would enter into what seemed like such a one-sided agreement. They were orcs, and as such, believed they could take anything they wanted.

But Moonoak, another voice of reason, said, "I no want to kill good humans or take der planets. Dat der homes." He nodded at Nuttybomb.

Nuttybomb concurred, "Done. Plenna mine. Cypra yours. We keep ships ova Cypra fo' now to protect orcs. You gimme better ship stuff and we be allies."

Jon stood up and offered a handshake. He even used Nuttybomb's vocabulary to seal the deal with, "Done."

Harry sighed, "Thank gods. We should go now."

Ucktock pleaded, "You just gots here."

Rabbit addressed his orc friend, "Uck, we have a war to fight."

"I guess we do, too." He smiled.

"I'm looking forward to fighting alongside you again," Rabbit stated with a back slap.

Handshakes crossed the table. Humania and the orcs were allies.

With their mission complete, the Troublemakers boarded their trusty ship. Rabbit, the last to get to the top of the ramp, turned to see Pretty. He smiled and waved, "Goodbye." The ramp ascended and sealed the bottom of the *Outcast*.

Nuttybomb approached Pretty and asked, "Sure you ok? Rabbit Harrison no hurt you?"

The *Outcast's* Strenu engines fired, the ship beginning to lift.

Pretty nodded, "No. Him no hurt me. Him wus real nice." She rocked back and forth, her hand rubbing her tummy which had grown over the last month. She bit her lip when she realized Nuttybomb had noticed.

Even at some distance, over the roar of the engines, Rabbit smirked when he and the other Troublemakers heard Nuttybomb yell, "Rabbit Harrison!!!"

The end

If you enjoyed this work, please leave a positive review where you purchased it, if possible. Thank you for your involvement in the Hyadeswars universe.